"JUST ONE NIGHT, JOSIE."

"I'm not going to stand around and try to talk you into it. If you want me, you know where to find me." He took a step away from her. "But do me a favor. If you don't want to do this, stop wearing panties with lips on your ass. And stop bending over. The two together would tempt a saint, and despite what patients might say, I'm no saint."

It was not the term she would have chosen for him either.

Her hands went to her behind, face burning. How long had he been able to see through her pants? "I only wear these on Saturdays. They're day-of-the-week panties, and Saturday they're lips."

"Oh, my God," he said, before his eyes dropped down below her waist as if he were visualizing a seven-day panty parade.

Josie froze with her hands still on her ass. She was reduced to the intellectual level of an amoeba.

"What are the other days?" Houston said, sounding very intrigued.

Then some little devil in her, the one that was annoyed he had been so casual and blunt with her, smiled at him. "Since you only wanted one night, I guess you'll never know."

BOOK YOUR PLACE ON OUR WEBSITE AND MAKE THE READING CONNECTION!

We've created a customized website just for our very special readers, where you can get the inside scoop on everything that's going on with Zebra, Pinnacle and Kensington books.

When you come online, you'll have the exciting opportunity to:

- View covers of upcoming books
- Read sample chapters
- Learn about our future publishing schedule (listed by publication month *and author*)
- Find out when your favorite authors will be visiting a city near you
- Search for and order backlist books from our online catalog
- Check out author bios and background information
- Send e-mail to your favorite authors
- Meet the Kensington staff online
- Join us in weekly chats with authors, readers and other guests
- Get writing guidelines
- AND MUCH MORE!

**Visit our website at
http://www.kensingtonbooks.com**

Houston, We Have A Problem

ERIN McCARTHY

KENSINGTON BOOKS
KENSINGTON PUBLISHING CORP.
http://www.kensingtonbooks.com

KENSINGTON BOOKS are published by

Kensington Publishing Corp.
850 Third Avenue
New York, NY 10022

All Kensington titles, imprints, and distributed lines are available at special quantity discounts for bulk purchases for sales promotion, premiums, fund-raising, educational or institutional use.

Special book excerpts or customized printings can also be created to fit specific needs. For details, write or phone the office of the Kensington Special Sales Manager: Kensington Publishing Corp., 850 Third Avenue, New York, NY 10022, Attn. Special Sales Department. Phone: 1-800-221-2647.

Kensington and the K logo Reg. U.S. Pat. & TM Off.

First Trade Paperback Printing: September 2004
First Mass Market Paperback Printing: November 2005
10 9 8 7 6 5 4 3 2 1

Printed in the United States of America

*For Pat and Jude, whose e-mails of encouragement
about my shark story were priceless.*

Acknowledgments

I want to thank Dr. Ola Ghaith, Dr. Loretta Isada, and especially Sandra Lawer for helping me fuse medical reality with my imagination. Any errors are entirely mine.

Author's Note

If you read my story, "Blue Crush," in the anthology *Perfect for the Beach*, you'll recognize Dr. Sara Davis, Josie's friend. This book actually takes place before that story, so you'll see poor Sara lonely and dateless. I hope you'll have fun watching her lament her single status, knowing that she's on the verge of meeting Kyle, the sexiest lifeguard on Acadia Beach.

Chapter One

Josie Adkins had to stop waving her hot little ass in Houston's face, or he was going to have to slide his hands across it and squeeze.

Which would fall squarely under the heading of sexual harassment. He could see the headline: *State of Florida vs Dr. Houston Hayes. Surgeon fondles resident and loses license.*

Sweet little Josie had no idea he was plotting ways to lick her like a cat does cream. She wasn't tempting him with her curvy behind on purpose, so he couldn't really blame her for the detour his thoughts had been taking on a regular basis.

But just how in the hell an orthopedic surgeon could be so damn clumsy was beyond him. And Jesus, was Josie clumsy.

So clumsy that at least six times a day he was subjected to the sight of her, bent full over at the waist, retrieving something she had dropped from the floor. Today was even worse.

They were alone in a semidark alcove, for the purpose of looking at a patient's X-ray, only Josie had done her usual butterfinger bit.

The film Josie had been holding had slipped out of her hand, hit the floor, and disappeared under the desk next to her. She was now on her hands and knees, wiggling around searching for it.

God help him.

No one with a body that lush and womanly should be wiggling on her hands and knees unless she was naked and it was part of foreplay.

"Whoops. It just jumped right out of my hand, Dr. Hayes," she said in a cheerful voice.

Houston counted from one to ten and back again until he was in control of himself and his bodily urges. He didn't know what it was about her that had him hiding hard-ons left and right and sweating through three pairs of surgical scrubs a day.

She wasn't his type at all. She was on the short side, with an odd haircut that made her light brown hair flip around at gravity-defying angles. When she smiled, twin dimples appeared and she looked about twenty years old. She talked constantly. He had heard other staff members affectionately refer to her as a dingbat.

Yet here he was, unable to look away, all too aware that her scrubs were worn thin in strategic places.

"It has to be here somewhere." She chattered on, her head half under the desk.

"What the . . . ?"

As she pulled her hand back, Houston saw she was holding a crust of moldy bread.

"Gross." She flung it down.

Time to leave a note for housekeeping.

Josie disappeared back under the desk—at least the front half.

The back half was still in full view.

He could see her underwear.

The thin scrubs hid nothing, and the position she was in on her knees pulled them taut, giving him a clear view of her panties. They were riding up just a little, sliding into the crevice between her cheeks, fitting close and tight. There was a little red lip print stamped on each side of her panties, and he wondered what she would do if he leaned forward and placed his own mouth right on one of those lip prints.

And bit her.

He was fascinated by the full curviness of her behind, and ached all over from the desire to taste her, to cup his hand between her legs and feel her heat pulsing through his fingers.

He wanted to know if there was a matching lip print on the front of her panties. So that if he kissed it he would feel her soft dewy mound give a little beneath his mouth.

It seriously annoyed him, this edgy uncontrollable desire.

Houston had never had a problem maintaining his professional distance with both patients and co-workers. If anything, he had been accused of being too reserved. Now this one woman, this tiny tornado of smiles and klutziness, had successfully breached his aloofness.

Impatient with his thoughts, he glanced at his watch. How long had she been on the floor? It felt like hours.

"Do I need to come back, Dr. Adkins, when you can make your X-ray films behave?" Visions of making her behave with his hand on her soft bottom flitted through his mind, playing like a porno video. He had meant it to sound like a cool rebuke, but it came out sounding suggestive.

Either of which seemed too subtle for Josie. She laughed from under the desk, like he was simply teasing her, then gave a little cough.

"Yuck. I think I inhaled a dust bunny."

Her head reemerged long enough to smile at him in reassurance. "Just give me a sec. I'll get it."

"Really, we can do this later." Since he had learned just about nothing could hurry her up.

Of course he could brush her aside and get the damn

thing himself. But he didn't want to hurt her feelings. Josie always tried so hard to gloss over her gaffes. Plus he was a total masochist who didn't want to deny himself the glorious view of her backside, even though he knew he couldn't, shouldn't—*wouldn't* act on his lust.

So Houston resented the distraction and cursed himself, but still couldn't tear his eyes away from her, not even long enough to pick up the X-ray himself.

"Almost got it." She gave him another blinding smile, head cocked to the right as she stretched her hand a little farther.

He put his hands on his hips and reminded himself, again, that getting involved with a resident would be a complete nightmare, no matter how freaking adorable she was.

"I need one of those rubber arms, like Stretch Armstrong, that really weird doll my cousin had when we were kids. Remember that?" she asked him.

He shook his head. Rubber dolls were the least of his problems right now.

"Well, it was kind of cool, in a bizarre sort of way, kind of like molded Silly Putty. What did you play with?"

Houston fought the urge to moan. Josie managed to mix innocence with that lush body, all tossed alongside her brains and her quirky personality. It was an unusual combination he was finding damn hard to resist.

Especially in this room that wasn't really a room, but a very small, very crowded alcove cut out of a corner in the hallway. Where Josie was just inches away from him.

"When you were a kid, I mean, what did you play with?" She kept feeling around on the floor. "Risk? World domination seems like your thing."

Should he be offended? "No."

"So what then? Nerf football? Twister? Chess club?"

He folded his arms and rubbed his chin. He'd forgotten to shave that morning and the stubble was irritating and itchy. He was well aware that if another co-worker had engaged in this ridiculous conversation with him he would have walked away.

"I played doctor." Let her figure out what exactly he meant by that. Except that Josie seemed immune to sexual innuendos.

"Here it is!" She pulled the film out and handed it to him.

Josie sat back on her heels and blew her hair out of her eyes. "Oh, well, that makes sense. Like Operation? That game that buzzed at you if you dropped the body part?"

Houston just stared at her as she brushed her knees off. He had read Josie's personnel file. On paper, she was only a few IQ points short of a genius. In person, she was a chatty, clumsy, sex nymph. Who had his nuts in a knot without even trying.

"Thank you, Dr. Adkins." He took the X-ray, shaking a dust ball off it, and wondered just when her residency would be over.

With a little luck she would leave Acadia Inlet Hospital for another resident rotation at least fifty miles away, taking her sweet ass with her. Of course, she had just started her second year of residency so it could be a year or more before she left.

Until then, he was going to have to work overtime at pretending she didn't make him go hard just by entering the room. He'd had two rules since he had broken things off with his last semiserious girlfriend four years earlier. No long-term relationships. No anything with another hospital employee.

It had worked so far. He dated casually, and when it was mutually agreed upon, had some no-strings-attached sex. Neither of which were done with someone he had to see every day in a professional capacity.

But when he joined the staff at Acadia Inlet three

months ago, he had met Josie. And suddenly his hormones seemed to think rules were meant to be broken.

Taking this position had seemed like a good career move, allowing him to focus on reconstructive orthopedics, and he liked the other doctors in the orthopedic group. It was an intelligent decision and he wasn't going to let one sexy little resident interfere with that.

Holding the film up to the light, Houston focused his thoughts squarely back on his job and was pleased to see evidence of his original diagnosis.

"Okay, exactly what I thought. Schedule surgery while I talk to Amber's parents."

Surgery for the second time on a fifteen-year-old girl didn't thrill him, but Amber had suffered multiple fractures in a gymnastics injury six months prior, and surgery on her ankle had been done in Atlanta.

The injury had healed and Amber had returned home to Acadia Beach to recover, but she was left with increasing pain and swelling. Houston knew a second surgery to release scar tissue and remove any bone fragments was the only way to curb a lifetime of debilitating arthritis.

"How soon?" Josie asked.

"Within a week."

"Okay. Not a problem. I'll take care of everything." A smile danced across Josie's plump lips as she played with the ID badge clipped to her waist.

She smiled so much it gave him a headache. No one could be that damn cheerful all the time. Yet she was, and damn it, he found that attractive. Everything about her was attractive to him, almost as if he *liked* her.

At that thought, he shot her a violent scowl.

The ID badge flew off her pants and hit the floor.

"Whoops."

There was no way that word should be sexy, but somehow it was.

Josie leaned down to pick up her badge right as he

turned to move out of her way. Her forehead connected with his thigh.

His pants were no thicker than hers and he could feel the warmth of her skin brush against him. Hot breath drizzled across his crotch as she gasped in surprise.

Houston took a fast step back. By sheer willpower he prevented an erection from popping up and embarrassing the hell out of both of them.

"Oh, sorry, my fault," she said, brushing her hair out of her green eyes. The movement made her shirt pull up, exposing a tiny ribbon of pale smooth skin above her waistband.

If he opened his mouth, the only thing that would come out would be a primitive growl, so he kept his lips clamped tight.

This time when she started towards the hall, she tripped. Over nothing, from his point of view. But as she stumbled, he reached out and grabbed her arm to steady her.

"Thanks," she said in a breathless voice, her moist pink tongue peeking out from under her shiny teeth. The corners of her eyes crinkled as she smiled.

If she had any idea how close he was to yanking down her pants and sliding into her, she wouldn't be smiling at him.

She would be running.

Or moaning.

Shit.

Houston dropped her arm. "You're welcome."

Annoyed, he turned his back on her to hide the hard-on that he could no longer keep at bay. He stood rigid and listened to her leave the room, her shoes squeaking on the tile floor.

He was never this greedy, this needy, this wanting. It made him feel reckless and vulnerable, out of control.

All feelings he despised.

The first of his rules wasn't one he was about to break. There wasn't ever going to be any woman who would entice him into wanting a relationship, or even more than one night. But Josie Adkins was well on her way to beguiling him to toss the second rule out the window.

He'd never slept with a co-worker, but then he'd never been this distracted by a woman's backside either. There were a thousand reasons why dating Josie would be a disaster. But the reasons against it dipped down to only several hundred when he thought about just having a quick, burning-hot affair with Josie.

Would an affair be wrong? Yes. But so was repairing Mrs. Kransky's kneecap while sporting an erection, which he was going to have to do in another minute, since his dick was not cooperating and deflating.

Sleeping with Josie wouldn't just be inappropriate, it would also be a mistake, of course.

Houston had made mistakes in his life, though nothing monumental or unfixable, including proposing to his first lover in a fit of Jack Daniels-inspired euphoria at age sixteen.

He'd skirted disaster on that one—and given up alcohol for life—and would on this, too, if he handled it with a little bit of discretion. As long as no one knew and it was just a night or two . . .

Houston grabbed the film and started towards the door. *No.* He would not give in to his base carnal urges.

Unless Josie gave him the slightest hint that she was interested.

Then he wasn't sure he could stop himself from taking a taste of those lips. All of them.

"It makes no sense!" Josie said to her friend Sara as she tried to peel back the wrapper on her cream cheese packet. "I mean, why is this happening to me? I can't go within two feet of Dr. Hayes without dropping something."

It only happened when *he* was in the room.

Left on her own, she was capable and confident. But when Houston Hayes approached her with his deep, penetrating stare and towering strength, blood pressure cuffs seemed to jump out of her hands and to the floor. Scalpels dropped and spun like bottles. Her hands shook, her hips knocked into gurneys and surgical trays, and she tripped over intravenous tubing.

It had to stop.

She was a grown woman of twenty-seven, with a medical degree, well-respected by the hospital staff and her patients. She was starting the second year of her orthopedic residency with relative ease and competence. Except for the Dr. Hayes–induced Dropping Medical Equipment Syndrome.

Sara raised her eyebrow and stirred cream into her coffee. "It's called sexual tension, Josie."

All Josie heard was sex. The top pulled back with a sudden jerk and the cream cheese container went sailing out of her hand. It skidded to a stop under the table next to her, where two male doctors were eating their dinner by the windows that boasted a view of the Florida coastline. She sat there stricken while Sara grinned at her. Josie was not amused.

"It's not sexual tension," she whispered urgently, standing to retrieve the now useless bagel spread.

That was a lie. No matter what he felt, it was definitely sexual tension on her part.

For one simple reason.

Dr. Hayes was a god.

Every inch of him—from his short black hair, to his gorgeous ice-blue eyes, and all down the length of his muscular, toned body—screamed power. Control.

A man who knew what he wanted and took it without any doubts or delays. The desire to be the taken had been creeping up on her steadily until she had found herself suffering from chronic klutziness in his presence.

So maybe what Sara said did make sense. But that didn't make it any easier.

Josie bent under the neighboring table and said to the pair of doctors, "Sorry, guys, I dropped my cream cheese." They moved their legs while she fished out the wayward package, neither surprised nor upset to see Josie on the floor collecting fallen items. Her colleagues at Acadia Inlet Hospital were starting to expect it.

"No problem, Josie," Mark Givens said with a grin, tucking into his hamburger.

His grin said it all. Everyone thought she was a royal idiot, incapable of holding onto a simple pack of cream cheese. How in the heck could she expect to be a surgeon if her fingers weren't steady on snack foods? Eight years of education and in a matter of three months she had jeopardized all of that.

Because of sex. Or lack thereof.

She blamed a certain orthopedic surgeon entirely. If he wouldn't stare at her with those probing ice-blue eyes, and stand way too close for comfort, she wouldn't get nervous. And when she got nervous, she dropped things.

She sat back down with Sara and sighed. "I'm ruining my career before I've even gotten started. Dr. Hayes is afraid to trust me with a scalpel, and who can blame him?"

Sara pulled to tighten her blond ponytail. "You're caught in a vicious cycle. He makes you nervous, so you act like a klutz, which makes him doubt your qualifications. Then you get more nervous, and on it goes."

Josie knew she was right. From the first day she had met Houston three months earlier when he joined the staff, she had been intimidated by him. By his confidence, his coolness, and his surgical skill.

"So what am I supposed to do? He won't even let me close a case, let alone conduct a surgery on my own. And I certainly can't go to the resident chief and complain about it." Josie felt even worse just thinking about it. "I'd look like a whiner and besides, what if Dr. Hayes tells Dr. Sheinberg I'm an idiot who needs my medical degree revoked?"

Becoming a surgeon was a lifelong goal, one she had been working towards steadily since high school. When her dad had died, himself a surgeon, she had been doubly determined to be successful.

Tripping over thin air and scrambling around on her hands and knees for X-rays wasn't the way to do it.

Sara tossed her spoon down on the table and grinned. "You know what they say if someone intimidates you. You need to picture them being powerless. Like standing in front of you in just their underwear."

Underwear? Josie's face began to burn. The sudden image of six-foot-three, tanned, muscular Dr. Hayes standing in front of her in a pair of black boxer briefs sent her senses into a tailspin. "Are you trying to torture me?" Her voice was a strangled whisper.

Sara shrugged. "Or you could just sleep with him. That ought to reduce him to human status."

While Sara made it sound no more exciting than a stroll down the produce aisle, it made Josie flushed and uncomfortable, even in the air-conditioned room. "That's even worse! I can't have sex with my orthopedic mentor."

There could even be rules against that, for all she knew, never having looked into the hospital fraternization policy. Besides, not that the guy was easy to read, but from what she could tell, Houston wasn't all that impressed with her. Intellectually or physically. Josie was used to men dismissing her on both counts, and Dr. Hayes appeared to be no exception.

She added, "I'm sure he would laugh hysterically at the prospect of sleeping with me. He doesn't even like me. At least I don't think he does."

He sure in the heck spent a lot of time frowning at her. Probably trying to determine how a clueless idiot like her had survived medical school.

And he never smiled. Not at her.

Of course there was that other look he gave her sometimes, the deep and penetrating look that made her want to glance down and check to see if her clothes were on. She had convinced herself she was imagining it, that it was the wishful thinking of a sex-starved imagination, but maybe she wasn't.

"Sometimes, Sara, I catch him staring at me, and I swear, he has The Look in his eye. But that's crazy, I must be wrong, I know I'm wrong." She fanned her face just at the thought of Houston's eyes sweeping over her body.

"What look?" Sara paused with her coffee mug halfway to her mouth.

Josie glanced around to make sure no one was paying attention to them and lowered her voice to a barely audible whisper. "The If-we-were-alone-I'd-rip-your-clothes-off look."

It wasn't a look she had seen often in her life, given that most men saw her as a slightly chubby, cheerful companion. Like a living Care Bear. But the few times she had seen that kind of sexual intent were burned into her memory.

Sara set her mug down. "Are you sure?"

"No, I'm not sure." It could be a total delusion on her part, brought about by poor sleeping habits and lack of sexual release.

After all, Dr. Hayes was *hot.* He could have any

woman he wanted, she was sure, so why would he want her? The two P's. Perky and plump.

"My life is ruined," she wailed. It was so like her to do something as idiotic as falling for the man who held her career in his hands.

"Don't be so dramatic, Josie."

"Easy for you to say." Tall and thin, with dark glasses, Sara looked studious and was taken seriously. "People respect you. I always have to prove myself over and over again before I'm taken seriously."

It was the curse of being cute. She was embarrassingly short, taller only than the average sixth-grade boy, and for ease of styling, wore her brown hair cropped. She had also been born with dimples, which didn't aid her cause.

Add to all of that her natural buoyant personality, and most people dismissed her as less than intelligent. Which was why it was so frustrating to be contributing to that prejudice by her own behavior with Dr. Hayes.

Sara blotted her lips with a paper napkin. "Do you ever worry that by becoming a surgeon, you're denying your natural self? That maybe you're meant to do something more . . . whimsical."

"Whimsical?" Josie sat back and wondered how she could ever have thought Sara was her best friend. "What do you want me to do? Twist balloon animals? Make hemp jewelry? I had a 4.0 grade point average in college. I graduated magna cum laude!"

She didn't care if her voice went a little loud. She was proud of that gold braid she'd gotten to wear around her neck at graduation.

Stirring another packet of cream into her half-empty coffee cup, Sara shook her head. "That's not what I meant. But you're also a social, cheerful person who is in a profession that is made up mostly of arrogant men who don't go in for conversation. It just seems to me that having to deny the gregarious and fun-loving side of yourself every day has you rattled."

Interesting theory and not as offensive as Josie had originally thought. But she knew what had her rattled, and it wasn't having to slow down her motormouth.

"Thank you, Dr. Phil. But I think it's a lot simpler than that."

She just wanted to jump Dr. Hayes's bones. Simple.

Josie shook her head. "While surgery may not exactly be fun-loving, even if I wanted to I couldn't back out now. People would think I was insane, and I would have to be, to toss out all those years of education and money. I just want Dr. Hayes to treat me like any other physician, like a *male* physician." If she kept telling herself that, maybe she would start to believe it.

"But how is that going to happen if I'm falling all over myself and blushing every time he's near me?"

"I don't even know what you see in him," Sara said, her brown eyes puzzled. "He's so cold."

What did she see in him that made her pulse jump and her hands shake? Beyond the handsome face and rock-solid body, that is. "He's brilliant, Sara. The man is absolutely calm during surgery, confident without being arrogant. He knows what he's doing."

She felt her insides turn to oatmeal just thinking about him. Her hand propped her head up on the table as she continued. "He's so focused on being a fantastic surgeon that he has this amazing tunnel vision. Nothing else around him matters."

Josie wished she had that level of concentration.

Sara wasn't impressed. "That sounds annoying to me. I always thought that was the nice thing about being a pediatrician. There aren't a lot of inflated egos running around my office."

"It's not annoying to me." She sighed a little, indulging in the fantasy of Houston turning those focused blue eyes on her, and placing his skilled hands somewhere between her medial thighs. Or in layman's terms, on her hot spot.

"I really wish you hadn't suggested the underwear thing. Now the next time I see Dr. Hayes I'm going to be picturing him naked." Who knew what she'd drop or fall on with that image in her mind. She'd be lucky if she didn't impale herself by accident.

Sara grinned. "It's just jealousy on my part. At least you're getting The Look. I haven't had a date in a year. The only penises I see are on eight-month-old boys."

Josie laughed. "Not the same, is it?"

"Hardly." Then Sara sat up straight and her eyes went wide. "Ohmigod, ohmigod, I *saw* it."

Turning a little in her seat, she said, "What? Saw what?"

"Don't turn around!" Sara hissed. "Dr. Hayes just walked in."

Josie froze, half-turned like she was in the middle of a bizarre yoga ritual. "Why not? What's he doing?"

"He gave you The Look. I saw it." Flapping her hands back and forth, Sara was acting like she'd just witnessed a UFO sighting. "Whew, the temperature just shot up ten degrees in here."

Josie felt the hairs on the back of her neck stand up and she pinched her lips as she faced forward again, determined not to look at Dr. Hayes.

"This is crazy." She pushed her unappealing plain bagel away. "I feel like I'm in the high school cafeteria, not the hospital. I'm fantasizing about this guy and I don't even know him at all. The only time we talk is when he's reprimanding me for my latest bout of idiot-itis."

"Sometimes you just don't need words."

Josie pictured Dr. Houston Hayes wearing nothing but a stethoscope, giving her an internal exam.

Oh, crikey.

Sara had no idea how profound her statement was.

Chapter Two

Unable to stand the feeling of Dr. Hayes's disapproving eyes on the back of her head, Josie fled the cafeteria a minute later. She brushed bagel crumbs off her shirt and studied the ground as she rushed through the doorway, determined to pretend she didn't see him.

In the hall, she said good-bye to Sara, who was on her way back to pediatrics. "Are we still going shopping tomorrow?"

Sara gave her the thumbs-up as she pushed the UP button for the elevator. "I need your moral support. Bathing suit shopping is the single most traumatizing experience in a woman's life. I can't think why I ever thought living next to the beach was a good idea." She gestured up and down her lean frame. "I always feel about as sexy as a number two pencil in a bathing suit. I'm just as flat as one."

"Oh, please." Josie rolled her eyes and laughed at Sara's exaggeration. Sara was thin, but since Josie had spent a childhood shopping in the Pretty Plus department, it was hard for her to dredge up a lot of sympathy. She tended to be round in strategic places like her behind and her chest, another undesirable result of being short. Or more likely it was related to hating exercise, and loving ice cream.

Whatever the cause, for the most part weighing more than the media portrayal of perfect didn't bother her. She had no interest in self-inflicted starvation, but sometimes she did feel a bit of longing for a man to give her the so-called Look. She was reasonably attractive, with a cute figure if you went for curves, yet guys always treated her with a best-buds kind of attitude and frankly, she was tired of it.

But being tired of it, and knowing how to fix it, were two separate things. She had no clue how to address the problem without completely altering her personality, learning the art of smoldering looks, and undergoing outpatient liposuction. Since none of those choices appealed to her, it seemed she was doomed to remain man's best friend.

With a final wave towards Sara, she pushed her way into the surgical recovery room and approached bed three.

"Mr. Davidson, how are you feeling?" Josie leaned over the gurney bed and studied his complexion, putting Dr. Hayes out of her mind with effort.

Even at seventy-two, Mr. Davidson was one of their livelier patients, and she was confident the knee replacement surgery he had just undergone would have him back on the golf course in no time.

Mr. Davidson's case had been the fifth or so total knee she had assisted Dr. Hayes on, and despite the fact that Dr. Sheinberg had allowed her to perform the surgery in the past, Dr. Hayes never did. She had been hopeful that Dr. Hayes would let her operate on Mr. Davidson, but he had merely taken over without a word. At this rate she'd need her own knee replacement surgery by the time Dr. Hayes decided she was ready to operate.

Mr. Davidson's eyes focused on her sharply, despite having awakened from the procedure only two hours earlier. "Doing fine, Dr. Adkins. Just a few more hours of sleep, then I'm ready to test this metal piece out."

She smiled, since she knew he was kidding. At least she hoped he was kidding. She checked his hemovac for blood. "You know you're going to have intense physical therapy ahead of you. No jumping up and dancing a jig now, you hear?"

He winked at her, his complexion rosy and healthy. "Yes, ma'am."

She gave his good leg a squeeze through the blanket. Charlie Davidson was a real character. "That's more like it."

It was times like these, when she was talking with patients, that she worried in the back of her mind that surgery wasn't for her. Not that she should be doing something *whimsical,* despite what Sara thought. But that she would be more suited to the people-oriented areas of general practice or pediatrics.

However, she had chosen surgery, specifically orthopedic surgery to specialize in, and there was no going back now. It just wasn't acceptable to change your mind in the second year of your residency. Of course, she hadn't really chosen surgery, her father had, but she had to make the best of it.

She knew that she would be good at it, and had handled her cases with Dr. Sheinberg well. Then Dr. Hayes had joined the ortho group and she had morphed into a stammering, clumsy comedy act.

Mr. Davidson said, "You know the only reason I'm even here is for the hospital food and to see your pretty face every day." He gave her a cheeky grin.

She couldn't help but smile as she checked his vitals. "That's an awful lot of pain to go through just to see me and to get a meal."

"What pain? I'm not in any pain."

"Wait until the anesthetic from surgery wears off,"

she warned him, once again amazed at the man's vigor. His blood pressure was just as it should be.

He shrugged. "Then I'll have the nurse get me those little blue pills. Those work." He impatiently shoved the IV tubing out of his way. "But enough about me. Let's talk about you. I see you're not wearing a wedding ring."

Making a notation of his vitals on his chart, she looked up, amused. "Don't you think I'm a little young for you?"

He laughed, which dissolved into a post-surgical cough.

"I made you cough," she said cheerfully. "That's good. It clears your lungs." She helped him to a sitting position.

"You're not my type," he said with a grin as he caught his breath. "Never went in for brunettes myself. No, I was thinking about my grandson. He's about your age, a lawyer, looks like that Tom Cruise fellow the girls are always raving about."

Josie dropped his chart back on the foot of the bed. Shaking her head, she held up her hand and laughed. "No, thank you."

She wasn't lonely enough to succumb to blind dates arranged by medicated patients. "Now, if you be good, the nurse will arrange for you to be moved to your room on the floor, and let your wife pop in to see you. I'll stop by first thing in the morning to make sure you're behaving."

With a wave and a smile, Josie turned around to leave and connected with something solid. She knew immediately it was Dr. Hayes' chest, since she had mentally catalogued every inch of his body.

Well, not *every* inch.

Some she'd had to leave to her very vivid imagination.

Her cheek brushed against his hard, muscular pectorals beneath his light blue scrub shirt before she darted back quickly to avoid further contact. Which had her colliding with her patient's bedside tray, spilling his cup of water and knocking his glasses to the floor.

"Oh! Sorry Mr. Davidson." She quickly retrieved the glasses and stood up in time to see Dr. Hayes sigh with long-suffering patience.

She suspected he was tired of her clumsiness. As if she were enjoying it.

"Mr. Davidson is doing well. BP and oxygen levels normal." She gave him a wide smile.

It was a skill she had perfected, smiling like a demented flight attendant even in the face of cold disapproval.

He ignored her and proceeded to check all the readings that Josie had just recorded on the chart. She stood there silently, feeling humiliation slide into anger. Surely he thought her capable of doing a simple BP read? A second-week nursing student could do that.

"How are you feeling, Mr. Davidson?" Dr. Hayes said in a clipped voice as his eyes ran over the IV bag and heart rate monitor.

"Fine, just sleepy. You're not going to ask me the same questions Dr. Adkins just did, are you?" Mr. Davidson's smile was considerably less warm than the ones he'd given Josie. "Because if it's all the same to you, I'd rather catch some shut-eye."

So there. Josie felt juvenile satisfaction.

"That's a great idea. We'll just see about moving you up to your room."

She'd beaten him to that, too. Josie said, in a patented cheerful voice, "I've already arranged it. Third floor is on their way to transport him."

He paused in the act of flicking his black hair out of his eye. "Well, aren't you the busy little bee?"

It shouldn't bother her, she knew. It was a casual

light comment he might have made to anyone, and she didn't imagine he intended to sound patronizing. But given her current mood of frustration, it rankled too much to let slip by without comment.

"Buzz, buzz," she said, capping her words off with another bright smile.

His eyes narrowed.

He gestured for them to leave, glancing at Mr. Davidson who seemed to be sleeping, or trying to anyway.

Conscious of Dr. Hayes following right behind her, she pushed through the doors of the recovery room and stepped out into the hall. She wondered if he intended to shadow her on her rounds, something he only did on occasion. Too bad she couldn't go home and clean the oven instead. With a toothbrush. That sounded about as fun.

A moment later he fell in step beside her, and touched her elbow. Josie came to a screeching halt, an embarrassing little gasp slipping out of her mouth. Yikes. Why the hell was he touching her?

"Can I speak to you a moment?" he said.

When she darted a glance over at him, he was frowning.

"Um, sure, of course." Like she was going to tell her boss no.

"In private."

Josie felt her lip drop down into the area of her chest as she stared at him. "No problem."

She was in trouble. There was no other explanation. He was going to fire her and suggest she take her drop-and-spill act on the road with Carrot Top.

"Your office?" she suggested, trying to sound like the mature adult she sometimes was. She couldn't prevent a little wheezing sound from escaping her mouth, though.

Dr. Hayes looked around the empty hallway and shook

his head. "That's halfway across the building. Let's just go in here."

And he opened the door to the supply room and gestured for her to step inside.

A darkened room.

Alone.

Again.

In private.

The underwear image returned, full force.

Her body flushed, and her nipples perked up.

He closed the door behind them.

Just think of something else, that's what she needed to do. Picture all those student loans that had to be repaid.

It wasn't helping. Josie was breathing hard and sweating between her breasts when Dr. Hayes turned around and gave her a slow, curious once-over.

Even when he flicked the light on, bathing her in artificial brightness, it didn't help dispel her anxiety. Sexual tension. Yep. Sara was right.

"Is something wrong?" she forced herself to say.

He folded his arms across his broad chest and reached a hand up to rub at his chin. Josie could see he hadn't shaved that morning, and he had an attractive, earthy stubble under his bottom lip.

"Are you getting enough sleep, Dr. Adkins? Are the shifts too demanding?"

Her first thought was that she had unflattering dark circles under her eyes, but then she realized he was probably referring to her klutziness.

"I'm fine," she said immediately, in what she hoped was a confident voice. "I can handle the schedule perfectly well, it's not a problem."

The shifts were brutal at times, but that was to be expected at this stage in her career. She had known all of that going into med school.

Chewing her lip she chanted to herself, *Don't fire*

me, don't fire me, please, I'll stop thinking lustful thoughts about you and will no longer sneak glances at your crotch . . .

"I have to admit I'm a little puzzled. On paper, you're an excellent physician, with top med school grades."

Josie relaxed a little. It was true. She'd worked her not-so-small butt off in med school.

"But I haven't seen any evidence of that in my time here."

Whoops. Staring at the floor, heart pounding, she hedged. "I don't know what you mean. Has a patient or staff member complained about me?"

He shook his head, stepping back a foot to lean against the shelving unit holding blankets and gowns. "That's not what I mean. It's just that you seem distracted. You're always fumbling around, dropping things."

Grateful for the dim room hiding her burning cheeks, Josie pressed her lips together and tried to figure out how to reassure him she wasn't a total dipshit.

"I'm not clumsy when it counts, with the patients, so does it really matter? My mother didn't name me Grace, after all." She gave a little laugh.

There was a prolonged silence.

Dr. Hayes narrowed his eyes, studying her so intimately that she fought the urge to squirm. And the man wondered why she dropped things. Her whole body was vibrating with lust under his scrutiny.

She always thought he would have made a great cop. Interrogation and intimidation wouldn't have been a struggle for him. Whenever he looked at her like that, she felt the need to confess to everything but third-world poverty.

"If you're having problems, you should discuss them with someone. Any one of the staff doctors would be willing to listen and help you." He tugged on his bottom lip in a gesture that made her mouth go dry.

What would it feel like to have that mouth on her? So serious, so concentrated, so determined? She shivered.

"I would listen, Josie. You could tell me if something was wrong."

His voice was low, persuasive, and at the sound of her name tripping off his tongue so softly, she swallowed hard. He had never called her Josie before. "I don't have any problems, Dr. Hayes, I promise."

"Boyfriend troubles, maybe? A recent breakup or a guy who . . . mistreats you?"

This conversation was going from awkward to absurd. He seemed determined to find an explanation for her behavior, but she could hardly tell him the truth. That she wanted him so bad he scattered her thoughts like pool balls in the first break of the game.

"No. I don't have a boyfriend. And if I did, I would never let that interfere with my work here at the hospital." And on that point she was firm. Never was she anything less than confident in her contact with patients, despite Dr. Hayes's unnerving presence.

She knew her job.

It was all those pesky things like walking and carrying that seemed to be a struggle for her.

He stood up, taking a step forward, towering over her, his manner coaxing. "Sometimes we don't mean for those things to interfere. But something . . . someone distracts us, and we find our concentration broken."

Crap, she was *caught*. He knew she wanted him to throw her down on the nearest gurney and have his way with her. This was horrible. This was like body odor. Embarrassing, and difficult to cover once it's been discovered.

"I . . ." she said in a breathless little voice that sounded like she'd been hitting the helium on her lunch hour. "I don't know what you mean."

"Don't you?" Another step and he was right in front of her, close enough to touch, in smelling distance. He wore no cologne, and his scent was a mix of antiseptic soap and musky man.

Which made her wonder what she smelled like to him. Probably like sweaty fear, or maybe sexually aroused, which she was. Geez, she didn't even know which would be worse. Under the circumstances, both were mortifying. Lifting her arm subtly for a little armpit air circulation, she cleared her throat as she touched her neck.

How could he have figured out she was attracted to him? How the hell could he know?

And what exactly was he going to do about it? Force her to confess she wanted him? She'd rather undergo a hysterectomy without anesthetic.

Unless, just maybe she was right about The Look and he *was* interested in her. Then she'd be an idiot not to tell him he made her ache with want, and despite her recent embarrassing track record, Josie was no idiot.

The trick was figuring out whether he was or he wasn't.

Houston knew he needed to stop. Put an end to this conversation and walk out with his rules intact.

But he couldn't. Josie was too appealing. She was ripe and round and breathing a little hard in the hushed small room, her eyes wide.

"I don't know what you mean, I really, really don't, I swear, nothing is bothering me."

Ignoring the way her words were tumbling over each other, he reached out and ran his thumb across her bottom lip, enjoying the soft full flesh under his touch. The gesture startled her, if the two-foot leap she made was any indication. But he didn't care.

"Dr. Hayes?"

"Call me Houston." He didn't want to be a doctor right this minute. He wanted to be a man. A man who was going to kiss the sexy woman in front of him.

He'd told himself he wouldn't kiss her until she showed interest, and so maybe alarm couldn't be classified as such, but she wasn't smacking his hand away either.

"Houston . . ." She licked her lips. "We have a problem."

His fingers stopped sliding across her cheekbone as Josie realized what she had said and giggled.

"I guess you've heard that one before, huh?"

There was a bright sparkle in her eyes, so adorable that he couldn't bring himself to be annoyed the way he usually was when someone made an Apollo 13 reference. "Once or twice." Or a thousand times. He'd lost count.

Leaning forward, he kissed the corner of her mouth, then the other. A little gasp left her, but she didn't move away. Her lips were soft and moist from wetting them with her tongue, and they fell open as he brushed over her a third time. Right in the center, flush on her mouth with his.

Josie sighed, her mouth receptive to him, relaxed.

She tasted like apple juice, sweet and ripe, willing, and he fought to keep his eyes open and his hands off her body as he pulled back.

This wasn't what he had intended to do with her in here. He had meant to clear the air, make sure she didn't have a more serious problem than chronic klutziness. But he couldn't be sorry that he'd kissed her.

Nor did he feel sorry for what he was about to propose.

"The problem, Josie, is that you're driving me crazy."

"I am?" She shook her head, flustered, eyes unfocused. "Oh, right, with all the dropping and the tripping. I don't mean to, you know, it just happens."

"That's not what I meant." He buried his nose in the hair by her ear and breathed in deeply. Strawberries. Damn. She was practically a fruit farm.

"I meant you're driving me crazy because I want you."

"Want me?" Her breath hitched, and he felt goose bumps rising on her jaw and neck, but she still didn't pull away. "Want me for what?"

That she could even say that, so innocently, made him hard.

"I want you for this." He plunged his hand into her short hair, drew her flush up against him, and gave her a real kiss. A lip-sliding, mouth-open, tongue-tasting kiss that had them both panting and wide-eyed.

"Oh," she said, looking up at him before darting her eyes over to the closed door to the hallway.

He could hear the standard hustle-and-bustle, voices carrying down the hall as business went on as usual in the hospital. This was risky, inappropriate, and he was still new on staff. He should care that someone could walk in at any second, but he didn't.

"Are you serious?" she asked.

Seriously out of his mind with lust. "Very. I'm attracted to you, Josie, and we need to discuss what we're going to do about it."

Josie gave an awkward laugh. "I thought you couldn't stand me."

Had she just missed the kiss he'd given her? "Hardly. Now tell me that you're attracted to me, too." So he could lean her against that door to prevent a possible interruption and kiss her again.

Josie worried her bottom lip with her teeth then gave another heartfelt sigh. "Okay, here's the thing. I am something of a klutz, but I've never been this bad before and it's all your fault."

Her fingers gripped his shirt and pushed him lightly to emphasize her point. "I feel like you're always watching, waiting for me to screw up, and I've had this sort of ridiculous crush on you."

Her cheeks were pink, eyes wide, and Houston kept quiet, liking the sound of this, wanting to hear where this could go. Desire punched him in the gut at her admission that she was attracted to him.

"Silly, really, because you're . . ." She waved her hand around in front of him. "And I'm . . ." Gesturing to herself, she blew a loud breath out of the corner of her mouth.

He had no idea what that was supposed to mean, and he was about to ask her, when she glanced toward the door again.

"But anyway, I don't think this is the place to discuss this."

Josie stepped back out of his reach. He took her hand, pulling her to a stop, not about to let her escape now that he'd gotten a teasing taste of her. She had admitted she was attracted to him as well, and that was just the green light he'd been looking for.

He knew he should let her go. He should forget he had started this and walk out of here with his sanity intact. Except that he would go crazy if he couldn't have Josie. The ache was too strong, too burning, deep inside where it plagued him and distracted him every minute in her presence.

He had to have her.

"Have dinner with me tonight. Then spend the night."

"What?" She stopped trying to tug her arm out of his hand and gaped at him.

So it wasn't pretty. It wasn't charming, it wasn't skilled or poetic or coaxing.

It was the truth.

Put baldly before her.

He didn't want any misunderstandings. This was sex and nothing more. This was about fucking her out of his system so he could get back to more important things like his patients.

Josie knew she should be big-time insulted. Houston was standing there, calm as you could be, offering her dinner and a quick dive under the sheets. She was too confused to know how to act, having no experience up until now with men proposing hot, passionate flings.

It seemed she had been right about The Look. But The Look didn't come with anything else. She was still convinced he didn't particularly like her, and it was even possible his attraction to her angered him.

All of which were serious red flags to grab her dignity and run out of this room.

Yet here she still was.

Turned on and seriously considering his offer. After all, how many times in her life was she going to have a gorgeous, dark-haired surgeon claiming he had to have her? She was betting this was the one and only.

Josie studied his face, looking for signs of dishonesty or entrapment. Maybe this was an ethics test. *Surgeon boss offers sex-drenched one night together, possibly jeopardizing your career. Do you take him up on it?*

"You don't mince words, do you?"

"I want you. You want me. I don't see any reason to wait." He ran his fingers through his hair. "It's getting damned awkward between us here at the hospital, don't you think?"

"And how would sleeping together fix that?" she asked in amazement, picturing herself slinking into the hospital after a night of carnal passion with Houston

Hayes. If she was nervous now, she'd be an absolute marshmallow then.

He smiled. *Oh, no.* He'd never smiled at her before, and it was a sexy, caressing little lift of the corner of his mouth. A smile that would have her pressed against the wall dropping her drawers if she wasn't careful. She gave another futile tug on her arm. He held her tightly.

"The sexual tension will be gone. We go out tonight, we enjoy each other, we come back and everything can return to normal."

That was rationalization at its worst.

His thumb rubbed the back of her wrist, and she swallowed hard. That kiss he'd given her had stolen every last vestige of common sense, his hot tongue sweeping reserve away and making her feel sexy, desired.

Josie had the overwhelming urge to give in, to take what he was offering and have a night of good, not-so-clean fun. But this was her career at stake. Her brain understood that even if her inner thighs didn't.

"I'm not convinced that would rid us of the awkwardness."

"It can't be any worse than it is now."

He had a point. "This is my career, Dr. Hayes." If she called him Houston, she just might lose it and fling herself back into his arms. "I can't let it get out that there's something between us. You're my boss."

Houston stiffened. "No, I'm not. Dr. Sheinberg is your boss, he's the resident chief. I'm just a co-worker who has more experience than you do. There is a huge difference, and I have no power over your position."

Oh, great, he thought she was suggesting sex for surgical opportunities. "That's not what I meant! It's just that I'm new here, and I don't want staff to think I just sleep around. That could taint my career."

"This will protect both of our careers. One night. We're both adults. We can handle coming back next week, and then all this tension will be gone between us."

His expression was wry. "That way no one will know. Otherwise I think there's a high probability one day we'll get caught here in the supply room."

And to put truth to his words, he tugged lightly on her hand, and her feet, shod in sensible white sneakers, moved forward without instructions from her, until she was right against his chest. His hands roamed over her back, down to her behind, and squeezed her cheeks with light pressure. Josie shuddered, wanting to bump forward against him, wanting his hands *in* her pants, touching deep inside her.

It was wrong to feel so aroused. She knew that. He wasn't even being all that nice, but she was shivering with excitement. Men who were used to getting their way weren't her usual style, but nothing was usual about her reaction to Houston. Since the day she had met him, she had been off balance, and despite the uneasiness of her feelings, she was like oven-roasted chicken. Hot and moist.

The look on his face, the set of his jaw, excited her, thrilled her that he could want her so much that he'd risk being caught.

Her nipples pushed through the thin cotton of her scrubs as he lightly ran his finger across her breast. She drew her breath in hard, and felt her head dropping back. There had to be a reason she should say no, but she couldn't seem to remember what it was right then.

"I love the way you smell." He trailed his lips along her neck. "And the way you taste."

A sudden unpleasant thought popped into her head. Maybe he had wanted a lot of other women in the hospital and she'd just never known about it. That was a lowering thought. "Have you done this before with any of the previous residents?"

His lips stilled on her skin. "No. You're the only one to even tempt me."

Then he laughed, soft and low, just under her ear. "But until now, all of the orthopedic residents I've run across have been men. Not a lot of women choose to be bone crackers. But no—no nurse, no doctor, no surgical assistant, has ever made me want to make out in a supply closet."

Josie was reeling. She was confused, overwhelmed, attracted to Houston beyond the rational, and she needed breathing room. She had to get away from him.

"I need time to think about it."

"Think about this, Josie."

Another crushing kiss fell on her lips, bruising in its intensity, shocking her with the possessive violence of it, and more so, her reaction to it. She felt telltale moisture between her thighs and a gnawing ache in the pit of her belly.

Both of his thumbs were moving back and forth across her nipples, flicking at the tight painful nubs until she was dizzy. It served to make her even less sure that they could spend the night together and return to work the better for it.

This desire was different, deeper than any she'd ever known, and one night might make her desperate for more. Not the other way around.

"How do you know one night will be the end of it?" she whispered when he broke off the kiss.

He shrugged. "I never want more than one night."

She should be appalled, disgusted by the thoughtless casualness of his remark.

Instead she found herself intrigued. That was a decisive remark to make when she could feel his erection resting against her thigh.

Curiosity gave way to determination to prove the arrogant Houston Hayes wrong.

With her, one night wouldn't be enough.

He would want more.

And he wasn't the only one who liked to be successful, especially when the odds were against her. Josie usually got what she wanted, too, no matter how hard she had to work at it or how long.

Chapter Three

Bob Andrews and Dave Jablonski were in the hall talking when Josie emerged breathless, even more scattered than usual, patting down her hair. Houston was right behind her, which made her blush when she realized there really wasn't any plausible reason for a doctor and a resident to be in a closed supply closet.

Both doctors looked up at her and she gave them a bright smile, hoping like hell no one would guess she'd just spent ten minutes getting felt up by Houston.

Dave smiled back at Josie. "Hey, Josie, we're all going to Coconuts for a drink in about an hour. Join us?" At the last minute he seemed to realize there was someone standing behind her. "Oh, you, too, Dr. Hayes. The more the merrier."

Josie noticed that everyone on staff always referred to one another by first names, with the exception of Dr. Hayes. She was starting to suspect he didn't want anyone to know he had a first name. Even his ID badge clipped to his waistband said merely Dr. Hayes. She knew. She'd looked.

Yet his name fit him. It was unusual, commanding. Erotic. Or maybe that was her hormones on overdrive again. But she suspected he used formality to maintain distance between himself and his colleagues, herself included until fifteen minutes ago. Now he wanted zero distance between them, clothing optional.

Which brought to mind a whole other unpalatable subject. Could she really bring herself to get naked in front of a man who by all rights should only exist in her fantasies? Forget sex. One look at her and he'd be mentally composing an article for the AMA on the overabundance of fat in the American diet.

"No thanks. The storm this afternoon kicked up a few waves, so I'm going surfing," Houston said.

She spun around in amazement. Surfing? Houston was a surfer? Not to mention that was the longest personal statement she'd ever heard him utter.

He was always all work, driven to perfection as a surgeon. He didn't engage in idle chitchat.

Even his kisses weren't idle. They, too, were skilled, concentrated. Perfect.

"Oh, yeah," Bob said with a nod. "Those waves are a solid five feet. Have fun out there."

Dave said, "Well, how about it, Josie? I don't think you're going surfing, are you?"

Relieved that no one seemed to notice the tension between her and Houston, she laughed at Dave's question. The most athletic thing she did was jump around in pain when she forgot her aqua socks and the sand on the beach burned her sensitive feet.

"No, no surfing for me. But I can't go to the bar anyway because I'm on call for ER."

"Okay. Maybe next time." They waved and continued on down the hall.

Which left her standing in the hall staring at the floor, no clue what to say to Houston. He had pressed her for an answer in the supply room. She hadn't given him one.

She knew what she wanted. But she still didn't know if it was the right thing to do. If she listened to her body and Houston's argument, she could ruin her career as a surgeon.

If word ever got out they'd had an affair . . . well, it would be ugly, no matter what he said.

Yet it was so darn tempting.

He spoke first. "You're quite the Miss Popularity, aren't you?"

"Excuse me?" There were about a million different interpretations to that statement, none of which were good.

He shrugged. "It's just that no matter what department we're in, everyone seems to know you."

She darted an amazed look at him. He looked almost bitter, despite his casual stance. Was Houston feeling left out of the hospital social circuit?

But that made no sense. The man shot out don't-come-near-me vibes on a constant basis. Not exactly the way to build friendships. He must just think of her as a charming little fluff who had flirted her way through medical school.

Or slept her way through medical school, given what he was proposing. Suddenly anger replaced a good portion of her nervousness. She was an intelligent woman, not a brainless bimbo.

"I've been here over a year now, and spent nine months doing ER orthopedic trauma, so I've met a lot of people. And set lots of bones," she added, hoping to beef up her resume in his eyes. "Plus I work a lot of double shifts to gain experience, and do two rotations a month for ER instead of one."

His eyes narrowed as he studied her, his hands on the hips of his scrub pants. "Are you sure you're getting enough sleep?"

"I told you, that's not what's been distracting me."

Sudden awareness flared in the air between them.

"Don't take too long to make a decision."

Josie felt like she had already made her decision. "I'll let you know as soon as I have."

"Well, I'll see you on Monday then. I'm leaving for the day." His blue eyes rolled over her, without hurry and with possession. "Unless you make a decision before the night is over. Then just page me."

"And you'll come running?"

He smiled tightly. "Something like that."

More likely it would be her doing the running.

It was embarrassing to admit even to herself how long it had been since she'd slept with a man. Given that most men saw her as a funny little friend, she hadn't dated tons. Over the years she'd had a few boyfriends, of course, but even those had been lukewarm affairs, friendships more than grand passion.

She and her boyfriend Luke had called it quits after realizing that while they spent almost every day together palling around, they could go two or three weeks without sex and neither of them even seemed to notice. Never had she experienced a melt-your-panties kind of passion.

Right now her panties seemed convinced Houston was the man to melt them and were halfway to liquid already.

Houston started to brush by her at the same time she turned to go the opposite way.

Josie found herself knocking into his chest again, stumbling from the impact, bouncing around the hallway like a pinball with hair. His warm hands came out and gripped her arms to steady her.

"Sorry," she said, trying to quickly move out of his grip. Only she tripped over his foot. Her shoulder hit the wall behind him and she gave a nervous laugh. "Oops. I guess I haven't got that clumsy thing under control yet."

"I know a cure."

That was the problem. So did she. Only that particu-

lar cure seemed destined to land her in even hotter
water than she was in right now.

"What? Ritalin?" she joked.

He didn't laugh. "Just one night, Josie. I can guarantee you'll enjoy it."

Enjoyment wasn't in question. She was getting hot
with him just breathing in the same hallway with her.
"I'm sure I will . . . would. It's just I'm not sure this is
a good idea, I have too much at stake and I'm already
screwing up lately by acting like a klutzy flake. What
if this makes it worse and I blow my entire career to
pot?"

Screwing up her fists, she took a deep breath as he
just stared at her.

"I'm not going to stand around and try to talk you
into it. If you want me, you know where to find me."
He took a step away from her. "But do me a favor. If
you don't want to do this, stop wearing panties with
lips on your ass. And stop bending over. The two together would tempt a saint, and despite what patients
might say, I'm no saint."

It was not the term she would have chosen for him
either.

Her hands went to her behind, face burning. How
long had he been able to see through her pants? "I only
wear these on Saturdays. They're day-of-the-week
panties, and Saturday they're lips."

"Oh, my God," he said, before his eyes dropped down
below her waist as if he were visualizing a seven-day
panty parade.

Josie froze with her hands still on her ass. Every
inch of her body was dripping with desire, shot clear
through her until she was in agony. She was reduced to
the intellectual level of an amoeba.

"What are the other days?" Houston said, sounding
very intrigued.

Then some little devil in her, the one that was annoyed he had been so casual and blunt with her, smiled at him. "Since you only wanted one night, I guess you'll never know."

Houston drove his Jeep across the sand at Acadia Inlet Beach and glanced at the water.

The sight was incredible. The waves of the Florida coast were normally mild-mannered, making for only recreational surfing as opposed to the competitive level of beaches in Australia and Hawaii.

But today they were high and glorious, and he couldn't wait to test them out. He parked next to half a dozen other cars and cut out the engine, taking in a deep breath of the salty air. He loved the beach. He loved the feel of the hot sand beneath his feet and the warm water lapping around him.

It soothed him. It was the only place he let go, the one time in his life when he was willing to sacrifice control and let the ocean guide him. But even then, surfing was a fight against nature, a determination to control the wave, the ride, the outcome of each time he lifted onto his board.

As a kid he hadn't known control, watching his father mistreat his mother, knocking her around and more often than not coming home smelling like stale beer and sweat. The day his father had left for good was the best day of his life, and at that moment Houston had taken control. Of his life, his mother's, and his little sister Kori's.

He had only been fifteen, but he had been single-minded from then on, determined that he would find a way to be successful, to support his mother and sister.

He had achieved that. He enjoyed being a surgeon, and he knew he was good at it. When he did something, he liked to be successful at it. Sometimes he wondered if that's why he had never considered marriage. He didn't like to lose.

A game, a challenge, or his heart.

He fought for control to the bloody end of every battle, and knew he was far too cynical to make anyone a good husband. So he dated casually and spent the majority of his time focusing on his career now that his sister had married one of Houston's oldest friends and his mom was busy being a grandmother.

Giving quality of life back to elderly patients was satisfying. He took himself and that responsibility very seriously, and he was meticulous in his methods, checking and rechecking himself and his co-workers over and over again. His patients trusted him to heal them to the best of his ability, and he never wanted to compromise that trust.

Houston had been aware over the years that his bedside manner was a little lacking, but it had never been easy for him to start up conversations with people. He wasn't a talker. It was something he had to work at, force himself to remember to smile and make conversation. Unlike Josie Adkins, who he thought could chat with a tree stump.

After leaving the hospital for the day, he'd stopped off at home and changed into a T-shirt and swimming trunks. He pulled off the shirt and tossed it on the seat of his Jeep, shaking his head just at the thought of Josie.

He must have lost his fucking mind.

Instead of counseling her, like he had intended to, he had kissed the hell out of her and asked her to spend the night with him. He was just about certain she was going to say no.

Josie was already hanging on to her residency by a thread, and was clearly nervous that an affair with him would snap that tenuous hold. He didn't understand her logic. If one looked at her med school records, she was brilliant. Her rapport with the patients was fantastic. Yet she was nervous, tentative, and downright clumsy, none of which could be explained by an attraction to him alone.

He suspected at times that her heart wasn't in surgery, and that she would be happier in a more patient-oriented specialization. It was why he had held back on allowing Josie control in the operating room.

She was an enigma he hadn't figured out yet.

Not to mention she was damn adorable. And he was more interested in stripping off her little dick-tease lip-print panties than psychoanalyzing her.

Grabbing his shortboard out of the back of the Jeep, he turned his mind resolutely back to the surf. Josie was back in the cool, sterile, hushed hospital, while he was out here in the glorious sun facing the best swells all summer.

"Hey, Houston!"

He looked up to see Dennis and Christian walking across the sand towards him. He'd been surfing with these guys since high school, and he'd never doubted for a minute they'd be out here today, even if they all had more responsibilities now than they'd had fifteen years ago.

"Hey, guys, what's up?"

"What took you so long?" Dennis scolded as he dropped his board in the sand, and then himself.

"A patient. What do you think?" His friend would never guess he'd been begging for sex from a hospital colleague and he wasn't about to tell him.

Houston prodded Dennis's leg with his foot. "What are you laying down for? I'm ready to go out."

"I'm sitting this one out. I'm whipped today."

"Don't be an old lady," Houston said in disbelief. "These are the best waves all year."

Dennis rested back in the sand and closed his eyes,

dropping his hands on his chest. "You don't understand. I'm married. Tammy kept me up all last night."

"Jesus, that's more information than I need." Not to mention he was still partially erect from his teasing encounter with Josie an hour ago. He didn't need sex talk right now.

"What, are you embarrassed? You've gotten a conscience or something? You used to be a big talker, from what I remember." Dennis snorted.

"Yeah, well, you can't talk about what you're not getting." Not getting on a regular basis, anyway. He did envy Dennis and Christian that.

His buddies laughed at him, while he grumbled and pretended to check the wax on his board. "Besides, I never was one to blab about what I was doing with girls. That was you."

"You need a life outside of that germ-filled hospital, Houston," Christian said. "Kori's got another woman all lined up for you."

Oh, hell. Houston frowned.

He'd been friends with Christian for twenty years, way before the guy had gone and fallen for Houston's younger sister, Kori. While Houston had gotten over his buddy sleeping with his baby sister, and had learned to appreciate that Kori was in good hands since she'd married Christian, it also meant that his friendship with Christian was always tied to his sister. Which he could do without.

But he had a definite soft spot for Kori, despite her tendency to think the answer to all his problems lay in marrying one of her friends.

He didn't have the heart to tell her that he was never getting married, and that while he wasn't above having some company for dinner, there was no woman he would ask out twice. More than one date, and they started to have expectations.

Expectations he couldn't live up to.

Besides, he hadn't met anyone yet who had intrigued him enough to want more than one date.

Except for Josie Adkins.

Whose alluring qualities centered around her lush curves and how soon he could lick every inch of them.

"All right, I'll go on the date with Kori's friend," he told Christian with a shrug.

Christian clapped him on the back. "See, that's what I like about you. You're so easy-going. And all this matchmaking business keeps Kori's mind off having another baby, which is what she really wants to do."

"Two aren't enough?" Houston loved his two little nieces, ages four and two, but damn, they wore him out. He had serious doubts about his personal ability to deal with that kind of constant diaper-ridden chaos.

"It's plenty for me," Christian assured him. "But Kori's a born nurturer, you know, and with Abby out of the crib, she's got an empty spot."

"Buy her a dog," Dennis suggested. "They shit just as much, but they cost less."

Christian laughed. "Yeah, I'll suggest it to Kori just like that. I'm sure that will win her over."

As Dennis and Christian argued the merit of Labs versus Irish setters, Houston found himself wondering about Josie. He didn't know her very well, but he suspected she fell solidly into the category of a nurturer.

Which disturbed the hell out of him. He should count himself lucky that Josie looked inclined to say no to his offer of a single night of passion. She wasn't the one-night-stand type, and he might have found himself entangled in a big old emotional mess that wouldn't have fixed the tension between them, but increased it tenfold.

Yeah, he was feeling lucky all right. Too bad his rock-solid and sadly neglected dick didn't agree.

He interrupted the dog conversation. "So you're really sitting out this wave?" he asked Dennis.

When Dennis nodded, he said to Christian, "That's enough bullshitting for me, boys, I'm heading out. You coming?"

As Christian nodded, Houston kicked off his shoes and dropped his towel down on the sand next to Dennis. He tossed his cell phone onto it. He wasn't on call, and he didn't really expect Josie to page him, but on the off chance . . . he sure in the hell didn't want to miss her if she did.

With a firm grip on his board, he went down to the edge of the water, squishing the wet sand beneath his toes. He bent over and attached his leash to his ankle. The device kept him and his board from being separated if he fell off.

Then he was on his stomach, paddling out, relaxing under the hot sun. Christian was next to him, but they didn't talk. This time was for silence. For just enjoying the ocean and listening to the melodic roar of the waves rising and falling in a timeless pattern.

There were shouts of excitement and groans as other surfers rode and crashed, but Houston blocked those sounds out and concentrated just on stroking back and forth with his hands lightly skimming the surface of the warm water. When he came to a wave, he lifted his waist and let the water pass between him and the board.

Josie was on his mind again, a disturbing floating presence in his thoughts constantly, confusing him with her unexplainable attraction.

She walked with a bounce. Nearly a foot shorter than him, she had to almost run to keep up with his stride sometimes. How would that petite curvy body fit against his?

Her full chest would press against his ribs and her mouth would glide across his bare skin, rolling over him with teasing little strokes. Then she would go down on her knees and pull his cock into that same sweet pink mouth and he would hold her head against him, tugging on that short silly hair of hers.

He groaned aloud in disgust. Imagining her giving him head was not doing anything but giving him a huge boner in his swim trunks. Since he was in the water, and his trunks were soaked, he was going to shock the hell out of his fellow surfers when he stood up.

Yeah, it was a damn good thing she wasn't going to call him. Forget about *her* morning-after reaction to a night together. He wasn't sure he trusted himself not to want more.

Pathetic. He commanded himself to put Josie out of his mind, and focus on the wave rising in front of him instead. It was a big one.

On the outside of the crest, he suddenly leapt onto his board and hunched down, feeling the spray of the thrusting water fly across him as he turned the board quickly back and forth using his leg muscles.

He was on top of the wave, soaring through the air, catching a view of the huge expanse of mustard-colored beach and feeling the tenuous balance between him and his board, resting on nothing but water.

It was exhilarating.

He lasted a solid eight seconds before the crest buckled and he dropped into the pit at the bottom of the wave. In another second the whole of the wave crashed over the top of his head, sending him catapulting off his board and sailing through the water.

Closing his mouth, he let the surf pummel him and knock him around until he, the broken wave, and his dangling board all washed ashore.

Not one of his finer endings to a run.

Rubbing the dripping water off his face, he unhooked his leash and reined his board in with a self-satisfied grin. That had been a blast.

"Whoa, Ice, total wipeout."

Houston looked up from his undignified position sitting in two feet of water to see three teenage boys grinning at him. He shrugged it off. The fall had been worth the ride. These guys knew that as well as he did. They were out here just about every day and had nicknamed him Ice since he was known for riding his board without a lot of movement. He suspected it also had a thing or two to do with his serious personality. He wasn't exactly known for hanging around shooting the breeze.

One of the teens didn't look like he'd been in the water that day and was sporting a big bandage on his foot. "What happened to you, Andy? Jellyfish?"

Andy grinned, tossing back his scraggly brown hair. "No, I got bit by a shark yesterday. Six stitches in my foot."

"Really?" Houston stood up and leaned against his board. "Does it hurt?"

"Nah." Andy shrugged it off. "It was like getting a big paper cut, you know? It was a little shark, just a three-foot black-tip."

Black-tips were common in the waters around Acadia Beach and were known for coming in close to shore in search of fish and mistaking human limbs for them. Usually they sank their teeth in, then released quickly, probably realizing they'd bitten something bigger than them.

"Well, no going into the water until those stitches are out, all right?"

"I hear you."

Christian came up beside them. "How many is that? Like six bites in the last few weeks?"

"Something like that."

Another one of the boys said, "They were talking about closing the beach, but I think that's crazy. Getting bitten by a black-tip's no worse than a jellyfish, and they never talked about closing the beach for jellyfish."

Houston thought he had a point. Shark or jellyfish, nothing was going to stop the majority of them from coming out here.

"Did you see that sign the Coast Guard put up?" Christian asked as he gestured to the sign. "Warning. Dangerous marine life has been spotted in this area." He gave a snort. "Give me a break."

Houston agreed. He wasn't about to give up on the best waves he'd seen in a long time just on the off chance of getting a nip in the heel. Until someone got bit by a serious predator like a bull shark, he was going to stay in the water.

He was headed back toward the edge of the surf, intent on another wave, when he saw Dennis gesturing to him to come over. Annoyed at the interruption, he jogged back to his friend. It was getting late, and he wanted to get a few more runs in before the sun disappeared.

The diversionary tactic was working. While in the air on his board, he had actually gone a whole minute or more without thinking about Josie. Which lately was a damn record.

"What's up? You coming out this time?"

Dennis nodded. "Yeah, but your cell phone's buzzing."

Shit. Houston stared at it, lying so innocently on his navy blue towel. It couldn't be her.

But it could be.

He went hard, tight with need and aching with tension.

Dennis glanced at him as he stood up and brushed off his swim trunks. "Aren't you going to see who it is?"

"Maybe." He shouldn't want this. It was a bad idea

for all the reasons Josie had outlined, plus the half-dozen or so he'd come up with on his own.

Yet he still wanted it. He wanted her. He could taste her kiss on his lips again, feel her curves pushed against him, and hear her anxious little breaths.

Fuck, he wanted her.

Dennis shook his head. "You need to get a life. You're starting to get weird, man."

Houston ignored him and bent over. He picked up the phone and read the text message.

Call me. Josie.

Yes. Giddy with relief and anticipation, he stuffed his wet sandy feet into his shoes and plucked his towel off the ground.

"Where are you going?" Dennis demanded. "You just got here."

The best waves all season suddenly held little interest in light of the alternative. He clapped Dennis on the shoulder.

"I've got a date. Sometimes even us single guys get lucky."

And he was planning on getting really lucky.

All night long.

Chapter Four

They had cancelled her second shift.

It was like a sign.

Divine permission to run off and indulge in a night of temporal lust with Houston Hayes.

Yet she hesitated.

Sara, who had stopped by to see if she wanted to go out to dinner, had a thing or two to say on the subject.

"I think you're insane if you don't do it."

"Well, thank you for your support." Josie ran her fingers through her hair as she pulled a pair of shorts out of her locker to change into.

They were grubby shorts. Sort of grunge meets *That 70s Show*. Normally Josie just wore her scrubs back and forth to the hospital on surgery days, but if she was going to meet up with Houston, she thought she should change. But these shorts that she'd unearthed in her locker weren't exactly going to set the man on fire.

Sara looked at the shorts in horror as Josie pulled them on. "Where are you going wearing those? To visit someone in prison?"

It was easy for Sara. As a pediatrician, she got to wear cute floral skirts and sundresses to work every day. Josie alternated between scrubs on surgery days and khaki-colored pants her mother would call slacks when she attended clinics.

"I'm going home. Alone." She wasn't going to call Houston. She couldn't.

It would be a mistake.

But such a naughty, good, orgasmic mistake.

She squeezed her eyes shut. Dammit. A picture of him in tight briefs, strutting towards her, ready to tear her clothes off, would not vacate her distraught brain.

The kiss had done her in. If he could make her pant with a kiss, she just knew he could make her scream with a strategically placed touch or two. And didn't she deserve to scream, after all? Didn't she work hard? Houston's plan to give in to all of their pent-up lust for one sex-drenched night would solve all her complications at work. Wouldn't it?

No, no, and no.

Sara pushed her glasses up. "We're back to the part about you being crazy."

"Sara, it's not a good idea. I can't risk it."

"Then let me have him." Sara grinned at her.

It was supposed to be funny. Just a joke. But Josie found herself feeling anything but amused. She didn't want Houston. But she didn't want anyone else to want him.

Who exactly was she kidding? She wanted him. So much that even now she was moist and swollen with need, just in anticipation. Even pressing against the front of her shorts felt arousing, and the zipper was only plastic, for crying out loud.

"Besides, how many times are you both going to have the same night off? It's like fate telling you to grab the bull by the horns and have sex with him. Dr. Hayes, not the bull."

She knew what Sara meant. And she was starting to think she was right.

Just one night.

A fantasy come to life.

Then everything would be normal.

Or she would totally fall for him, become addicted to his touch, and spend the rest of her residency trotting behind Houston begging for more.

Of course she had more pride than that. Usually.

She nibbled her fingernails in indecision. "Oh, I can't decide. It's like staring at a big piece of chocolate cake when you're on a diet. You know you shouldn't, you know you'll be sorry, but it will taste so damn good."

"Do it, Josie." Sara put her hands on her hips. "Have a little chocolate cake for all of us who can't. I'm like in Communist Russia. There's no chocolate cake even available to me."

Josie grabbed her dirty scrubs and pulled her backpack purse out of her locker. "Let's go. I'll go to dinner with you and think about it."

They started down the aisle towards the door, Josie's mind not on her feet, but on Houston and his marvelously skilled surgeon's hands and what they could do to her body.

She caught her bulky gym shoe on the metal rung of the aisle bench and went sailing into the lockers with a vibrating crash.

A little stunned from the impact, the sting of locker slat marks on her cheek, Josie looked at Sara.

Sara shook her head.

Josie sighed in defeat. "Fine. I'll page him." Maybe Houston could screw some sense into her.

Houston paced across the ceramic tile of his living room, waiting for Josie to answer the phone.

After six rings, she answered. "Hello?"

If she could sound that breathless, that erotic, just from answering the phone, Houston wondered what she would sound like when she was coming. He clamped his eyes shut and said curtly, "This is Houston."

"Oh, hi, this is Josie. Josie Adkins."

Like he didn't know who she was.

"Thanks for calling."

Then silence.

"Is this a hospital call or a personal call, Josie?" With his luck, she'd have a medical question and his gonads would have been in an uproar for nothing.

Another lengthy pause. "Personal."

He stopped pacing, his swim trunks still damp and stuck to his skin. Droplets of water trailed down his legs, and in the cool air-conditioning, his testicles drew up.

"Good answer." He started towards his bedroom, intent on changing and getting to wherever she was as quickly as he could without access to super powers.

"I'd like to see you. Tonight." Her voice sounded different than he was used to. The cheerful perky was gone, replaced by a soft, eager temptress.

It had the effect of a lap dance on him.

"Tonight is now, Josie. I'll pick you up in ten minutes."

Propping the phone up with his shoulder, he stripped his sticky shorts off and kicked them into the bathroom, off the carpet. Naked, he went to his dresser for some boxers.

"Where are we going? What should I wear?"

Something see-through and easy to get off.

She added, "What are you wearing?"

Glancing down, he caught a glimpse of his erection. "Actually, right this minute I'm not wearing anything."

She gasped. "Nothing? You're naked?"

Painfully so. Houston pulled out his underwear and a pair of soft, faded jeans. "Totally naked."

"You're joking right? This is some kind of phone sex joke."

That sweet adorable innocence, laced with naughty interest, caught him in the gut every time. She sounded horrified, yet more than a little curious.

"No, this isn't phone sex. If it was, I'd be saying dirty things to you."

There was a pause. He waited, muscles clenched. He gave her three seconds to ask, sure she would.

One . . . two . . .

"Like what things?"

His mouth went dry. "I'd ask what you're wearing. I would describe where I would touch you, tell you how hard I am . . . things like that."

"Oh." She cleared her throat. "But you're not going to do that, right?"

Houston squeezed his hand around the phone and tossed his pants on the bed. He'd never be able to zip them up right now. "Maybe I will. Or how about I tell you what I'd like to see you in?"

He didn't wait for an answer, captivated by the thought. "I'm picturing you in a short denim skirt, the kind that barely covers your ass, and drops so low on the hips I can see your pelvic bone. It molds to your curves, and in the back it's so short that I can reach both my hands up inside."

And touch hot skin.

Her answer was hard breathing in his ear.

"And those lip panties, don't forget those. I want my mouth on your lips, Josie." Each and every pair, both on the panties and on her.

He didn't picture Josie in the silk classy bra and panties displayed in the window at the mall. The kind that cost damn near a hundred bucks for the set. Even on a date, Josie would wear the funny little matching sets from the department at Target meant for teenage girls.

There was no explanation for why he found that

such a turn-on, but he had the painful pressure below the waist to prove it.

"Then on top, you're wearing one of those white shirts, I don't know what they're called, but they're loose. With one of those little ties right between your breasts. And I can see through it."

First, he envisioned her wearing a bra, breasts spilling over. Then he switched and pictured her with no bra on underneath, pink nipples and darker areola taunting him through the wispy fabric.

Come and get me, she'd say, since this was his fantasy and he could damn well picture her saying anything he wanted. His hand dropped below his waist and covered his throbbing cock, pressing it to stop the agonizing pain.

"I don't look good in white," she said. "Make it hot pink. Tight. No bra."

Shit. His hand squeezed. "Okay, I can do that."

"And maybe I shouldn't wear panties at all. That way when your hand reaches under, you can just touch me. I'd like that." Her voice had gone low again, wispy, sultry.

This wasn't the reaction he'd expected. She knew how to do this just right. It made him reckless, out of control. Eyes closed, his hand moved up and down without thought. Each stroke made his ache tighter, his desire hotter. He wanted more, her, but he couldn't stop. She had him ragged, desperate.

He murmured, "I'd like that, too."

"Are you coming?"

His eyes flew open. He saw his hand on his jutting cock, felt the shuddering pulses, and went hot with annoyance. What was he doing?

Did she know? Her teasing little voice sounded pleased.

Pulling his hand back, he said, "What do you mean?"

"Aren't you coming over? Tonight is now, remember?"

He took a deep breath and blew it back out. "Right. Give me directions and I'll be over in ten minutes."

Hopefully by then he would be able to zip his pants.

Houston listened to her babble on and on, giving detailed overzealous directions, and had to acknowledge that for the first time since he'd lost his virginity, he was thinking with the wrong head.

If Josie hadn't watched Houston perform countless surgeries, she would swear he was blind.

Looking at herself in the mirror, there was nothing she could see that would attract a man as good-looking and intelligent as Houston Hayes.

Having tried on every single article of clothing she owned, she was down to the least unappealing, a simple pair of beige shorts and a blue-and-white striped tank top. And flip-flops.

No wonder she was single and perpetually dateless. Any woman with an ounce of sexual sense knew you didn't go on a date with a surgeon in rubber shoes. But the problem was, she only had work sneakers, a pair of black pumps she wore to any occasion that required a dress, and the flip-flops.

She suddenly felt rounder than usual. Her thighs were rubbing together and jiggling as she walked, and a quick glimpse at her backside had her questioning how she even got through doorways with that thing following her around.

Her hair was charged with static from ripping so many shirts on and off, and her skin was the lightest shade of white on any Floridian under the age of sixty-five. Plus the locker she'd fallen against at the hospital had left a red bruise on her cheekbone, and her attempts to conceal it had her looking like she'd been eating oatmeal and missed her mouth.

It was not with a whole lot of confidence that she answered the door when the bell rang.

Houston had on jeans, a navy blue T-shirt, and sandals. She'd never seen him outside of the hospital, and he wore the beach-bum casual look well.

"I don't have a skirt," she blurted out, though she had wished with every ounce of her being that she did after their arousing phone conversation.

Houston smiled, his teeth very white against his thin lips, and she was aware of how infrequently he smiled. Good thing though. Because when he did, she was ice on a hot skillet.

"That's okay, as long as you're wearing the lip panties," he said.

He had quite the fixation on those underwear. Not that she minded. "They're still on."

His eyebrow went up. "For now."

Hello. Josie fisted her hands in the hem of her tank top. "Do you want to come in?" *And take my panties off?*

"If you don't mind, I'd like to grab some dinner. I haven't eaten, and I know a little out-of-the-way place that the tourists haven't found."

It would prolong her agony and horniness, but maybe she could order a glass of wine to loosen up a little. Right now steel was more flexible than she was. It was one thing to talk sexy on the phone with her eyes closed, but not so easy staring Houston in the gorgeous face.

"Sure, that sounds good."

Her flip-flops made little stick-and-slap sounds as she walked with him towards his car, and Josie was acutely aware of the silence between them. She hated silence, had always been a talker, and truthfully, something of a babbler. Her mother claimed it was from being an only child, where she had to provide the majority of conversation with herself.

Whatever it was, silence made her nervous. When people were happy, they talked, and Houston rarely pried his lips apart. Except when he was kissing her. They'd been wide open then.

She fanned herself discreetly. "So how was surfing?"

"Fine. Good waves."

Waiting for him to expand on that, she nodded politely. After sixty seconds she realized no expansion was forthcoming. He unlocked his Jeep and she climbed into the passenger seat, tossing her backpack purse on the floor.

"So . . . I've never been surfing. I always thought it sounded fun, but you know, I'm not very athletic at all, and I've heard so many horror stories about swimsuits being knocked off and shark bites and sunburns that it just never seemed like a good idea."

Oh, good. She was babbling. Glancing to the right, she studied the fast food restaurant in front of her and rolled her eyes. And she wondered why people thought she was a ditz?

"I've never had my trunks knocked off." Houston didn't take his eyes off the road. "And if you like the water, you should try it sometime. It's like being on a roller coaster."

"Yeah?" She stole a long peek at his profile. Yep. Still a god. His nose hadn't suddenly grown a bump. His eyes weren't muddied. And his jaw hadn't softened like she kept expecting it to, thereby explaining what the hell he was doing with her. "Maybe you can teach me how to surf."

He shook his head. "I wasn't volunteering. I have no desire to accidentally drown."

"Hey! What's that supposed to mean?" She could surf if she wanted to surf. She had just never thought standing on a board over water, suspended in the air, was a particularly good idea.

He pulled into a parking spot and turned to her. The corner of his mouth lifted. "It doesn't mean a thing. I'd love to see you surfing. I would pay *money* to see you surfing."

Well. Amusing, was she? His big-butt entertainment?

"Hey!" Offended and not sure what to say, she reverted to juvenile and stuck her tongue out at him. To her surprise, he reached out and caught it, holding her tongue captive between his thumb and index finger.

"Ahmm," she said, before she realized that talking without tongue mobility was impossible.

Those ice-blue eyes watched her with equal parts lust and humor. "I can think of better things to do with your tongue than sticking it out at me."

He released her, but before she could close her mouth, he drew the tip of her tongue between his lips and sucked. A shudder raced through her, desire sharpening below her belly. She let out a breath on a sigh, feeling out of control already, dominated by the position as he drew on her. Josie wanted to both push him away and pull him in further.

Her arms came up, hovering in indecision, her eyes drifting shut. Speaking of drowning.

Houston let go of her and moved back. "Do you like crab?"

Sucking huge gulps of air in, her hands pressed against her stomach, Josie just stared at him. "Huh?"

His thumb pointed to the weather-beaten restaurant in front of them. A swinging sign proclaimed Barnacle Bill's Crab Shack. It could have said Our Food Sucks for all Josie cared. She was still pondering that odd mating game he had just played with her tongue, not at all sure she liked it.

"Sure. Crab is fine, as long as they don't mind flip-flops."

Houston shook his head. "Not at all. It's mostly deck seating anyway because the back of the place butts up to a private stretch of beach."

Josie followed him into the dim interior, then out the back door onto the deck, crowded with tables and diners and staff maneuvering in and out with trays. After a quick consultation with the hostess, Houston took her elbow and led her to a table in the corner next to the railing and featuring a view of the sun setting over the ocean.

Josie sighed as she sat down. "I love watching the water. And it's nice to get out of the air conditioning."

Despite the fact that she wasn't hurting for meat on her bones, she tended to get chilled in excessive AC, and much preferred a balmy breeze and eighty degrees to sixty-eight-degree airtight rooms.

"Are you from this area?"

"No, not exactly. We moved here from Michigan when I was thirteen."

"Then I'm surprised you don't like air conditioning. We get all those tourists here from up north. It hits seventy and they're sweating, squirting water in their faces with battery-operated misters, and moaning about the humidity."

"Just like when we go north and a cool breeze blows and we're pulling on sweaters, and the locals are all running around in shorts."

Houston smiled. "I guess so."

Josie fingered the menu in front of her and studied Houston. He puzzled her, with his reserve and his burning eyes, and she felt very young and gauche sitting across from him. She had never drawn the attention of serious men, and had always dated guys who fell squarely under the heading of class clown.

Houston was older than she was, efficient with his words, and she knew absolutely nothing about his personal life. Except that he wanted to have sex with her.

Just once, so Lord, she'd better make it count.

Grabbing her menu, she fanned herself and tried to retrieve her thoughts from the bedroom. "So what's good here?"

"Crab," he said.

Well, duh. Josie blushed. "Well, I'll have that then." And a big bag to hide her face in.

Houston was aware he was making her uncomfortable, that he was staring with no shame whatsoever, and that it bothered her that he didn't run on at the mouth, but he couldn't help it. She had him burning.

Every inch of him was aware of her and he could only be grateful for the table hiding his hard-on. The wind ruffled her hair, sending the short strands sticking straight up, and her eyes were bright, shiny with embarrassment, and what he hoped like hell was sexual interest. Her cheeks were dusky pink against her pale chin and neck, and her lips were open a sliver, showing off their wet, plump undersides.

The spot where he wanted his tongue.

"How old are you, Houston? How long have you been a surgeon? I'm twenty-seven, almost twenty-eight, you know."

Her words tumbled over one another as she waited, twisting the napkin in front of her between rigid fingers, and Houston sat back in his chair, frowning a little at her attempt to chitchat. Something he was never good at.

"I'm thirty-three." Old enough to know better than to be sleeping with a co-worker, not that it seemed to matter.

"I was at a hospital in Daytona for five years before I came here." He knew she wanted more, and he wanted to tell her more, but he had no idea how to do this, how to open up, how to have a conversation that wasn't artificial and superficial.

With his buddies, it was different. They just hung out together and surfed and lifted a box when someone needed help moving. With his mother and his sister, well, he loved them beyond anything, but he also protected them. He didn't tell them his business. Instead, he made a point of talking mostly about their business, or when pressed, discussing medicine, which was a safe topic.

Josie wasn't like other dates he'd had. She had a guilelessness about her that unnerved him at the same time it struck a raw nerve. He was both attracted to that and repelled.

She scared the crap out of him—or, more accurately, his intense feelings for her scared the crap out of him.

He found himself scratching his jaw, trying hard to think of something to say. "I chose orthopedics because I like working with the older folks. They don't have the fear of the younger patients, and they're so damn grateful to you for making their life a bit easier. It's a good feeling."

Josie smiled, mouth full of straight teeth, and he could see he had pleased her with that answer. And for some reason, that pleased him.

He shifted in his seat, feeling self-conscious, and was grateful for the waiter asking for their orders.

Josie was still wearing that expression a minute later when the waiter left, and this time Houston told himself to enjoy it. He had a cute, sexy woman smiling at him and he was worrying about it? That didn't say good things about his mental health.

"So you're twenty-seven," he said, feeling that those six years between them stretched long and jaded. Or maybe age had nothing to do with it, and he was just cynical and selfish and had always been that way. "Why did you decide to be a surgeon, Josie?"

He was curious about her answer. Surgery really didn't seem to suit her.

"Well, my dad was a surgeon." Josie chewed her lip and stared at the table. "He died when I was fifteen, and it made him so proud to know I was going to follow in his footsteps."

Josie looked up with a soft smile. "And like you, I enjoy helping people. I'm a people person. My mom always said I never met a stranger."

Unlike him, who lived surrounded by strangers, all because he never made an effort to be otherwise.

Josie's pert little nose was wrinkled up, freckles dusting her cheeks on either side, and the temptation to slide into self-disgust faded. He smiled at her. "You're definitely a verbal person."

She laughed. "That's a polite way to put it."

"Not really. I like listening to you." It surprised him, but it was true.

A little flush crawled up her neck. "Is your family close to here, Houston?"

Josie leaned forward and propped her face up with her hand, her leg crossed and swinging to the side of the chair. The tips of her healthy breasts rested on top of the table, momentarily distracting him.

"They're right here in Acadia. My mom, my sister and brother-in-law, and their two little girls. That's part of why I took the job here, even though I was only twenty minutes away before."

When confronted with questions about his family, he always gave the pat answers. Listening to himself and his stilted responses, it occurred to him for the first time that even if he ever wanted a relationship, it would be damn near impossible to expect a woman to fall for him.

A friendly dolphin was probably better company.

He tried a little harder, not stopping to wonder why he cared. "My nieces are four and two, Miranda and Abby, and they're these little bundles of sticky energy."

"Tell me something cute they've done."

"What do you mean?"

"Come on, everyone has a cute story about kids. Tell me something cute." She was sipping the soft drink the waiter had brought to her, and her tongue slid up and down the straw.

"Well . . ." Houston pictured Miranda and Abby, their dark hair tumbling across their faces, little rosebud lips curved in smiles or pouts or stubborn determination. "They call me Unca Ouston, which is kind of funny."

Josie laughed. "Does their Unca Ouston spoil them rotten?"

"Not at all." He took a swallow of his beer. "And no matter what my sister thinks, that inflatable ten-by-ten bounce house for Miranda's fourth birthday was not excessive."

"Oh my God." She shook her head, clearly amused.

Houston settled back in his chair, spreading his legs out. This wasn't so bad, this getting to know someone stuff. He almost felt relaxed with Josie, a feeling he usually only accomplished on a surfboard or eating his mother's lasagna.

"I'm an only child. I wish I had nieces and nephews."

"Whenever the urge strikes, you can borrow mine. Just be prepared to get really familiar with diapers and Dora the Explorer."

"Do you want kids, Houston?"

He had always hated when women asked him that. It implied they cared what his answer was—that they were planning, hoping, assessing. Usually he tossed off a stone-cold no and watched their expressions change. Some women questioned why, some insisted he'd change his mind, and others looked at him like he had admitted he kicked puppies.

But they all left him alone after he assured them that he was a cold-hearted selfish bastard who had no interest in devoting his life to ungrateful brats. No woman had ever heard him speak the truth. That he desperately wanted to be a father, that he would love to have a tiny warm body clasped against him in trust, but that he was terrified he wouldn't be any good at it.

His own father hadn't exactly provided him with a model to imitate.

Something, he didn't know what, made him open his mouth and tell Josie Adkins the truth. "Sure, I'd like kids."

She nodded thoughtfully. "I can see that. You'll focus every ounce of yourself on that child." She brushed her bangs off her forehead. "Lucky kid."

Except there never would be a kid, and it suddenly pissed him off. He shrugged, affecting unconcern. "Except I won't have a kid without a wife, obviously, and I won't be getting myself a wife."

"Anytime soon, you mean?" she asked, meeting his gaze without wavering, her little round cheeks plumped out with soft drink.

"Ever."

Brown liquid squirted between her lips and dribbled down her chin.

Chapter Five

Josie was dead. She was a goner. In trouble, wrecked, a ship smashed against the rocks at midnight.

Despite her best intentions to not fall for Houston, she was doing just that.

He was walking next to her on the stretch of beach in silence and she was stuffed with crab and wine and good feelings. The pauses in conversation were no longer bothering her quite as much, though she did say ten words to every one of his. He just wasn't a talker.

His other assets more than made up for it. During their dinner, she'd seen glimpses of him that had never surfaced in the hospital. The concern and loyalty he felt for his family, his love of the water and surfing in particular, and his passion for his career.

And of course, desire for her.

That had been there through the whole meal, an arc of sexual tension between them, awareness of where the night was going to end. In bed. Through every inconsequential conversation and medical chatter, the knowledge that he wanted her naked and under him was always there—alive, pulsing, keeping her off-balance and strung out with physical need.

Holding her flip-flops in her hand, Josie let the sand sift between her toes and watched the round red sun dropping down over the western horizon. The night was quiet, the mournful jabber of seagulls the only sound except Houston's steady breathing and the loud yammering of her excited heart.

"I thought this beach was private," she said, stepping close to him to avoid a piece of driftwood.

"It is. My condo association owns it." He pointed to a cluster of white houses attached to each other. "Right up ahead there is my place."

Oh, yikes. Panic slammed her in the gut. They were walking there. They were almost there. Another five minutes and they'd be there, in his condo, and there would be no reason not to do what had been talked about at such great length in the supply room.

She coughed, feeling like her crab might rise for a second viewing of her mouth. "It looks like a nice development, right here on the beach. Wow. Lots of windows for the view, and everything."

Houston stopped walking. He turned to her. She expected him to take her hand, to reassure her. But that wasn't Houston, and she should have known that.

No, he took her mouth, with one hand in the back of her hair, eliminating the distance between them. The kiss was determined, skilled, hard, and urgent. She lost her hold on her flip-flops, and they tumbled to the sand as she also lost any sort of grip on her control.

That went the way of the waves, washed out to sea and dashed apart.

Not that she'd ever planned to resist him, not that she'd ever thought for one little teeny-tiny second that she was running the show. Houston was far too dominating and used to getting his way. While she may have entertained split-second thoughts of charming him into more than one night, she knew it was wishful thinking, an illusion of power.

He wasn't a man who was charmed into anything, and she wasn't a woman who had a fabulous track record of doing any sort of charming. She used her brains, worked hard, and when necessary, used a little wheedling and begging and self-deprecating humor.

Right now her brain wasn't even working as his mouth closed over hers wet and firm, his hand holding her right where he wanted her, and Josie opened her lips, felt his tongue, and clung.

Houston broke the kiss and let her go. "Grab your shoes, we're almost there."

Blinking, wondering how he could switch gears so fast, she gazed at the ground stupidly, chest heaving. He'd said something about her shoes. They were at her side on the ground, liberally dashed with sand.

Right. Flip-flops. Pick them up.

She bent over.

Houston swore, reached down, and scooped up the sandals before she could. "No bending over until we get there."

It hadn't been her plan to intentionally arouse him. But maybe because it was the only way she felt she had the upper hand, she had the urge to be a little impish in the face of his fascination with her behind.

Catching him off-guard, she bumped the flip-flops in his hand, tumbling them back to the ground.

"Oops." With a grin, she bent over. All the way over. Without bending her knees more than was necessary.

She waited for the swearing.

"Damn it, Josie," he said.

Her grin grew broader. One of these days she was going to ask him what exactly he found so appealing about the two lumpy throw pillows she called her butt. But for now, she was just enjoying teasing him.

Then he ripped control right back by reaching out and grabbing hold of her backside, his fingers firmly planted across each of her cheeks.

She let out a yelp. "Houston!" She hadn't expected

that, and while the beach was private, there were forty condos within eyeball range.

"Don't start something you can't finish, Josie," he said, and his hands ran up and down on her.

She didn't know how he could do that, paralyze her with just one little touch. She couldn't move, didn't want to, and let him stroke over her possessively as the now-familiar ache started to build between her thighs.

Around and down his fingers went, under and through her legs until the tip of his finger was tantalizingly close to the juncture of her thighs. Her shorts flooded, her legs stiffened. Her nipples jumped out and begged for attention, and while her brain said *Good God, not here,* her body said *Anywhere you like, gorgeous, just don't stop.*

She gave a whimper like a dog needing to go out, and waited to feel embarrassment, but she was clearly having a delayed reaction, since all she felt was blinding lust.

He slid back and forth, his large hand crowding between her legs, brushing up against her clitoris through the taut fabric of her shorts.

"Not here," she begged in a futile attempt at modesty, aware that she wasn't really up to resisting him if he pursued the matter. But a token effort would make her look less desperate. If she wasn't going to fool herself into thinking she gave a damn if half the population of Florida assembled stadium-style and watched, at least she could try and fool him.

"No one can see. I'm right behind you, blocking your body. No one can see that my finger is between your legs," he whispered in her ear as he caught the edge of her shorts with his thumb. "I could slip it into you and no one would be able to tell. It just looks like I'm hugging you."

He was going to do it and she was going to moan and bite her lip and come right there on the beach. In full view of anyone looking. And somehow she really doubted a man leaning against a woman with his hand moving back and forth between her legs would be interpreted as an affectionate hugger by any passerby.

This would be setting a bad precedent. If she gave in and shattered all over Houston's hand on the beach, who knew what else he'd think her capable of? He'd have her dangling from a chandelier naked if she wasn't careful.

Forcing her eyes to stay open, she swallowed hard and tried to ignore the little teasing back-and-forth motions of his finger, the way he played with the edge of her shorts, darting under, brushing her underwear.

"I think they would be able to tell," she panted, clamping her thighs together to keep him at bay. Which only trapped his hand, pressing him more firmly against her. Oh, man alive, that felt good, and she savored it for a long slow pulsing second.

Then with the willpower she had relied on to study in med school and to work twenty-four-hour shifts, she stepped forward, out of Houston's reach.

He didn't say anything, but she heard the rush of his breath, felt his stillness. A breeze off the water ruffled her hair as she turned around. Houston stood straight, taut, his muscular arms at his sides. His jeans were straining to hold his impressive erection.

But he didn't acknowledge that, didn't make a joke, or crack a smile, or shift himself in his pants like other men she knew would do. He reached into his pocket and pulled out his keys, spinning the ring, holding them around his index finger.

He wouldn't beg. She had figured that out by now. He wouldn't push her or coax or charm. He would just wait, knowing she wanted him, until she was doing the begging, compliant and wide open to him.

But he couldn't quite achieve the remoteness she was used to seeing from him in the OR. He was just as edgy, though he knew how to control himself better than she did.

He took one step towards her. "Next time you bend over like that to tease me, I just may be tempted to smack your ass instead of touch it."

Josie gasped. She gaped. She covered her butt with her hands, as if he might grab her and give her ten whacks right there on the beach.

He was joking, of course. Wasn't he?

Of course he was. And she was repelled by the thought, not turned on and curious and leaning towards him like a sun-starved houseplant to the window.

Nor was she entertaining any thoughts of bending over just to see if he would actually follow through on his threat.

If she did have any thoughts in that direction, any tiny, small, ridiculous thoughts, she ignored them and patiently waited for her brain to provide her with speechmaking capabilities again.

It was a little slow coming.

Houston didn't know what in the hell was the matter with him. He had never struck a woman during sex or otherwise, had never once even entertained the idea. He had always been a traditionalist in the bedroom, choose top or bottom, in and out, let's go.

But Josie had him contemplating all kinds of twists on the old tried-and-true. Watching her stare at him like she'd suddenly found herself on a date with a self-proclaimed serial killer, he managed a small smile.

"Not hard, of course." He should back off, apologize, tell her he'd lost his mind momentarily, but he had an aversion to admitting he was wrong. It made him feel weak. And besides, he really did want to grab onto her ass and give her a little spank for putting him through so much sexual torture.

Memories of his father suddenly leapt into his head. Images of that bastard's hand knocking his mother down onto the kitchen floor, along with Houston's hatred for the man whose DNA he shared, rose swift and sure. Along with hatred for himself that he could ever be anything like that sorry excuse for a human being.

Josie made him lose control. Control he'd worked all his life for. And what if, when he lost that control, he learned parts of him were closer to his father than he ever cared to acknowledge?

Standing there in the fading sunlight, Houston stared at Josie and wondered if he had to pull the plug right then and there. She was too damn dangerous.

But then she smiled, perfectly straight teeth flashing at him, her dimples deep and adorable.

"That's probably not a good idea," she said, tugging the bottom of her shirt down. "I'd probably end up pitching forward, landing on the ground, and knocking my teeth out."

The solemn seriousness with which she spoke amused him, breaking his sour mood. He might be afraid of Josie, but hell if he could resist her. "Well, we don't want that. It'd be a shame to mess up such a model smile."

He touched the tip of her nose. "Anything else I should know about you before we go in? Any medical conditions or physical limitations?"

Her lips pressed together and she tilted her head. "I can't touch my toes."

Houston laughed at the unexpected answer. "I'll keep that in mind." And he reached for her hand, pulling her next to him so they could walk.

He tucked that little soft pale hand in his and tried not to notice that he never did this with a woman, that he was already crossing into an intimacy with Josie he had never shared with anyone else.

Shit, he hadn't held a female hand since he was seventeen and at the prom. And then it had only been because he'd had to for the pictures. He touched women, of course, but only as a prelude to or as part of a sexual encounter. He didn't hold hands, rub shoulders or backs, kiss hello and good-bye, aside from his mother and Kori.

No one touched him back, either. Women sensed he didn't want that, or if they didn't they learned soon enough. He didn't snuggle and he didn't spend the night, and when he showered or took a bath, he was always alone.

Which suddenly felt very cold and isolating.

He wanted to touch Josie and have her touch him back; he wanted to feel all of her, in his arms and flush against him. He wanted her to let him bury himself inside her soft round body until he felt the way he should, content with his life.

He would be inside her. But he told himself the rest was a bunch of BS, his extended state of arousal making him needy and weird. He *was* content with his life.

There was no room for anything else in his guarded heart.

Yet he found himself caressing that feminine hand in his, giving a light squeeze, enjoying the way she bumped his arm as she walked, her eyes tilted up to his with anticipation. With a pure unrestrained pleasure that wiggled under his defenses and made him want to smile.

Something was happening and it wasn't good. Houston's hand in hers was causing rapid heart rate and compromised breathing and she wasn't prepared for this side of him. This sort of nice, almost tender, contented silence that made her want to scream in agony.

God, this was a mistake. She couldn't do it, couldn't remain aloof and worldly and nonchalant in a "let's just be lovers" way. That was for thin women with long French-tipped fingernails, whose boobs required a Wonder-Bra boost in their Ann Taylor dresses.

Not Josie. When a man touched her whoo-hoo she couldn't ever go back to thinking of him as a disinterested co-worker.

So she babbled. Long, and eloquently, about nothing.

"It's a little warm tonight, at least ninety still and here it is mid-September." She stopped just short of adding a golly-gee. "That's why I keep my hair short, you know." Of course he didn't know; she was making absolutely no sense. "It's usually so hot here."

Silence. She waited five seconds, then opened her mouth again.

"Have you ever thought about getting a tattoo?" She lifted her hand that was still in his and touched the tip of a finger to her bare shoulder. His knuckles brushed against her flesh, making her shiver. "I thought maybe I would. Right here. You know, like a rose or something, but actually, that would look awful on me now that I think about it. I'm too pale and well, sort of like cottage cheese. I guess a rose would look like a blob of blood on me."

Houston didn't say a word, not a single blipping word to save her from herself, and he led her up the path to a condo with a coral colored door. His hand didn't leave hers as he deftly put the key in and turned the lock. She wondered if he sensed she might bound off like a quivering rabbit if he let her go.

"Um . . ." Her mind blanked. She wanted to say something intelligent, suave, mature. But since she was none of those things at the moment, she said nothing.

The door drifted open. Houston turned to her. His head bent, his mouth dropped over her shoulder, and he pulled her skin between his lips and sucked. She gave a startled sigh. The hot tip of his tongue rolled over her, outlining the bone and muscle, and she shivered again, desire spiraling through her body.

She was ragged, ready, tense, and nervous for him to touch her, but desperate for it at the same time. She had been waiting since that afternoon when he had first kissed her, really just about since the minute she'd first met him, and now she just wanted to get on with it. Appease her body and get back on an even footing.

Houston murmured against her skin, "Not cottage cheese at all. You're like cream, milky white and sweet and I want to lick you up."

Fine time for speech to desert her. It seemed around Houston she either talked too much or stood mute and wide-eyed like a Precious Moments figurine. She just nodded. *Yes, please. Lick me up.*

His fingers played with the bottom of her tank top, brushing across her belly, while his tongue trailed along her shoulder and up to her neck, leaving her skin wet and tingling.

"Shouldn't we go inside?" They were still hovering in the open doorway, and though Houston's front door was private, surrounded by some shrubbery and facing only one other condo, Josie still felt conspicuous.

"Why?" He lifted her tank top up over her breasts and roughly yanked it past her head before she could even react. "Are you shy?"

She gasped, feeling shocked to the tips of her toes that she was left standing on his doorstep in her bra. It didn't matter that it wasn't particularly revealing and that bikinis showed more skin. The point was it was her *bra*.

Houston covered her mouth with his before she could squawk at him, his tongue teasing across her bottom lip the way he had just tasted her shoulder. She wanted to pull away, to deny him, to demand they go inside, but really, no one could see and what did it matter when he was making her feel so damn good?

A large skilled surgeon's hand had snaked across her breast, covered only by the lacy white bra she'd thought to drag out of her drawer at the last minute, forsaking her usual industrial-strength cotton underwire. Josie had seen his fingers at work, saw how they could manipulate and control and heal with intricate precision, and he was doing that to her now, stroking the pad of his thumb across her distended nipple while his mouth took hers over and over.

When his lips dropped down Josie didn't think to protest, just let her head go slack and felt the wet anticipation as he sucked lightly on the swell of her breast.

"I love your body," he said, switching to the other breast. "You're so lush and curvy, with so many places to hold and suck."

His arms had wrapped around her, drawing her closer into him. While enjoying the attention, Josie remembered her fears about baring all in front of him. "I'm overweight."

Ice-blue eyes locked with hers. "Says who?"

Wasn't overweight the definition of lush and curvy? "The world. I'm short, I'm round, I have a good thirty pounds stuck to various parts of my body that should not be there."

When he just frowned at her, she wondered why she was spoiling what was proving to be the most erotic experience of her life. "I mean, I know I'm not fat or anything like that, it's just that I'm too pale, too soft, too *much* to be considered really pretty," she finished lamely, feeling a blush dart across her face.

She hadn't meant to do that. Dr. Houston Hayes wanting her was a fantasy come to life, and she was questioning it like a twenty-million-dollar lottery winning.

Houston stepped back, into the entry of his condo, but still only a foot or two in front of her. He studied her, assessing her with a bold, unapologetic stare.

"I want you so bad, I've been making an ass out of myself over you all day. I'm having dreams about your body and what I can do to it, and how many ways I can fuck you."

Josie blinked at his crude language.

"What would you want to have less of?"

He reached behind her and unhooked her bra, dragging it down her arms roughly so that her breasts tumbled forward like melons in the grocery bin. Yes, she wanted less of them. They were useless and in the way and anytime she could compare something on her body to produce, it wasn't sexy.

Houston threw her bra on the front stoop where her tank top was, behind her. Oh, great, she was naked and the door was still open, her clothes out of reach. But amazingly, she didn't really give a crap, so fascinating was the look on his face, and so wet were her inner thighs.

"Would you want to have less of these?" He cupped her bare breasts as Josie gasped and her heaviness filled his questing, kneading hands.

"Because then I couldn't do this." He took her in his mouth, rolling his tongue over her nipple, wetting her and making little sounds of enjoyment like he was licking a particularly good ice cream cone.

Josie grabbed the door frame and clung. So okay, maybe he had a different perspective on the whole thing. "That's true."

"What about here?" He touched her hips. "Less here and I'd be afraid I'd hurt you when I'm driving into you."

That image assaulted her and Josie moaned. Rolling her shoulders back, she took a step forward, giving him permission to do just that. Drive into her. Anytime he wanted. Preferably sooner than later.

Houston stuck his fingers through the loops of her shorts and tugged her the rest of the way to him. Her chest collided with his and he kicked the front door shut behind them. Then his grip was on her backside, holding, caressing, teasing her with wandering strokes that crept between her legs and into the dip dividing her cheeks.

"And less here, and what would I have to fantasize about?" His mouth found her ear as he whispered, his breath tickling her skin. "What would I spank when you get out of line and bend over without asking?"

She sighed, tilting her head when his tongue slipped inside her ear, making her ache with the hypnotic movements in and out. She squeezed her thighs together, clenching her inner muscles as she anticipated him moving in her the way his tongue was.

"You have a woman's body. And a woman should not look like a twelve-year-old boy, not like those starving heroin models do."

Houston ran his hands across her waist, his mouth on her neck, and Josie knew that he was genuinely attracted to her.

For the most part, she was content with her body, but Houston had a way of making her doubt herself as a doctor and a woman. He was so confident, never the least unsure in what he did, and she felt sometimes like she was being consumed by him and his overwhelming personality.

Yet at the same time, she had never felt so desired, so appreciated, so wanted in her whole life.

Her shorts were being unbuttoned, and she noticed he didn't fumble at all. Whether that was from being a surgeon or from being experienced in removing women's shorts, she didn't want to know. Well, she did, for sick, self-torturous reasons such as wanting to believe she was the only woman whose butt he had waxed so enthusiastically about.

One night, he had said. He never wanted more than one night.

Josie gasped as his erection ground into her, burning through the barriers of his jeans and her panties. Another hard thrust left her gasping.

"Jesus, Josie, I want you so much."

About to answer, her words were cut off by his groping fingers jerking between them. Her eyes rolled shut. The khaki shorts fell down past her knees when he gave them a brutal shove.

Good thing he was a doctor, well versed in CPR, because she almost passed out from anticipation.

"Oh, damn," Houston said, feeling like he'd swallowed an orange whole.

Josie's panties did have a lip print on the front. A wide red lipstick set of lips, right smack in the middle between her thighs. Not high, above her belly button, but low, over her rounded mound and right about where her clitoris would be.

"Give me a kiss, honey," he said, and he dropped to his knees in front of her.

She gave a startled cry and tried to take a step back, but he wasn't having any of that. He grabbed that gorgeous ass firmly and hauled her right up in front of him. He breathed in her scent, soft and clean, mixed with the sweet smell of passion.

Behind those lips he knew he'd find Josie slick with want, curls dampened and clitoris gleaming with moisture. So when he placed his mouth on the silk-screened lips, he was picturing what was behind it and how it would taste, and Josie's cry of pleasure matched what he felt.

Houston loved the way his hands sank into her

sweet backside, the way she was soft and real and eager, and that when his mouth moved over her, her legs enclosed him on either side in a musky cocoon. He ate at those lips, kissed and bit and sucked, soaking the panties with his mouth and her desire until he could taste her tangy wetness even through the cotton.

Her hands were tight on his shoulders, digging in with hard, short nails and Josie panted, murmuring something that sounded like a plea for help over and over. Which drove him nuts, and he gripped harder, his cock straining and pulsing in his jeans as he sucked the front of her damp lips, finding the soft give between her folds. Pressing his tongue there.

"Stop!" she said, giving his head a half-hearted shove before stumbling backwards.

Houston groaned, wiping moisture off his mouth, ready to ask her why in the hell he should stop, when Josie let out a scream, and not an orgasmic one. Her arms flailed, which didn't help his hard-on one bit given that she was in her panties and nothing else, and she had a rack to rival a Hooters waitress.

Paralyzed by the sight of breasts bouncing a foot in front of him, he didn't react quickly enough. His mountain bike, which had been propped up against the wall of the foyer behind them, caught the impact of Josie reeling backward. The bike hit the ceramic tile, clipping Josie in the leg and pitching her forward in a heap. She landed in a tangle of legs with lots of jiggling and wiggling.

Jesus, Josie needed accident insurance. "Are you okay? What the hell happened?" Still on his knees, he lifted the bike off her and settled it back against the wall before turning to assess her.

"Whoops." She giggled, her cheeks pink, her arms propping her up, lying a little on her side. "I forgot my shorts were stuck around my ankles and I tripped."

Relief flooded through him that she hadn't broken an ankle or anything.

She'd just tripped. The urge to laugh was strong and he closed his mouth tightly for a minute, enjoying the erotic shape of her breast from the side, the way her waist dipped in, the full rounded curve of her luscious hip. "Did the bike hurt you? Are you sure you're okay?"

"I'm fine." But her hand stole down to rub her leg and he could see a long red scratch on her pale calf.

"Let me see." It was a physician's response to check the injured, to run his hand along her and assess. But for hell's sake, it was just a scratch, which he could see, and the way his hand was moving had nothing to do with being a doctor.

He just didn't want her hurt. That's why he found himself leaning over and giving her a kiss right there, a tender boo-boo-all-better kind of kiss that he gave his nieces.

Because he didn't want Josie hurt. And he worried that he would somehow hurt her.

She kicked the shorts off her ankles. "It's not even a laceration, there's no blood. It's just that Josie the Klutz struck again."

But she didn't look embarrassed. She was smiling at him, moistening her plump lips, reminding him that he had yet to feel those lips anywhere on him besides his mouth. He wanted more, he wanted her to taste him everywhere, to draw him into her mouth between those pink lips and flick her little tongue across his cock.

"I was supposed to be fixing that, wasn't I? Cure you of your klutziness?"

Her ample chest rose quickly. "That's right."

The sight of her lying there, ready and aroused, made him groan. Josie's body was built for sex. Not for modeling, not for Olympic sports, but for pleasing a man, plain and simple.

Placing a knee on either side of her legs, he leaned over her, arms propped by her hips, so that he could stroke her wrists with his thumbs. "Why did you want me to stop then? I could have made you come, Josie. With your panties still on."

Those expressive green eyes fluttered shut. "I know. That's why I wanted you to stop."

He dropped a light airy kiss on the tip of her nipple. Her breasts were beautiful, full and round, with large nipples the color of peaches against her fair skin, making him want to clamp his teeth around them and suck.

"Houston."

"Hmmm?" Gut feelings weren't to be taken lightly. He had known it would be a damn good idea to take her tight nipple into his mouth, and when he did, tasting her salty sweetness, he knew he was right.

"Will you kiss me again? On the lips."

Now he was the one closing his eyes. He counted to ten and tried to breathe. The tone in her voice left no doubt as to which set of lips she was referring to.

When he opened his eyes, she was pushing those gorgeous tits out towards him, an expectant little smile on her face, her panties bunched from her fall, slipping down past her hipbone.

Then stealthily her finger strolled across the front of her panties, and tapped right on the lip print.

Damn.

"Josie, I'll kiss you wherever you want. All night long."

He bent over.

Chapter Six

Josie figured it was just her luck that she'd fall in the midst of staving off an orgasm and bring a bike down on herself. The scratch on her leg stung, but she hardly noticed, too busy enjoying the look on Houston's face.

Despite her babbling, her thunder thighs, and her constant supply of stupid human tricks, Houston was attracted to her. More than attracted. He was on the verge of foaming at the mouth, which made her feel sexier than she'd ever had in her life.

And speaking of his mouth. What he could do with it should be taught to all men on their twenty-first birthday. He deserved some kind of commendation on behalf of all women for those maneuvers, and she would be the one to present him with his prize.

He was leaning over, his black hair descending between her legs as Josie realized he meant to honor her request. Suddenly changing her mind, she scooted back out of his reach before he could get to her. One more touch and she was going to combust, and she didn't want things to end anytime soon. Tomorrow would be too soon, let alone sixty seconds from now.

"Where are you going?" He was stalking her, moving forward on his hands and knees, backing her into the wall, looking powerful and determined.

They hadn't yet made it out of the hall, and Josie hit the cool wall with her back and pressed her hands across her breasts, suddenly aware how uneven their state of undress was. Just why was she naked and he was wearing everything?

She clamped her legs together. "Take your shirt off, Houston."

He did without question, leaning back on the balls of his feet and dragging it over his head in one quick motion.

"Oh, man." Damp panties still clinging to her, she moaned. Because he was incredible, every toned and tanned inch of him; biceps not bulky but strong and powerful, chest with just a smattering of dark hair dead center.

"Just to warn you," he said, standing up, moving his hand towards her head.

"Yes?" Josie sucked in her breath. He was going to guide her mouth down onto him, she was going to take his jutting erection between her lips and lick like crazy . . .

"Don't move, there's a shelf right next to your head."

"What?" Distracted, Josie let him pull her forward and up. She half turned to see a collection of personal photos propped on two shelves inches from her head.

That's all she needed was to send his snapshots the way of his bike. But Houston didn't look concerned. Urgent was a better way to describe him. He started pulling her down the hall to his living room with long single-minded strides, hand clamped on her wrist. Houston fascinated her, a complex and controlled man, and she was seeing more and more facets of him. So far all of those facets pleased her, particularly the one that seemed to think she was a goddess naked.

Which made her want to see what other reactions she could get from him.

So when he stopped in front of his couch and turned back to her, she bent over, stretching the tips of her fingers to her ankles.

"What the fuck are you doing?" Houston's voice was outraged, tight, and oh-so-turned-on.

Just right. "I told you I couldn't touch my toes. But I didn't really know that for a fact. I'm just checking. Close, but not quite." She was a little breathless as she bounced, straining towards her feet, her breasts tumbling down her belly.

Denim hit her behind, rocking her forward. His erection slid right between her cheeks.

"You look so sweet and innocent, but you know exactly what you're doing, don't you?"

Hands on her waist, he started to grind her backside against him, and Josie gave a gasp of approval. "I'm not doing anything."

"You're playing games with me, aren't you, you little tease." He was nibbling her shoulder as he pressed against her, hot and hard. "Want to be spanked, do you?"

She'd forgotten about that. Her hand strolled around to her unreachable behind, covered as it was by him. Somehow she had no trouble picturing him carrying through with his threat. A little turned on and shocked by her own reaction, she tried to pull away, but he held her tight. "No, Houston, that's not what I meant. I was just teasing."

Something she didn't think Houston was subjected to very often, at least not at the hospital. So she wasn't sure if he was teasing in return or was ass-smacking serious.

One hand holding her breasts, the other cupping her mound, he pulled her back, securely held to him, the denim of his jeans soft on her hot skin. "So you admit you were playing the tease then? Fine, I won't give you a spanking. But if you want to play games, we should try doctor instead."

Oh, God. She went still, afraid to move, afraid she might have an orgasm with his fingers just moving across the front of her moist panties and his erection nudging into her backside. He was fondling her nipples with careless abandon and she ached everywhere for him.

Her stethoscope fantasy leapt into her head. "Doctor? I guess you'd be good at that."

He kissed the back of her neck—slow, hot presses that sent shivers down her spine.

"I'm very good at it. So here's how we'll do it, since we're both doctors. You show me yours, then I'll show you mine, and we'll take turns examining each other."

Josie wiggled against him, unsatisfied and impatient, sorry she had bent over in the first place. Without her ill-timed teasing, he might be inside her already. "What's my co-pay?"

Houston laughed at Josie's unexpected response, leaning his chest forward to press against her smooth, bare back. She felt delicious all tucked up along his body. "Since we're taking turns, I think we can skip the co-pay. Besides, I don't remember that being part of the game. Didn't you ever play doctor when you were a kid?"

His tone was light as he stroked across Josie's belly, skimming lower and lower, but he was burning. The idea of having her down on his bed, exploring every inch of that tempting body, had him on the edge. He had almost lost it, right into his jeans, when she had bent over and showed him those lip-print panties stretching across her glorious backside.

Her head shook back and forth, soft hair brushing his

chin. "No, I was what my dad called a butterball, and a tomboy. I was always tagging along with the boys, but not a one of them wanted to play doctor with me."

Not the answer he wanted. It ticked him off that she seemed to not realize how sexy she was and that being called a butterball at eight had nothing to do with her adult body. She wasn't thin, that was true, but she was full of shape and character and had the kind of hips that a man could grab onto like he was now and thrust into with abandon. No bones on her to poke at him, and her breasts were real, functional, instead of decorative knobs.

Nothing sagged or drooped or rolled, but sat there perky and lush, taunting him to taste and enjoy.

And he wanted to enjoy her more than anything.

"Truthfully, I never played doctor, either, but then I never had you around before. Something about you and your gorgeous body, Josie, I just can't resist." He slid his hand inside the front of her panties and cupped her as he rubbed his thumb across her curls. The heat rolled out of her, her breath hitched. With a casualness he didn't feel he moved his finger to rest inside her folds, to flicker across her clitoris.

She was wet. Ready.

"I love your body," he said in a low voice as he stroked her, up and down, slipping the tip of his finger just inside her to tease. Her body hugged him, held on, moist and eager, her hips rocking forward.

He leaned over her shoulder to watch his hand covering her, to see her nipples puckered and her fingers digging into her thighs. Next to his ear, little hot gasps of delight left Josie's mouth.

"I want to worship your body, touch and taste every inch of it, show you how it fascinates me."

Normally Josie's voice was high-pitched, cheerful, full of energy, and an almost naïve exuberance. Now it had dropped an entire octave, grown husky and sultry, yet still so full of that eagerness he loved. "We can do that anytime," she said. "Now is good."

It certainly was. He pulled his hand back. She let out a sound of disapproval that was silenced when he stripped down her panties with a yank, going on his haunches to lift first one foot out, then the other, holding onto her smooth, pale ankles. He caressed her feet, noticing how short and rounded her toes were in a cute, very-Josie kind of way.

The panties in hand, he tucked them into the pocket of his jeans. She wasn't getting those back.

Since he was moving around to her front, she saw him and gaped. "Why did you put those in your pocket?"

"I'm keeping them." He went back down in a squat, resting his thumbs above her knees. He kissed her thigh, trailing upwards, noticing the sheen of moisture on her inner thigh.

He trailed his finger across the glistening flesh, then raised it to his lips and tasted, closing his eyes as the rich musk of her desire touched his tongue.

"Why do you want my panties?" Josie gasped, hands grabbing onto his shoulders, hips backing away from his touch.

He held her tighter.

Unwilling to look at Josie, he nuzzled his nose in her thigh and searched for something to say that was the truth, but not the whole truth.

Those panties belonged to him, because he couldn't see her again after tonight, and he wanted a little tangible reminder of what they were doing. Because this was it, one shot, one night of burning pleasure like he'd never experienced before. Then he had to pretend it hadn't happened, because she was already crawling past his defenses, and another date would do him in, he knew. He would fall for Josie, and then he would inadvertently hurt her or she him.

Tossed on the rocks. Crashed and burned.

Reaching for her soft brown curls, he murmured, "Trophy," then moved his tongue across her swollen clitoris.

And just like that, she came with a whimper. Stunned, he held onto her pulsing body, gripping hard, still moving his mouth over her to draw out the climax she seemed to be fighting. Intense and hard, in mere seconds it was over, her fingers relaxing on his shoulders. As her bucking hips slowed down, Houston gave one last lingering lick then pulled back.

He gave a soft laugh, kissing her pink thigh. Damn, she was incredible. He loved that he could push her to the edge so quickly, and she was everything he had envisioned and more. There weren't games with Josie, despite the teasing back and forth, because he didn't have to guess what she was thinking. Her thoughts would always be written all over her face, or spoken directly to him with that guileless honesty of hers.

So he glanced up the length of her body, past the rounded belly and glorious breasts, expecting her to be wearing that sly smile of the satisfied, and purring contentment. And she was. But more prominently, more frightening, was the tender look of intimacy she shot him, a look that went straight into his chest and squeezed his heart like a rotten tomato.

Oh, hell, she liked him.

Damn it, damn it. He knew this was going to happen. He should have told his cock to lie down and behave, and now instead she looked like she wanted to pet him and pack his lunch.

He squeezed his lips shut so he wouldn't say something asinine, like he wanted her to stay the night, share his bed, and breakfast, and a whole string of tomorrows.

"Thank you," she said, with a genuine gratitude that annoyed him.

How could he have sex with her and not look back when she was *thanking* him?

Her knees bent, and she slid down in front of him onto the floor. Her nipple swayed before his mouth. "What now, Houston?"

Well. He could be an idiot and send her home. He could gather what little shreds of decency he possessed and make soothing gentle love to her to make up for the way he was going to ignore her.

Or he could push her back on the carpet and drive into her hard and fast, since she was there and willing and tomorrow was a long night away.

He started to put her away from him. It would be smartest if she just left now, before they sunk deeper into relationship muck.

"Wait." She bent over him and unzipped his jeans, lifting him out of his briefs with trembling cold fingers that sent shuddering jerks of desire through his cock.

He swallowed the lump of lust that rose in his mouth. Again he tried to give her a gentle shove. He wanted to do the right thing. Let her get the hell out while she still could, and protect herself from the emotional wasteland he had always known he was.

"Before you put a condom on, I want to taste you."

And her mouth closed over his cock, just the way he had imagined, her spiky hair sticking into his stomach, her pale shoulders rounded. Teeth scraped his skin and he groaned, low and loud, his balls tightening, his gut cramping, his legs stiffening as the agony of her touch washed over him.

Damn, she was incredible. Up and down she was moving over him, her fingers on his hips, pulling him forward so that her moist mouth closed fully over him, his cock slipping deep down her throat.

That was it. All he could take. He didn't have the will-power to push her away a third time. For now, to-night, she was his, and he was taking her. Hard.

Josie licked the tip of Houston's smooth skin, catching the bead of clear sticky fluid there, thoroughly enjoying the taste and feel of him throbbing inside her mouth. She sighed in pleasure as his hands landed on her shoulders.

Then the next thing she knew she was flat on her back.

"Spread your legs," he ordered, then didn't wait for her to do as he asked. Instead, he took her right knee and dropped her leg wide open.

Josie felt hot all over, so ready that she didn't feel an ounce of embarrassment that every inch of her imperfect body was splayed out like an all-you-can-eat buffet in front of Houston.

Houston took her left knee and shoved it forward towards her hip, his expression tense, ice-blue eyes darkened with desire to a rich azure. He was ripping open a condom and shoving it on with more haste than finesse, and she saw a wild edgy abandonment that she had never expected to see from him.

It made her respond in kind. Without thought, she used both thumbs to spread herself, hoping to encourage him.

"Oh, fuck," he said.

Her eyes drifted shut as she murmured, "Yes."

His weight fell on her legs as he held her down and then he was there, rushing inside her, going deep with an urgent thrust. Josie felt her inner muscles quiver as she fought a scream, grinding her teeth.

"You like that?" he said, eyes fixed on her as he pulled back and slammed into her again.

She didn't speak, her breath stuck in her throat, every thrust of his drawing her closer and closer to the edge. It was more vivid, raw, than anything she'd ever experienced, deeper and intense, shattering pleasure swirling through her. Her body squeezed around him as she nodded violently up and down.

Jaw clenched, he said, "I can't hear you. Tell me that you like it."

Josie's head whacked the coffee table leg as his quick motions propelled her backwards, and caught there by the furniture, she moaned again. Immobile she could feel even more, every hard inch of him stroking through every part of her, and she didn't hesitate.

"Oh, yes, I like it."

His mouth captured hers, his teeth scraping along her bottom lip. His blue eyes had darkened, clouded over. "Prove it. Make noise for me, Josie."

If he insisted. Hands hooked on the waist of his jeans, breasts brushing against the hair on his chest, it wasn't an effort to moan for him. To groan and grind and whimper and claw until she was moaning loud enough to crack the mirror in the hall. Then it didn't matter that her knee was still bent awkwardly and her head smashed against the table, she felt a tightening below her belly and knew that she could come again.

Houston wasn't doing anything but sliding into her over and over again. Yet it was more than she had ever imagined she would share with him, and the fierce concentration on his face made her feel absolutely seductive. Lifting her hips, she met his thrusts, felt the burn of her back on the carpet, and knew that she had been right.

This was a mistake, because there was no way she could look at him again without remembering this feeling of him pushing deep inside her body, gripping her knee, his cool mask of disdain torn away. Stupid, stupid, stupid, yet she reveled in every stroke, every thrust that she arched to meet, and she knew she was about to come hard.

And she thought he should know that. "Houston, oh, don't stop. I'm going to come."

Her eyes stayed open long enough to see his nostrils

flare and the corner of his mouth tilt up in a satisfied smile, before her vision blurred and she climaxed.

She tried not to claw at him, honestly she did, but he wasn't letting up, and she was desperate, passion exploding through her entire body as he drove her into the carpet.

"Yes!" she yelled, shudders continuing to tear through her, muscles twitching with release.

Houston paused, then filled her deep as his own orgasm met the tail end of hers. Josie found the strength to lift her mouth to his to capture the shaky moan he gave through gritted teeth. While he pulsed into her, he ignored her kiss, mouth clenched too tight to respond. Then without warning his tongue slid past hers, rough, possessive, teeth nipping at her lips.

Arms rubbery, Josie collapsed back on the carpet, head half under the coffee table, but he pursued her, kissing her cleavage and rolling his tongue down towards her belly button.

She panted, exhausted, boneless, but Houston's grip on her thigh didn't loosen. His mouth strode everywhere over her body, while he stayed buried inside her, movements so intense she wondered if she'd imagined his orgasm.

The fierce possessive domination of his lips and hands on her sent shivers through her, delicious aftershocks rocking her vulva. But then he pulled back, emptying her, and Josie let her hands droop to her sides with a satisfied sigh. Maybe if Houston did this to her every day, she'd never drop a darn thing again. She'd just walk around the hospital smoking a cigarette and purring.

His hands were stroking her sides, lightly now, tickling her, and she giggled, shoving at his hands. Houston moved his grip to her behind and pulled her out from under the coffee table, eyes roaming over her.

"Checking for injuries again?" she asked, legs shaking a little as she drew them together. Her muscles weren't functioning properly.

"Did you hit your head?" Fingers ran through her hair, marching across her scalp tenderly.

"I'm fine." She smiled at him, telling herself that was genuine concern on his face. She brushed across his chest hairs with lazy fingers. "In fact, I think I'm cured."

"Oh, really?" He sat half-up, resting on his hand as he shot her a phony look of suspicion. "You're never going to drop anything ever again?"

"Well, I don't know about *ever.* No one is ever really one-hundred-percent recovered." Maybe she could convince him to cure her on a daily basis.

Houston's hands were roaming actively, urgently. "Let's go to my bedroom and we'll see if I can get you even more relaxed."

A finger teased around her clitoris and all she could think was *bring it on.* Taking advantage of the opportunity while it existed was what any intelligent woman would do.

Houston pulled back his finger, damn him. He stood up and reached for her hand, clearly expecting her to say yes. Which, of course, she was going to.

Josie's breath hitched. "Yes, Doctor," she said in a soft, obedient, aroused voice that made Houston want to grind his teeth in gut-twisting agony.

No need to worry about getting it up again so soon. He was so hard he could harvest wheat by turning sideways.

Forget the bedroom. Fifteen feet was too far away. Josie had the most arousing effect on him. Even when he'd climaxed, he hadn't felt finished, had just wanted to eat and lick every inch of her over and over until she agreed to never leave.

Which was more than one night.

Damn it.

Houston shoved his jeans down hard. One more time. Then he had to let her go. Had to make her leave. But first he was going to make this last time count.

He reached for another condom while Josie, clearly guessing his intent, lay back down on the carpet, arms over her head, eyes bright with anticipation.

After discarding his briefs and rolling on the condom, he clasped her smooth knees, stroking over her warm flesh. Then dropped her pale legs open. Wide.

He held her so hard, when he moved his fingers he saw pink streaks on her flesh, and he coached himself to relax, to slow down. But her nipples rose and fell as she breathed deep in anticipation, peeking at him from under long, fawn-colored eyelashes, and there was nothing relaxed about the way he felt.

Though her mouth was open a little, she didn't say a word, and Houston marveled that he had actually made Josie go silent.

His mouth went dry as he stared at her inner thighs spread out for him, damp curls pressed against her flesh.

There, ready, waiting for him, to touch and taste and sink into.

"Josie," he said tightly, bending over in front of her, kissing up the length of her thigh.

"Yes, Doctor?"

Oh, man, she was killing him with that. That teasing little breathy voice, sounding not one damn bit like she did in the OR. During surgery she was chatty, full of questions, and cheerfully muttering to herself through every task she did. It had always annoyed him no end.

This flirtatious shit she was doing now was way too appealing.

And he didn't know what in the hell possessed him, but he said, "You might feel a little pinch . . ." before closing his lips around her clitoris and sucking.

"Oh," she said, hips rising off the floor. "Oh, oh, Dr. Hayes."

Clearly Josie wanted to play.

"Hold still," he whispered against her dampness. "I'm almost done."

He ran his tongue along the length of her, dipping inside her smooth folds, enjoying the way she jerked beneath him. One more greedy lick across her clitoris and he pulled back.

"There, all done."

Her frustrated expression made him grin.

One hand reached out and stroked his chest. "I don't feel any better," she said. "Isn't there something else you could do?"

He could think of a lot of things he could do. "Well, there is something, but it's a rather drastic procedure."

Goose bumps darted across her skin, and she wiggled under him, raising her hips in a blatant offer. "Some cases need aggressive measures."

Houston could stare at Josie all day, just pet and worship her body twenty-four, seven. He loved the way her soft belly curved out, and rounded down to her hips. Loved the way her breasts fell to her sides a little, and the pale underside of her arm when it was raised above her head.

For months he had been attracted to her, fantasizing about her and trying to convince himself that he wasn't. Now that she was here, lying on his floor, spread out for him like a sweet, wet treat, he found that no fantasy had prepared him for reality.

And he had been lying, or just plain stupid when he told her that one night was enough. He didn't think he could ever tire of running his fingers along her delicate flesh and listening to her little sighs of pleasure. Of watching the corner of her mouth lift up in a smile, or her tongue reach out and dampen her plump bottom lip. It was a habit of Josie's he wasn't even sure she was aware of.

"It's that bad, is it?" he asked, pressing his tongue into her belly button, distracted and aroused and annoyed that she tempted him so completely to make such a total ass out of himself.

Bad, in an incredibly good way. Josie felt like she had fallen into another woman's body. A body that knew things she'd never claimed to. How to come in five seconds or less was the knowledge that astonished her the most.

Josie was one of those time-consuming women who needed lots of manual stimulation and full concentration on sex-slave fantasies to have an orgasm. There had been more than one occasion in the past when she had been waiting for her ex to check his watch or complain of a finger cramp.

She knew it was because she was always self-conscious, way too aware of her body and its various flaws, to relax and just feel pleasure.

There was always too much white skin and jiggling thigh in her view to let it all go and feel nothing, think of nothing but how she and her partner were trading satisfaction.

But with Houston, she wasn't having a problem. Whipped cream was tenser than she was.

Houston's willingness to tease and play games was a contributing factor. It surprised her, but she realized it shouldn't. One of the things she'd always admired about him was his ability to focus, to concentrate solely on one thing, achieving perfection.

Usually she was witnessing that during a hip replacement. Today she was seeing his attention focused on making her insane with desire.

It was working.

"It's bad, Doctor. I can't go on like this."

He had the nerve to laugh. To nudge against her with his penis, but not enter her. To flick his thumb across her nipple, her lip, her nose. To sink a mere inch inside her, then pull back.

"That's not funny."

"Who's laughing?"

"You are."

The grin fell off his face, his head moved slowly back and forth. "Jesus, the things you make me do."

Any words she might have thought to say were cut off. Josie rolled her eyes shut when he slid into her again, softer still than the previous time, pausing only half embedded in her. It was a delicious tease, to feel him throbbing inside her motionless, and she moaned, making the sounds of approval she knew he wanted.

"Houston, do you like it?" Fairly sure she knew the answer to that, she still wanted to hear him say it.

But he didn't say it. He just nodded, then sank deeper until his hips were resting against her, and she was taking all of him.

There was no reservation, no thought to her cellulite or pouchy stomach, just mindless, enthralling pleasure seeping through every inch of her and out her pores.

"Damn it," he said sharply, his teeth clenched.

"What?" Josie let her whole body go slack as he filled her over and over, hot friction, with a slow, deep rhythm that rocked her breasts up and down against his chest.

He shook his head.

She didn't pursue it, feeling the climax creeping up on her, surrounding her, dragging her into satisfying sensual fulfillment, and like a lazy river it rolled over her, taking her under.

A whoosh of hot air blew across her chest, and she saw Houston had been holding his breath. And his own orgasm, which he finally let go as hers shattered. His head dropped over her shoulder and his hips moved faster, pushing her back into the carpet with hard thrusts.

Josie lifted her body to meet his, wanting to show him how good he felt to her, wanting him as sated and pleased as she was. For all he wanted her to yell out, he was quiet, controlled, but then she didn't expect otherwise.

A shudder and a curse told her he was depleted, and he slowed his movements to nothing as Josie sighed in satisfaction.

The kiss on the shoulder was something she didn't expect, and she felt a tiny sliver of hope hovering in her, that maybe she was different to him. More. Which was exactly what she shouldn't be considering. It shouldn't matter.

But it already did. Maybe it always had.

She wrapped her arms around his neck, enjoying his weight on her as he rested over her, not looking at all eager to pull away.

Chin buried in her hair, his voice was low. "I was supposed to show you my bedroom, wasn't I?"

Josie kneaded the corded muscles in the back of his neck. "Is there something good in there to see?"

"Damn right."

She laughed, then stopped short as the demanding buzz of his hospital pager went off.

"I'm not on call. I'll just ignore it." Houston withdrew from her.

Josie maneuvered her knees together, wincing at the sore muscles in her thighs. That particular muscle group didn't see a whole lot of action, she was sorry to say. Not for three sets of ten on a thigh machine, and not for regular sexual activity.

Houston's cell phone started to ring. He frowned as he ran his fingers through his hair. "Coincidence."

With a sigh, Josie sat up and began to accept the fact that she probably wasn't going to get to see Houston's bedroom after all. The hospital was trying to reach him.

It was confirmed when his personal phone started ringing.

"Shit," was his opinion, but he stood up and walked naked over to the end table and snatched his phone.

Josie waffled between intense post-coital satisfaction and regret that the night was prematurely over. She'd wanted to see his bedroom and anything else he might be inclined to show her. Like how to make her eyes roll back in her head for the fourth consecutive time.

"Yeah, okay," Houston was saying. "I'll be there in twenty minutes."

Josie started looking around for her clothes, crawling across the floor on all fours towards her shorts, which were lying inside-out a few feet away.

Houston stopped her progress, startling her into squawking as he grabbed her hips and pulled her back against his erection.

"Hospital?" she whispered, even as he started to rock forward and back, his penis fitting right between her cheeks.

"Yes. One of my patients fell and broke her hip."

"You should leave then." She panted as he stroked against her, slipping into her slickness with the teasing tip of his rock- solid body.

"Yup. In a second."

But that second drew out to a long, pleasant minute, and Josie bit her lip, the soreness in her leg muscles forgotten. "Mmm."

Then Houston pulled back, giving her backside a little pat. "Damn. I really do have to go."

"I know." Recalling herself, Josie scooted forward and sat up, still on her knees.

Houston was pulling on his underwear and reaching for his jeans. "I'll get your clothes."

Josie watched him retrieve first her shorts, then her shirt from the front stoop. She clutched her knees awkwardly, wishing there was a way to cover her naked self. She didn't want to distract Houston any further.

Well, she did, but it wasn't ethical. His patient was in pain and needed his surgeon, and Josie couldn't justify making him wait so that she could take a shot in the ass.

Houston handed her the bundle of wrinkled clothes and cleared his throat. "I'm sorry."

"Don't be." Giving up hope of modesty, she wiggled into the shorts, trying not to think about her panties still tucked in his pocket. She zipped gingerly. "It's part of the job, as I well know."

She smiled up at him. "And at least we both, well, got there. You know. Were finished, sort of. Twice, too." She blushed as her thoughts shredded into incoherent babblings as she realized she couldn't bring herself to say orgasm or come out loud.

"In your case three times," he said with smug satisfaction.

The faint blush tinting her face turned into a rushing river of red heat. He'd just had to point that out. Like she was a cheap date who couldn't hold her sex.

"Don't be embarrassed," he said, clearly not understanding that it was too damn late to stop that. "I would be giving you a fourth right now if I wasn't called in."

The words were on her tongue, to ask if he was offering a rain check, but she didn't say it. She just rolled her eyes at him and buttoned her shorts. Picking up her tank top, she stared mournfully at the large neck. "You stretched out my shirt."

"And I'd do it again."

She'd let him. Lifting her arms up to pull on her shirt, Josie had the pleasure of hearing Houston suck in his breath.

"You would?"

"Oh, yeah. Anytime."

Josie quickly donned her tank top without her bra, not wanting to wiggle into it in front of Houston. Any movement like that and the bra would likely wind up back on the floor.

But his words made her pause. Anytime? Here it was. The awkwardness. When she second-guessed every word out of his mouth, probing for hints of a future, a relationship, or at least another orgasm between them.

This was what she had feared in the supply room, and it was just as uncomfortable as she'd imagined.

"We'll have to walk back and get my Jeep from the restaurant, then I'll drop you off on the way to the hospital." Houston stepped into his jeans and zipped his fly.

"Great." Not great. Tense, mortifying, and awkward, with a feigned casualness that fooled neither of them given they both still smelled of sex. Great? Not at all.

"Here are your shoes."

"Great." Their fingers touched as he handed over her flip-flops, and Josie pulled back quickly.

"I'm going to grab a bottled water on the way out. Do you want one?"

"Great," she said for the third time, realizing there were four-year-olds with a better command of language than she was currently displaying.

Then his hands were on his hips and Josie saw that his cool mask of indifference had slipped back into place. Dr. Hayes was standing in front of her, not Houston.

"So, we have an understanding about tonight, correct? This won't affect our working relationship."

"Not at all." Because she was never going to go to work again. God, what the hell had she been thinking? She couldn't stand next to this man in the OR and pretend he hadn't been inside her playing a naughty game of doctor and wet and willing patient.

She wanted to run outside and bury her head in the sand, except that would leave her ass sticking up in the air.

Standing there, rumpled and pantyless, shattered and sex-satisfied, Josie had to ask. Before they went back to being Dr. Hayes and Dr. Adkins, who avoided and never made eye contact and practiced polite nods in place of actually having to speak.

"Why won't you let me do a case on my own? I have experience, you know, and you refusing to let me take the lead looks bad for me. I need to know your plans for the remainder of my residency."

Houston paused while pulling his shirt on over his head. He stared at her through the stretched neck hole. "God, Josie, don't make me talk about work right now."

His reticence annoyed her. He was allowed to be enigmatic while making decisions about her career, but she was supposed to confide in him, rely on him to guide her, while she just smiled like the dingbat everyone thought she was.

"It's just a simple question, Houston, and if we're going to go back to the hospital tomorrow and act like nothing has happened between us, at least I'll have a better understanding of where my career is going and what I can expect from you in the future."

Houston stared at Josie, a step away from the living room carpet where he had stripped her and made her come, and wondered what the hell he was supposed to say now.

This was why he didn't have relationships with co-workers. It seemed like women didn't understand that work and play were two different things, and that you didn't bring up the one while engaged in the other.

Of course, he had pursued Josie at the hospital, breaking his own rules. And she had a valid point, which pissed him off even more.

"Josie." Agitated, he thought about the patient waiting for him at the hospital. Thought about how Josie had looked minutes earlier, lying beneath him, calling his name.

The tank top she'd pulled on covered nothing and her breasts were lifting, taunting him, the fabric caught on one plump nipple, her navel showing. The lip print panties were bulging in his pocket, reminding him that she was deliciously naked beneath those shorts.

He wanted to spread her again, to taste her damp curls, open her before him and see her wet desire. He wanted her open all night for him, every night, like a twenty-four-hour Dairy Mart. *Damn it.* He squeezed his hands into fists before reaching over and yanking her shirt down lower, his knuckles brushing her nipple.

She gasped. His cock started to swell again, but he ignored it.

Reminding himself that she was a colleague, a doctor, and that she hadn't been put on earth for his sexual pleasure, he collected his thoughts and spoke in as controlled a voice as he could manage. "Fine. This isn't really the time for this discussion, but since you insist. The problem is that you have no confidence in your ability. I'm not going to be comfortable with you conducting surgery without me until I see that you're ready."

Given the grip of her knuckles on the hem of her shirt, and the narrowing of her eyes, he figured she wasn't pleased with his answer. But he'd been honest with her, and now he wanted her to drop it.

"How do I prove I'm ready?"

He paced back and forth in front of her. Josie being

ready wasn't a tangible thing, and he wasn't sure he could define it for her. When she just *was,* taking charge without hesitating. When she didn't wait to ask him for permission, but called a patient her own and didn't doubt herself.

"I don't know. Stop hesitating. Stop fluttering around like a damn bird."

Okay, so that probably wasn't the best choice of words.

Her eyebrows shot up. "Fluttering? You think I'm fluttering? I suppose you think I should be doing something more whimsical as well instead of being a doctor." The words spat out of her mouth.

Anger coming from Josie startled him. He pulled back from her a little, not sure what the hell to say, his brain not functioning at top capacity. Too much blood diverted to his erection for the last hour.

Her finger stabbed the air. "Forget it, buddy. I'm not quitting, I'm not going to go away and become a nurse, and I won't join the circus."

Join the circus? As what? A monkey trainer or a cute clown? "Uh, I wasn't implying you were laughable."

Josie made little huffing sounds and skittered her eyes away from his. "I want to be tall and thin and dimpleless so people will take me seriously."

Houston pictured Josie like she'd described and decided he wouldn't be the least bit interested in her if she was cool and controlled and never showed her teeth. He liked Josie's spark, her smile, her energy, and her big heart.

And her ass was a thing of beauty. Jesus.

But he didn't know how to reassure her, and he didn't know words that made women happy, and he was a workaholic. Sex he could handle. Sex was good. But the rest of this was over his head, and he had just known that being with Josie would sink him into relationship quicksand.

All he could do was tell her the truth. "Josie, you're not tall, and you've got dimples, and that's who you are and you're damned sexy. If you want people to take you seriously, you've got to be the one to do it first."

"What do you mean?" she said, kicking at the carpet.

"I mean, get the doctor attitude. Stroll into that OR like you own the place. Confident, arrogant."

She didn't say anything, just worked her toes back and forth, collecting a little pile of gray carpet fuzz.

"When you doubt yourself, so does everyone else."

The look on her face was killing him—that sad little resigned expression, green eyes wide and moist. He had to get the hell out of there, away from her and her needs and wants, away from *his* needs and wants, back to the hospital where it was all simple and everything made sense. And where he didn't have to feel anything, but just did his job with a cool detachment that made him a stellar surgeon.

"Why don't we discuss this on Monday? We can schedule an appointment to talk in my office, and we can plan the rest of your residency. We'll call in Dr. Sheinberg for a little strategy session." So he could avoid doing this here, now, when he felt vulnerable and she looked so fuckable.

Josie gave a nod. "Fine."

Houston studied her, running his eyes up and down the luscious length of her body, aware this was probably the last time he could look at her with frank appreciation. "I had an incredible time, Josie. I'm sorry things got interrupted."

But . . . Josie waited for the but that never came. No *let's do this again, let's pick up where we left off.* Nothing.

He chucked her chin.

Her chin. Like a kid at an autograph signing. Like a

chunky wannabe surgeon who he was trying to dismiss.

Then he said, "Thanks."

If he had said, "Thanks for the boff on my living room floor" she couldn't have felt lousier. Praying for sophisticated words to miraculously leave her mouth, she forced a shrug.

"No problem." The problem was there wasn't a single sophisticated bone in her pear-shaped body, and while he wanted to distance himself, she suddenly wanted to adhere to him like a blood-thirsty leech.

"Anytime, just call me," she added like a desperate fat girl looking for a prom date, and she hated herself for it.

The smile fell off his face. His lips pursed together. There was *pity* in his eyes. "We can't . . ." he started to say, but she cut him off by brushing past him towards the door.

She was an intelligent woman, with a medical degree, who was cute and upbeat, damn it. She didn't need his pity sex. She had gone into this with her eyes wide open knowing exactly what he wanted, and she would walk away with her head held as high as possible from the height disadvantage of five-foot-one.

"The hospital's going to wonder what happened to you." She jammed her feet into her rubber flip-flops with hands that only shook slightly. "Don't worry, Houston, tonight never happened."

Chapter Seven

Houston lay on his beach towel, furious with himself. He'd done exactly what he hadn't wanted to do. He'd hurt Josie.

She had stared at him Saturday night, her big green eyes wet with unshed tears, telling him she'd forget their night together had ever happened, and he had felt like the biggest pile of garbage north of Miami. A goddamn smelly landfill, leaking and dripping and festering.

Things between them hadn't gone at all as planned. He wasn't supposed to like Josie as a person. He was supposed to have screwed her out of his system with casual sex between consenting and emotionally unattached adults, not spending every waking second feeling guilty. And lonely.

For Josie. For her laugh, her smile, her silly little run-on sentences.

His decision to sleep with Josie had been made by his dick, and his dick had led him into disaster.

He was not husband material, and Josie was a settling-down kind of woman. It was better this way. He had cut ties before her emotions were really engaged.

She might have been a little hurt Saturday, especially since he'd been called to the hospital early in the evening, but she would get over those feelings a hell of a lot easier than if he had strung out an affair with her over months like he was tempted to do.

Houston pushed his sunglasses onto his head and sighed. He could rationalize with himself for hours—in fact, had been—but he still felt like shit. And he still wanted to scoop Josie up into his arms and offer her another round of the dirty doctor.

Christian nudged him on the leg with his foot. "One more run, H, then I've got to call it a night. Kori will have my hide if I'm not there for bedtime stories."

Dennis laughed. "Sounds kinky."

Houston forced himself to rise off the sand where he had been lying prone like a patient on a shrink's couch for the last half-hour. Dusk was darkening the sky, and he wanted one last run himself.

Out on the water, he could convince himself that it would all work out, that Josie would handle herself at work on Monday with aloofness and maturity and that he would see her through new, lust-released eyes.

Which was a joke. If anything, his lust had reached Himalayan levels. He wanted her more than ever now that he knew how incredible she was. How giving and sexy.

But he couldn't have her. She was exactly the kind of woman who could drag him under and take away his control and he would never let that happen. Ever.

He sighed again.

Christian glanced at him. "What's up with you? You sound like a teenage girl."

Now *there* was a mortifying comparison.

Dennis flicked Houston in the chest with a towel. "Sounds like our bachelor boy has fallen hard. Who's the girl, Ice?"

"There is no girl," he said shortly, picking up his board.

Dennis laughed and Christian looked more curious than ever. "Sounds like love to me, buddy. Have you messed it up already, or she doesn't know you exist yet?"

Oh, she knew he existed. Had felt his solid cock stretching her moist inner walls as he brought her to a screaming orgasm.

"None of your damn business," he said, than started towards the water.

Laughter followed him. Christian clapped him on the shoulder. "Don't let Dennis bug you, he's just messing around."

"He doesn't." A short, perky woman was bothering him, not Dennis.

"If you want to talk, hey, I'm here, man."

They reached the edge of the water and it lapped at Houston's feet. He knew his brother-in-law was only trying to help, but the last thing in the world he wanted to do was admit out loud what an ass he'd been to Josie.

"Thanks," he said, and started paddling out.

"See you back on shore." Christian waved to him as he headed out on his own board.

Houston hadn't gone to the hospital that day, so he hadn't seen Josie since the night before when he'd dropped her off at her apartment. She had been unnaturally quiet, and that had spoken volumes. He wasn't looking forward to going into work tomorrow.

Lost in his brooding thoughts, he had to look twice when he thought he saw a dark shadow moving to his left.

"You're seeing things, Hayes," he scoffed at himself and kept an easy rhythm going with his hands. He had probably imagined it since his brain was only half on the task at hand anyway. Or it could be a dolphin, or a big fish, or just a shadow on the water.

Yet he couldn't shake the sudden feeling of unease that something big was in the water with him. He glanced left and right. Christian was too far to the left to hear him. No one was to the right of him. Narrowing his eyes, he studied the water, but didn't see anything.

Still, he was on the verge of turning his board around and heading back when he saw it. A gray dorsal fin popped out of the water, vibrating back and forth, indicating extreme agitation.

That was no black-tip. That was a bull shark, and Houston was already pulling himself up instinctively onto his board, drawing all his limbs in tightly.

Bull sharks were unpredictable and vicious. Sometimes they left you alone, and sometimes they attacked without warning, taking you under the water in a powerful bite.

There was nothing between him and the shark but the water and the board. Salt water was no goddamn protection.

Fear rose like bile in his throat. "Christian!" he shouted, scanning, scanning the water, hoping like hell the thing would just swim off.

Then his board was bumped from beneath.

Josie was studying an X-ray film alongside Dr. Bennett, the radiologist on rotation that night. Unlike Dr. Hayes, the short, slightly rounded Dr. Bennett was not intimidating. Nor did he treat her like a glorified assistant.

Plus she hadn't slept with him on his living room floor. And she didn't have the slightest urge to make out with him in the small room.

"What do you see, Dr. Adkins?" Dr. Bennett rocked back and waited for her to make the diagnosis.

With confidence she ran her pen along the film that showed the elderly woman's ankle joint. "A spiral fracture to the tibia, a fractured fibula, and a broken talus across the neck here."

She glanced to see his reaction. He was nodding in agreement. She smiled. It wasn't relief she felt. She had known she was right. It was satisfaction that someone else was witnessing her being professional as opposed to clumsy.

"Whose patient is she?" Josie asked.

"Dr. Hayes. What's his schedule like? He might want to do this in the next couple of days."

All she knew about his schedule was that it didn't involve her. In the hospital or out, because she had every intention of avoiding him as thoroughly as possible. "I have no idea. We'll just transfer her to the third floor and work it out when Dr. Hayes comes in."

Her pager went off in her pocket. "Excuse me, Dr. Bennett."

"See you later, Dr. Adkins." With a friendly wave, Dr. Bennett pulled the film down and left the room whistling.

She followed him out of the room and started down the hall for the staff phone. She had a headache—a nagging, throbbing, behind-the-ears one that had been plaguing her since she'd woken up that morning, after a fitful and unproductive night of sleep filled with sensual dreams of Houston.

Which she should be grateful for in a way, she thought. Since in her dreams was the only time she was going to be getting any action ever again.

"This is Dr. Adkins."

"ER needs assistance, Dr. Adkins."

Josie felt her heart leap in anticipation. When she was on call for the ER they didn't always need her, and she wished they would. Every time she saw a case, she grew in confidence and experience. This could be another chance to prove herself capable to Houston and avoid the little career guidance counseling he wanted to subject her to the next day. She'd rather poke her eyes out with dull butter knives than sit in front of his desk while he told her all of the ways she had screwed up.

"What is the injury?" she said crisply.

"Surfer attacked by a shark. Heavy bleeding, possible shock, possible muscular and vascular damage. Victim is on his way in now."

"Eww." She voiced her unprofessional opinion on being bitten by a shark. "Sounds nasty. I'm on my way."

As she shifted through her mind all of the complications that could arise from having a dozen knife-like teeth sink into human flesh, she found herself thinking about Houston. He was a surfer. He'd had the day off.

The thought had her jogging down the hall, which suddenly felt three miles long.

It couldn't possibly be Houston, of course. It would be an amazing coincidence if it was him, since she didn't even know if he was surfing. He could be out on a date for all she knew, or stocking up on veggies at the grocery store. Or he was out there on the water riding a killer wave, looking cool, calm, and utterly untouchable. No shark would dare attack Dr. Hayes. He would stop it in its tracks with one of those deadly stares.

Yet she found herself suddenly running down the hall in her urgency to get there.

Josie saw his name on the board as soon as she walked in. Hayes. Top of the casualty list.

It was him. Of all the people in the water that day, it was Houston who had been attacked. Her feet slowed as she swallowed hard. Shark bites could be really horrific, with massive amounts of tissue loss. Even whole limbs.

Just yesterday he had been kissing her, stroking between her thighs and today . . .

The ER nurse came up behind her. "Dr. Adkins. Room three. They just brought Dr. Hayes in."

"How is he?" she asked as she started to jog down

the hall, grabbing a clean gown to pull on over the scrubs she was still wearing.

The nurse called after her, "I don't know. He lost a lot of blood, that's all I heard. The paramedics are with him now. Dr. Matthews is in room one dealing with a cardiac arrest, so you're the only doctor available."

Oh, fun. Being in a small beach town, Acadia Inlet Hospital kept a bare-bones emergency staff for normal Sundays. One physician and two or three nurses, with ortho on call.

Not only was she about the least qualified staff member to be dealing with a serious injury, she was personally involved with the patient. Or had been the night before. Houston had made it clear that was as far as any involvement was going to go.

Taking a fortifying breath that only made her stomach churn, she flung the curtain aside and brushed past the middle-aged nurse, Shirley, at the end of the gurney. Two paramedics were bent over Houston.

The taller paramedic with blond hair looked up. "Hey, Dr. A. Long time no see."

"Hi, Ernie." During her ER on-call days she'd run into Ernie and Brent regularly enough. "How is he?"

They stepped back for her to take a look, and she stopped dead in her tracks, her stomach moving beyond churning to roiling. Houston was unconscious, his face an unnatural white, and his lower leg was saturated with blood.

Ernie clapped her on the shoulder. "He's stable. Only wounds are the right hand, calf, and shin, but he's bleeding like a stuck pig. Good luck with him."

Brent read off heart rate and blood pressure as she swallowed hard and stepped forward, pulling on latex gloves. Her instincts and training took over. Quickly she peeled back a T-shirt from the leg that was soaked with blood. The wound was still bleeding, though sluggishly.

It was encouraging news that the lower leg was the only wound, and there didn't seem to be significant tissue loss that she could see at first glance. Josie relaxed her shoulders, not even realizing until that moment how tense she had been. She hadn't been sure she could handle a more severe injury, but she could deal with these wounds.

"Put a line in him, please, Shirley. He needs an IV and blood typing. We're going to need to do a transfusion once we stop the bleeding."

Assessing the pallor of his face and the blue tint to his lips, she added, "Get some blankets."

She tossed the soiled shirt in the biohazard bin and told the paramedics, "You guys can head out. We'll take it from here. He looks pretty stable, all things considered, and it sounds like you got him here in record time."

"Hope he does all right," Brent said as they left the room.

Josie hoped he did all right as well. One minute he'd been so cool and in control, teasing her, and now he looked pale and vulnerable. The woman in her, the one who had gone and forgotten they were nothing to each other, just co-workers who'd had a one-night stand, wanted to brush her fingers through his hair and trace those blue lips.

Which would look real professional. As soon as the nurse was done inserting the IV, Josie straightened her shoulders. "Grab those blankets and I'll get some saline to wash out the wound."

She listened to Houston's uneven breathing and allowed herself to rub his arms rapidly, rationalizing she was working to prevent shock. But it made her feel better that he was warm to the touch, his heart rate strong and steady.

"You're going to be okay," she whispered, no longer caring if she sounded professional or not. She didn't feel professional when he was bleeding all over her shirt.

Pulling out her penlight, she pulled back his eyelids and checked his pupils for dilation.

Houston focused on her and blinked. "Josie?" His voice was faint, but determined.

Her hand shook a little as relief surged through her. She was mortified to realize that tears had welled up in her eyes—tears she bent over and viciously wiped away so he wouldn't see what an emotional dip she was being. "Shhh. Yes, it's me. Just relax while we get you cleaned up."

The nurse came back and draped a thick, heated blanket over him and murmured to Josie, "I sent his blood for typing, and the saline is right behind you."

"Great." She turned to grab it when his hand pulled weakly at her, trying to stop her.

"What is it?" she asked, giving in to her sudden tender urge and tucking the blanket tighter around his chest.

"Where's Tim Sheinberg?"

Her relief turned to hurt. He wanted to know if a more senior orthopedic surgeon could be brought in. He obviously didn't trust her to know how to care for his injury. Even injured and half-unconscious he could insult her.

She spoke as lightly as she could manage. "Probably at home watching TV. He's not on call tonight."

"So call him anyway. You're not ready to do this on your own, or to stay detached."

If he hadn't been bleeding, she would have smacked him. It was his fault she wasn't ready to handle major cases, and his fault she was emotionally involved. Sleeping together had been his stupid idea, one he had pursued heavily if she remembered correctly.

Josie tried not to let her irritation show, especially since Shirley was watching and listening with interest.

"I am certainly qualified to give you stitches, which is all you need."

Her sympathy and tenderness evaporated, she changed the subject before she told him exactly what she thought of his attitude. "How much pain are you in? We'll give you some diamorphine."

Maybe it would improve his disposition. Permanently.

He groaned.

She took that to mean the pain was severe. "Shirley, would you get that, please?" He would need it for when she dug around in those wounds checking for debris.

Unfortunately, there was no time to wait for the drug to take effect. She flushed out the wounds with the saline and grimaced when sand and other foreign objects came out in a rush. Now that the blood flow had slowed considerably, she could see there were eight puncture wounds in a crescent-shaped pattern on his calf, consistent with the teeth of a shark, as well as vertical lacerations on the shin and foot.

Closer examination of the largest wound revealed a tooth fragment. She removed it and tossed it on the table next to her.

"What are you doing?" His eyes were watching her, his words slow and thick. The immediate effect of the painkiller Shirley had injected into his IV was evident in the relaxed grin on his face and the way his eyes struggled to focus.

"Taking a shark tooth out of your leg."

"Cool."

There was nothing cool about it, but she told herself it was the drug talking.

"Did you give me something?" He rolled his head back and forth. "I feel strange."

He looked strange, too, eyes unfocused, and she was amused in spite of herself. Relaxed and loose weren't adjectives she'd normally use to describe him, but that's what he was now. "Yes."

She didn't look up as she trimmed excessive loose tissue off of the edge of several of the wounds. "We gave you a painkiller."

"No." He moaned again. "Can't take those. Does funny things to me."

"Shirley, can you give him a tetanus shot while I suture some of these wounds?" Some were wide and needed suturing, others were narrow but deep and best left alone to heal to prevent the risk of infection. Only one had suffered any significant tissue loss, and even that was fairly minor. Houston would just have a large dimple in his calf once the wounds had healed.

He was obviously a very lucky man. The shark hadn't inflicted any significant damage. With the blood loss staunched and Houston awake, she was confident that her initial fears were unwarranted. There didn't appear to be any muscular damage and no major arteries had been severed by the bite. He was going to be as good as new in a few weeks.

"There's two of you, Josie."

"Close your eyes, Houston."

"Then I won't be able to see your pretty face."

Hello. She paused in her work, startled by his comment. She reminded herself the man was out of his mind with pain and drugs, though they hadn't given him that much diamorphine. But he still obviously had no idea what he was saying.

She couldn't help but feel a tiny bit pleased. Even though the compliment was given under the influence, she wasn't above taking it. *Pretty* sounded better than *fluttering like a bird,* which was how he'd described her the night before. Finishing with the scalpel, she reached for the needle the nurse had readied.

"Oww," he complained as Shirley gave him his tetanus shot.

The nurse, who Josie now could focus on since the immediate dangers appeared to be over, was shaking her head. "He complains about a simple injection, but he's got two-inch puncture wounds all over his leg."

Josie smiled at the woman with salt-and-pepper hair, glad for her practical and efficient presence. "It's good to see you again, Shirley. How are the kids?"

"Oh, they're fine. The older two are having fun at college, and the youngest is adding to my gray hair by joining a garage band."

Josie smiled. "Sounds loud. Thanks for the great work here. You're always efficient."

"Just doing my job." Shirley looked pleased.

"Do you mind?" Houston said in a petulant voice.

"What?" She finished stitching the first gash and moved on to the next, skipping one that wasn't as bad.

"You're not at the damn water cooler gossiping, you're stitching me up. Pay attention."

Tugging a little harder on the thread than was necessary, Josie gritted her teeth. It figured he was a lousy patient.

"I have it under control, Dr. Hayes."

"Oh, it's Dr. Hayes now?" he murmured. "That's not what you called me last night."

Josie snapped her head up. Geez, had she heard him right? Given that Shirley's mouth was wide open in astonishment, she must have. She wondered if he was hallucinating, but that wasn't normally a side effect of diamorphine. However, one never knew how an individual would react to a drug.

It was probably best to just let that little remark slide. She bent back over his leg, heart thumping hard.

"Josie."

"Yes?"

His voice was still warbled, and she wondered what drug-induced statement would come out of his mouth this time. Hopefully it wouldn't involve any vivid descriptions of her coming on his carpet.

"I'm sorry if I hurt you. I didn't mean to."

The embarrassment of having Shirley as a witness was worth hearing that. Even if Houston had no idea what he was saying. Her hands slowed down and she tried to swallow the lump in her throat, which clung there like a large grape.

"It's hard for me to get close to people, but if I was going to, it would be with you."

Her leg jerked back and hit the metal table with a loud bang, rattling the equipment lying on it. She gaped at him in shock, even though she told herself he was not in his right mind. He was watching her earnestly, his mouth pulled down in a frown, his blue eyes glazed with pain.

Those damn tears were back, which meant she really was unqualified to do her job. Swiping at her eye with no attempt at discretion, she frowned at him. "Go to sleep, Houston."

She didn't want to hear any more. Or rather, she wanted too much to hear more. A little seed of hope had sprung to life in her heart, and that was a bad thing. Because when Houston was off the drugs, he'd grind that hope beneath his foot.

Ignoring Shirley's questioning look, she went back to work, wishing she could just staple his leg and his mouth shut and get the hell out of there.

Houston obviously didn't like her answer. He was beginning to show signs of agitation. He was trying to sit up, and Shirley was pushing him gently back down. His hand snaked out and tried to grab Josie's, which at the moment was occupied stitching his flesh back together.

"My father. It's not your fault." His eyes closed for a minute and he sighed.

When he spoke again, his tone had changed, become flirtatious. "You know, I really like your hair."

Shirley smothered a laugh behind her hand. Josie felt a flush rushing up her neck.

"And your tits, and your hot, round a—"

Josie cut him off, her voice about three octaves higher than normal. "Let's get him some Augmentin, Shirley, and arrange for him to be moved to a room. He'll be ready to go in about twenty minutes."

Glancing at his wet swimming trunks above his wounds, she added, "He needs these trunks taken off, they're soaking wet."

"You can take my trunks off." A loopy, sexual smile crossed his face.

"Shirley can do it while I talk to your relatives."

His head rolled back and forth. "You do it. It's not like you haven't seen me naked before."

Geez, oh Pete. So much for discretion. Within thirty minutes this juicy piece of gossip would be making the rounds of the hospital faster than the SARS virus in Beijing. Josie wanted to hide under the bed, and couldn't quite bring herself to meet Shirley's curious stare.

Finishing her last suture, she told him firmly, "The nurse will handle it."

Eager to get away from him and his colorful descriptions of her body, she dropped the needle on the tray. "Is there someone in the waiting room I should talk to?"

He nodded. "Yeah. My buddies. They'll be worried. Tell them I'm fine, will you?"

Fine was probably overstating it. "Sure. Let me finish up here, then we'll get a unit of blood going. You just lie back and try to rest."

His eyes remained closed but he didn't seem ready to fall asleep yet. "So I'm okay? No devitalized muscle?"

"No. You'll have some really interesting scars, but I

expect you'll recover." Josie backed towards the door, rolling her shoulders.

"I'm finished. I'll go talk to your friends, then I'll be back."

Houston didn't answer, finally having given in to the effects of the painkiller and fallen asleep.

"Did you see his hand?" Shirley asked.

"No." Josie frowned, stepping back to the bed. Houston's right hand was covered in blood under a bandage.

How could she have missed that? She mentally berated herself for not being as thorough as she should have been. She had a vague memory of the EMT mentioning it to her as well, which made her even more of a bumbling incompetent.

But her annoyance faded to horror as she moved his hand to get a better look at the wound. It looked like someone had vigorously rubbed sandpaper back and forth over his palm. Which, in a manner of speaking, they had. Shark skin was about the texture of sandpaper.

Which would be well and good except in the center of his palm, arching towards his thumb, was a laceration that extended deeply into the flesh. "Oh, no," she whispered.

"What's wrong?" Shirley asked, narrowing her eyes.

Josie's heart sank. She looked at Houston, who was sleeping fitfully. "It looks like he's severed some tendons and the median nerve in his hand."

"It will heal, right?"

Josie nodded, pulling her own hand back, her stomach churning with fear for Houston. "Yes, but there's a high probability that he will lose some control of his thumb and his index finger."

Which would be a minor inconvenience to the average person.

To a surgeon, it would mean the loss of his career.

Chapter Eight

Josie stood silent for a moment, eyeing Houston's hand.

Maybe she was wrong.

It was the only time in her career she had wished to be wrong.

With a deep breath, she resumed her examination. It confirmed her original diagnosis.

Not only was she certain the tendon to his thumb had been severed, the cut extended far enough that she suspected the two tendons in the index finger had suffered the same fate, as well as the median nerve.

"Shirley, have someone page Dr. Williams, will you? Dr. Hayes needs to undergo surgery." Dr. Williams was an orthopedic hand specialist Josie had met on several occasions.

"I'm going to splint his thumb and index finger together until Dr. Williams can get here and take a look." Josie worked quickly, immobilizing the digits, her hands doing the task by rote, while her mind raced.

What was she going to say to Houston?

He never stirred as she taped and bound the splint. She surveyed her work, then packed the hand with ice to stem the flow of blood to the damaged area. Shirley had left to have Dr. Williams paged, so Josie was alone with Houston.

Her eyes strayed to his face, so pale against his strikingly black hair. His mouth was open a smidge and she watched him breath deeply in and out, the restless sleep of the injured and medicated.

Barely aware that she did so, she reached up and brushed his hair back out of his eyes. His forehead was clammy.

"Dr. Adkins." Shirley came back into the room.

Josie pulled her hand back so fast she hit the instruments tray again. She sighed to herself. She was incapable of rational behavior around Houston, it seemed. Awake or asleep, he had the most humiliating effect on her.

"Yes?" She cleared her throat and strove to sound professional. If she actually achieved it, that would be a first.

"Hey." Shirley touched her arm. "You okay?"

Josie gave a nervous laugh. "I guess there's no chance you didn't hear anything he said?"

Shirley shook her head. "Sorry. Caught every word of it. But my lips are sealed, if that's the way you want it."

Heck, yeah, and then some. "Thanks, Shirley. I appreciate it."

Reluctant to leave him, she stood there staring at him.

"He's going to be okay, Dr. Adkins. He's a tough guy."

"I know." Josie forced herself to take a step back, both physically and emotionally. "Is Dr. Williams on his way?"

"He's going to be a while. He's at home with his kids, who have the chicken pox, and his wife is at the grocery store. He's calling her to come home, but it will probably be forty minutes or so by the time he gets here."

She peeled off her gloves and gown and tossed them

in the bin. "That's fine. It's not an emergency, as long as Dr. Hayes has the surgery in the next couple of days. But I thought Dr. Williams would want to take a look right away."

Not that looking at it was going to fix it. The tendons in the hand lie close to the surface, vulnerable to lacerations of the kind Houston had suffered. Only surgery could fix it. And Josie knew that coupled with the loss of feeling from the severed nerve, the probability of regaining full function in the affected area was slim.

More likely, there would be reduced mobility and lifelong problems with arthritis and inflammation. Worst-case scenario, the thumb and finger would no longer bend. Plain and simple, you can't bend a finger that you can't feel.

Not good news for a man like Houston, who loved his career and being in control.

With a last look at his immobile form, she left the room. In the hallway, she put a hand on her stomach. She felt like tossing her guts in the hazardous waste bin along with her gown, even though she was reasonably sure she had conducted herself well in there. The leg wounds she had dealt with competently, and she had prepared the hand for Dr. Williams to examine.

Then why did she feel like her stomach was tied into slipknots?

Possibly starting with the fact that her feelings for Houston were muddled and confusing, to say the least. Then ending with the fear that a man who was a brilliant surgeon might no longer be able to share that talent with his patients.

A shiver coursed through her, and she took a deep breath to steady herself before proceeding forward.

The waiting room contained the usual assortment of crying babies, the elderly, and a family sitting solemnly together, a middle-aged woman crying. Josie expected they belonged to the cardiac arrest Dr. Matthews had been dealing with.

There were also two men about Houston's age, wearing T-shirts, swim trunks, and sandals. She approached them. "Are you here for Dr. Hayes?"

"Yes." The man with blond hair stood up quickly. "How is he?"

"He's fine." Relief crossed both their faces as she continued. "He lost a lot of blood, but the wounds to his leg weren't as severe as they could have been. No arteries were severed, and there doesn't appear to be any muscular damage."

She paused a second, then decided to give the abridged version of his hand injury. It was Houston's right to hear about his injury first before his friends did. "He'll probably be having surgery on his hand to repair some damage, but it's a standard surgery and he should sail through with no problems."

All of that was true. The surgery was routine, though complex, and Houston wouldn't be in any danger from the procedure itself. She simply neglected to give further details.

"Thank God." The man ran his fingers through his curly blond hair. "I'm Christian Drake, by the way, Houston's brother-in-law. I was next to him on the water, but I didn't see it happen. And when I saw him on the beach, he was bleeding so much." Christian shuddered. He jerked a thumb at his dark-haired companion. "This is Dennis Madsen."

"Nice to meet you both. I'm Dr. Adkins." Josie was distracted by a disturbance at the door. A tall brunette rushed in and gave a frantic cry of dismay before launching herself at them and bursting into tears.

Startled, Josie stepped back a foot as Christian caught the woman and began making comforting sounds.

"Shh. Kori, it's okay. Houston's going to be okay."

Dennis gave Josie a rueful look. "Christian's wife. Houston's sister."

"You're sure he's okay?" the woman asked, tears streaming down her face. "I mean, a *shark?* God, it's just awful."

"Ask the doctor if you don't believe me." Christian gestured to Josie. "Kori, this is Dr. Adkins."

Josie smiled, trying not to notice the fact that Kori was wearing a black bikini top, tiny little shorts, and wedge sandals. She was tall and lean, without an ounce of fat on her anywhere, her skin a golden bronze, and her long dark hair flowing down her back. Josie felt like a pale, chunky elf next to her.

"Is Houston really going to be okay?" Kori demanded anxiously.

She forced herself to smile. "He's going to be fine. He won't be surfing for a while, though."

"Thank you, Doctor," Kori said through her tears, then pointed her finger at her husband. "You can forget about surfing anymore, Christian. Just forget it."

"Kori, don't overreact."

Josie ran her fingers through her hair, exhausted and feeling a tad this side of uncomfortable meeting his friends and sister. It occurred to her there were really valid reasons for not engaging in personal relationships with co-workers. She couldn't distance herself, couldn't stop her thoughts. How would his friends look at her if she announced she'd spent the night with Houston? Or almost spent the night, if they hadn't been interrupted.

Probably wouldn't believe it, she thought ruefully. Chances were she wasn't his usual type.

"Houston's asleep right now so he's not up for visitors. We're going to schedule surgery, but I really don't know when. You should probably leave and get some rest for the night. Why don't you leave a number with the triage nurse where we can contact you, and we'll call you when he's awake."

After answering a few more questions, and facing a fresh bout of tears from Kori, who hadn't heard about the surgery, Josie was able to head back to Trauma Three. Dr. Williams was walking down the hall in jeans and a T-shirt and she intercepted him.

"Dr. Williams."

He nodded. "Dr. Adkins."

She watched as he rubbed his jaw and rolled his head, tension obvious in his stance. Dr. Williams was normally upbeat and talkative. To see him so serious was a little disturbing, and she wondered if she had been wrong to page him at home.

"Sorry to drag you back here on your night off." Half her job as a resident seemed to be interpreting the actions and mood of the staff doctors.

He gave a shrug. "It's been a hell of a week. The kids have chicken pox, which means my wife has been stuck in the house for the last six days, which isn't making her pleasant to be around. She finally ran off to the grocery store, since there's nothing but ketchup to eat in the house, and I had to call her back before she made it to the bread and dairy aisle."

He rolled his eyes. "She wasn't real happy, let me tell you. I was glad to get out of there and escape her wrath."

Josie knew Dr. Williams was a family man through and through, and guarded his days off fervently to spend time with his kids, but in this case she sympathized with his wife. Being in the house for days on end with kids and no milk for cereal didn't sound like a picnic.

"You know, you might want to stop at an all-night store on your way home and pick up the milk and bread. It will go a long way towards forgiveness."

He nodded. "You're brilliant. I never would have

thought of doing that. Maybe she'll be so grateful she'll actually do some of my laundry. She's been so busy entertaining the kids, who are crabby beyond belief, that I've been wearing the same socks for three days."

Josie fought the urge to look down at his feet.

Then Dr. Williams stopped outside Houston's room and his tone turned curt and professional. "So what have we got?"

Aware there was only a curtain separating them from Houston, she whispered, "Severed flexor pollaris longus. And he bagged a nerve."

Dr. Williams shook his head, his expression more serious than she had ever seen it. "That's not what I wanted to hear." He jerked his thumb towards the other side of the curtain. "Does he know yet?"

"No." She bit her lip as she imagined the reaction the news was going to get.

He flung the curtain aside. "Well, it's not going to get any easier the longer we wait. Let's get it over with, shall we?"

Houston heard the voices murmuring on the other side of the curtain. His leg ached like hell and his hand felt numb. He shook his head to clear it.

He glanced around. He was in the ER. That made sense. He'd gone a round with a shark and had lost. The bump, the bite, then paddling himself to shore. He remembered all that.

It was what came afterwards that was foggy. He had been flat on his back staring up at Josie, her perky green eyes trained on his leg.

Then nothing.

They must have given him a painkiller.

Which normally had the effect of a semi-truck barreling into him at ninety miles per hour. He was extremely sensitive to drugs. He couldn't even take over-the-counter decongestants without passing out.

Mike Williams strolled into his cubicle. "Hey, there, Hayes. Heard you had a wipeout and I had to come and see for myself."

He forced himself to smile. "It's not a wipeout when a shark drops in on your wave."

Mike chuckled and flipped the blanket off of his leg. Josie peered over him with Mike. Houston was suddenly aware that he was wearing nothing more than a hospital gown, which had ridden up to nearly his waist. If they twitched that blanket around any more he was going to be flashing them.

He had enough problems right now. He didn't need to add an inappropriate hard-on to the list. He'd been dreaming of Josie when he was dozing in and out of consciousness. Dreaming that she was in his bed, doing those delicious things to his cock with her tongue.

Houston didn't like the fact that Josie could arouse him without even trying, even while he was drugged up and unconscious.

Nor did he like being flat on his back. How in the hell did patients stand this? He felt like he was laid out on a slab in the morgue.

"Quit gawking at me and help me get this bed up." He rolled over, careful to tuck the blanket first to prevent skin exposure, and searched for the button to raise the bed.

Only to find to his astonishment that his right hand was wrapped in a splint. It had also been packed in ice, which had now fallen into his lap from his movement. "Damn! Get this ice off of me."

He had meant Mike. Not Josie. But she moved first, before he could even think, and suddenly her hands were on his waist, retrieving the ice pack. Actually, they were lower than his waist. In his lap. With nothing but a paper thin hospital gown between her fingers and his skin, and he was tenting the fabric with a partial boner.

If this wasn't humiliating he didn't know what was. Yet Josie looked cool and efficient, the picture of the unperturbed doctor. He should feel grateful, but instead found himself irritated that she was undisturbed by his near nakedness. Just the night before he had been tasting between her thighs, and now she was giving him a blank clinical stare.

"Can I get another blanket?" he snapped.

Mike and Josie shared a look.

"What?"

"It's true what they say," Mike said. "Doctors make the worst patients. Now can you stop whining for a minute so I can take a look at your leg?"

Josie spread another blanket over him from the knees up, her slender fingers tucking gently on either side of his waist. Her curvy body leaned over him as she worked, and he caught a whiff of the light, sweet lotion she wore.

He turned away from her, repelled yet pleased that she took the time to touch him so tenderly.

"So, how's my leg? And why is my hand splinted and packed?"

His mind was still moving like river mud from the painkiller he assumed he had been given, and he was having trouble thinking clearly. He recalled his hand being chaffed by the shark's rough skin, but that wouldn't warrant a splint.

Josie cleared her throat. "Your leg is fine. Eight two-inch puncture wounds, which I sutured, and multiple lacerations. You shouldn't have any problems with those healing. Stay off the leg for several days, and you know the drill for sutures. We'll take them out in about a week."

Houston tilted his head to look at her. Josie's words sounded reassuring, exactly what he had been hoping to hear, yet she didn't sound right. She sounded nervous. Unnatural.

Something was wrong, and he wanted to know what it was. "Is that it?"

"Oh, and I found you a souvenir." Reaching back onto the counter she held up a shark tooth. "From your leg."

He fought the urge to shudder. As if he wanted to remember that mouth coming at him, those teeth sunk into his flesh.

"What exactly did you give me, by the way? I don't remember anything at all. I'm really sensitive to pain-killers."

For some inexplicable reason, she blushed. "Diamorphine."

A horrible suspicion overcame him, one that would explain Josie's obvious discomfort. "Did I, ah . . . say anything unusual while I was out?"

The blush deepened.

Oh, God. He had. He tried to get his brain to cooperate and reveal his words to him, but it refused. There was nothing but a big blank.

"I don't think so," she said, her eyes not meeting his.

That was not reassuring. Though he couldn't imagine what he would have said, unless he'd come on to her or something, given what he had been dreaming about. Maybe he had actually asked her to suck his . . . *hell*.

But he didn't have time for regrets, distracted by Mike's examination of his hand. He didn't like the look on Mike's face.

"What's wrong with my hand? I thought I just scraped it."

Mike didn't say anything as he rebound the splint he had undone. Then he looked up and met his eye.

Houston's stomach hit the floor. "Mike? What the hell's going on here?"

"You've severed your FPL and median nerve. We need to get you into the OR."

Once when he was a kid, Houston's dad had shoved him out of the way, and he had fallen on the edge of the coffee table, forcing all the air out of his lungs and leaving him stunned and disoriented.

This felt like that.

He heard Mike's words. He knew what they meant. He just couldn't believe it.

"Are you sure?" He propped himself up on his elbow, and focused on his hand.

Impatiently, he attempted to wiggle and bend each finger. Neither his index finger nor his thumb moved.

"Oh, my God." Houston started to claw at the binding with his left hand, as if seeing the damage for himself would somehow alter the reality.

The reality that was sitting down hard on him.

He couldn't move his fingers.

If he couldn't move his fingers, how in the hell could he operate?

Mike's hand landed on his chest. "Take it easy, come on. We'll get you prepped and into OR and we'll patch you right up."

Houston stopped pulling at the adhesive on the splint and understood for the first time why patients sometimes looked at him with complete loathing. Mike's reasonable, calm voice made him want to ram a fist down the guy's throat. Take it easy?

How exactly was he supposed to take it easy when his life was ruined?

Then he met Josie's eye, and what he saw there was far, far worse. Swimming in her green eyes was compassion and something that he had only seen once before in his life—pity. Then it had been the neighbors feeling sorry for his mother when they heard her husband swearing at her, humiliating her.

At the time he hadn't thought he could feel any worse.

He had been wrong.

His elbow gave out, and he sank back onto the bed, stunned.

This was worse. For a man who demanded life obey his commands, this was the worst of all.

Then he prayed that Josie would leave the room, because her pity left him as paralyzed as his injured thumb.

Chapter Nine

Three days later Josie sat in her car outside Houston's condo and dialed Sara on her cell phone.

"I can't go through with this. He's not going to appreciate my just showing up on his front step when he's recovering."

"Josie, you were the last woman to sleep with him. It would be rude if you didn't check up on him. He got bit by a shark, for heaven's sake."

"I could just send a card." Not that Hallmark made a *Get well soon from your shark bite;* signed, *Your one-night stand co-worker* card.

"You can't send a card!" Sara sounded horrified. "That's tacky."

Josie was feeling pretty tacky anyway. "Fine. But he's going to tell me to go away."

"So you either go away, or you stay and make him wish his parts were all functional."

"What's that supposed to mean?" And she knew all his parts, save his hand, were very functional, but that didn't mean she should do anything about it.

"He has it bad for you. You have it bad for him."

"And?" There had to be more wisdom forthcoming.

"So, you can give up, let him blow you off, or you can fight for him. Make him want more with you."

Oh, because *that* was so simple. "He doesn't want

more with me." More sex, more talking, more dates, more anything.

Except under the influence of diamorphine he *had* said that if he did, it would be with her . . .

"It's worth a try."

Josie turned the air conditioning up higher, aiming it at her armpits, and pondered that. Maybe Sara was right and it was worth a try. Everyone knew that on drugs or alcohol people were given to bouts of confession and soul-searching honesty, which would mean Houston had probably meant what he had said. So why shouldn't she try to catch Houston's interest?

At the very least, she wanted back in his bed again. Or in his bed for the first time, since they hadn't actually made it to the bedroom on Saturday.

It was like med school. No one had expected her to be a doctor, except for her dad, but she had made the decision and she'd stuck with it, and it had worked. She loved caring for patients.

She wanted Houston. If only for an affair, so be it. She was a big girl, in several ways, and she could walk away when it was over, with enough material to fuel hot dreams for the next twenty years or so until menopause.

He had said if he could get close to anyone, it would be her. Well, she'd show him close.

Bending over, Josie blotted her nose on her shirt to dull any shine that might be hanging around, and ran a finger through her choppy hair. Nervous about dropping by unannounced, she had gone to the mall and bought a denim skirt in an attempt to look something other than scruffy.

It now occurred to her it would serve her new purpose even better, since he had said he wanted to see her in a skirt. He had suggested no panties, and barely covering her ass as well, but one out of three wasn't bad.

The T-shirt she was wearing was a little on the tight side, too, and she decided maybe it would be therapeutic for him. Aid his recovery, get the old irons back in the fire.

The news from Houston's surgery had been as expected. Both the FDP and FDS tendons to the index finger had been cut, and the FPL to the thumb, as well as the branches of the median nerve. Dr. Williams had retrieved the tendons from the forearm, where they had snapped back, and reattached them. He had then used a microscope to sew the nerves back together.

So really, this wasn't all about her. She was being a friend, that's all. Houston needed a distraction, and if that involved oral sex, who was she to say no?

As she got out of the car and headed up his walk, she tried to imagine what he was going through and couldn't. If she were to lose function in her hand, the medical field wouldn't exactly mourn the loss. Houston was different. He was a brilliant surgeon, and loved it.

He had to be feeling frustrated, angry, scared. In pain.

But helping patients in recovery was one of her specialties, something she excelled at and enjoyed. She could help Houston recover, take care of him, be a friend. Give him an orgasm.

Her hand hit the doorbell hard. If he would let her.

A woman in her fifties, tall and trim, answered the door. She gave a friendly smile. "Can I help you?"

This she hadn't counted on. Josie hadn't stopped to think—big surprise—that he couldn't possibly be alone, having just left the hospital the day before.

"Hi," she said, rubbing the back of her neck. "I'm Josie Adkins, a, uh, friend—colleague—of Houston's. I just wanted to see how he's doing."

The door swung wider and the polite interest turned to genuine pleasure. "Come in, come in. It's so nice to meet you, Josie. I'm Francesca Hayes, Houston's mother. Houston's in the living room, watching TV, and I'm sure he'll be glad to see you."

Josie could argue that, but she just nodded.

Houston's mother had a faint trace of an Italian accent and a welcoming smile. She leaned forward and whispered, "He doesn't do so well with being injured, you know, and he's growling like a bear."

Josie could well imagine Houston had no patience for being dependent on others. She stepped into the condo and started down the hallway after his mother, hoping she knew what she was doing.

"Shit."

They both heard Houston swear and the leather sofa squeak as he moved around.

Josie froze, a little unnerved, but his mother made a clicking sound with her teeth and called, "What's the matter?"

"I dropped the fucking remote and I can't pick it back up."

Oh, yeah. Bear was an understatement.

Francesca glanced back at her and gave a shrug of apology. "Houston, watch your mouth! You have company."

"Dennis has heard me swear before."

Josie stopped at the end of the hall and peered around his mother. Houston was on the couch, sitting up sideways, legs out straight in front of him. The wound on his leg was dressed, and his right hand was fully wrapped and splinted. He was wearing loose navy and green boxer shorts and a white T-shirt.

Her mouth went dry. He looked so delicious, so masculine, so pissed, as he leaned over the side of the couch and tried to retrieve the remote with his left hand, balancing precariously.

"It's not Dennis, it's your cute little friend Josie."

Josie cringed at the word "little."

Houston's head snapped up.

What was in those pale eyes besides surprise? Pleasure, impatience, curiosity? She couldn't tell. He was unreadable again, his face revealing nothing more than if he'd been wearing a surgical mask.

"Dr. Adkins," he said. "What a surprise."

His tone infuriated her, anger ripping through her without warning. They weren't at the hospital. She had slept with him two feet from where he was sitting, right by that very coffee table only four days earlier, and she'd sewn his chewed up leg back together. He could call her Josie.

The retort on her lips was swallowed, mindful of his mother standing there watching them both.

"I wanted to see how you're doing." She smiled brightly. "I thought maybe you could use some help from a friend."

Before Houston could even respond, his mother touched her arm. "That's wonderful, what a sweet offer! Are you busy right now, *cara*? I want to run to the store, since Houston doesn't have a thing without mold in his refrigerator. But I don't want to leave him alone, you know. Would you mind staying with him for an hour?"

Houston looked belligerent, revealing his feelings on being left alone with her. "Mom, I don't need a babysitter. You can go to the store whenever you want."

Said the man who couldn't even pick up the remote. She'd love to see him trying to fix something to eat, or walk to the bathroom without falling on his face.

"I'd love to stay, Mrs. Hayes. Take your time." Josie went around the coffee table and picked up the remote. She set it by Houston's left hand, brushing her arm against his, pausing to smile at him.

Eyes narrowed, he watched her. "Thank you."

His mother was already heading for the door, scooping up her purse. "Oh, thank you so much, Josie. I'm sure Houston will appreciate having someone to talk to besides his old mother."

"My pleasure," she said, as the front door opened and shut.

Josie couldn't help but quirk her lips a little as she perched carefully on the coffee table. "Your mom seems nice."

His expression softened just a little. "She's a hell of a lady." Then he rolled his eyes. "But she's driving me nuts."

Like Josie imagined she was right now. "So, can I get you anything? A drink? Coffee? Tea?" *Me.*

If it had been anyone else, she would have questioned him about his injury, inquired how he was feeling, expressed her sympathy. Instinctively, she felt all of those would irritate Houston. So she strove to be cheerful and matter-of-fact.

Normally impeccable, his black hair looked like he'd struggled to comb it with his left hand and given up, and his right hand was resting protectively on his waist.

He groaned. "Oh, God, don't you start mothering me too."

Josie glanced again at him, only lower this time, running her eyes across his rigid thighs as she licked her lips. "Mothering you wasn't exactly what I had in mind."

He caught the innuendo, as she'd known he would. The sound of his breathing changed. "Oh, really? What did you have in mind?"

She didn't answer him directly, but leaned back a little, resting her arms on the table. "You know, you're going to be on medical leave for at least a week or two."

His jaw twitched. "I'm well aware of that."

"So there's no one to notice any tension between us."

Just a lift of his eyebrow. "What are you suggesting?"

Here it came. She forced the words past her lips, heeding the need, the rolling, sliding, wet desire flowing between her thighs like rushing lava. "That we don't have to stop at one night. That we can have a string of one-nights together."

Josie swallowed hard. "Until one of us says enough."

This was unexpected. Houston had been unnerved to see Josie standing in his living room next to his mother, and puzzled at the strange longing that had tripped across his consciousness.

Followed by anger, that she would follow him here, see him like this, trapped on his own couch like some damn invalid. He didn't need Josie Adkins and her temptations right now, not when he was facing the fact that he had no feeling in his hand. That no matter how he ignored it, how he hoped and ranted and cursed, it was probable that he could never conduct surgery again.

That Mike William's words, *almost fully functional,* meant that someday after six weeks in a splint and months of rehab, he could expect to learn how to button his own shirt without assistance and lift a glass, but that fine motor skills like writing weren't likely.

But Josie, Josie, Josie—sweet and sexy Josie, with the words that stumbled in their haste and the pale, rounded body that lured him. He couldn't resist her. He hadn't finished with her. There were so many more things he could do to her.

Not like this though. Not stuck here, a gimpy, stitched-up, gauze-padded mess of a man. He wanted her to come back, when he was whole, and play their dangerous game again. Dangerous because they could get caught. Dangerous because he could find himself wanting more and more.

He shifted his legs to the floor, hiding a groan when his injured leg tugged and pulled, the skin itchy and tight under the bandage, the muscles burning. It felt less vulnerable to sit up, feet on the ground.

"I'm not up for it at the moment, but in a couple of weeks I think we can work something out."

That skirt she was wearing was riding up, and Josie looked to have forgotten she was wearing it. Her knees were parted, her thighs spread out in front of him, a peek of white panties teasing him.

"I don't want to wait a couple of weeks," she said, cheeks flushing, eyes wide, breath tight.

Neither did his cock. It jerked forward at her words. "Is that why you're flashing me your panties?"

Confusion crossed her face. The dusky stain on her cheeks darkened. Her legs came together tightly. "Oh! I wasn't doing that on purpose."

He grinned, feeling the upper hand shift back to him. "I thought it was meant to be an offer." Then he added, a curious thought popping into his head, "What are Wednesday's panties? What do you got on under there?"

Flowers, stripes, hearts?

"They're bull's-eyes."

What little control he'd thought he had disappeared, shaken loose under those words. Did she mean targets? Little circles ringing each other right on her . . . *fuck.*

"Show me."

"No!"

"Are they on your ass? Your front?"

"Both."

"Turn around. Show me your ass."

"They're like the lip ones."

"So let me see. Pull your skirt up."

His leg throbbed, his cock throbbed, and he suspected he was acting like a prick, but Josie stood up, taking a deep breath. Her fingers fiddled with the bottom of her skirt, then she inched it up, wiggling to work it past her curvaceous hips.

She turned around before he saw anything, but quickly bunched the skirt at her waist, bent one knee, and waited.

Houston felt as faint as he had on the beach, bleeding into the wet sand. Bull's-eyes ringed each side of her ass, red lines that blurred in his vision, taunting him, making his hand itch to land right on that spot.

"Where the hell did you get those?" he murmured in awe. "A sex shop?"

"Of course not! They're just theme panties—they're supposed to be cute, not sexual. Geez, like I'd buy something from a sex shop. I don't exactly have the butt for teddies and thongs."

Houston loved that Josie started these little games with him, then chickened out, panicked, tried to backpedal.

She was already shoving her skirt back down.

Only a foot in front of him, it was no effort to reach his good hand forward and under the skirt, catching it before it fell straight down. He snaked around between her legs as she went still, around to her soft batch of curls. He circled his finger over her.

"Is there a bull's-eye here, too?"

"Yes."

He nibbled the spot on her back thigh closest to him, right below her panties. Then he pulled his hand back and spanked her, right on that front target, cupping her after the blow.

She gave a cry of shock.

Heat poured out from beneath her panties.

"What was that for?"

"For suggesting you wouldn't look good in a teddy or a thong."

"It's true."

Houston held her there, his thumb marking the imagined dead center of the bull's-eye, and he ignored the sharp pain in his calf. "When was the last time you put one on?"

"I don't know, maybe when I was eighteen." She tried to wiggle away from him.

He wanted to hold her, to keep her there, to feel her panties grow moist beneath his hand. But a sharp stab in his calf had him swearing silently.

Letting her go, he sank back onto the couch, wishing his leg to hell. God, the way it pulsed, hot and itchy, made him furious. But he hoped Josie had no indication how much pain he was in.

"Then you don't know whether you look good in something sexy or not."

Josie turned around and plopped on the coffee table again, making sure she didn't hit his leg with her knee. "Why are we always talking about my body?"

Because he was obsessed with it. Because it factored heavily into the majority of his dreams every night and because she looked like an Italian master had painted her in curvy perfection.

"What else should we talk about? You're the one who came here with the offer to have wild sex whenever we want, with no commitment, for the next few weeks."

That had her rubbing her hands on her knees and her skin flushing in ruddy, uneven patches of pink so that if he didn't know better, he'd think she'd come down with a fever.

"I don't like the way you do that," she said with a frown.

"Do what?" Between the need for a painkiller and the memory of those bull's-eyes, he had no energy left for deciphering that statement.

"Make me deliberately uncomfortable whenever

you're uncomfortable. And the way you have to keep reinforcing to both of us that you're always in charge."

Josie watched Houston's eyes, which had been filled with pain and lust, murk over with confusion. "I don't do that," he denied, shoulders stiffening at her suggestion.

"Yes, you do. You're always catching me off-guard with suggestive comments, teasing me about spanking, complimenting my body. It keeps me off-balance and you in control."

He scoffed. "It's called flirting."

The words were spoken to the ceiling as he shrugged, sounding casual but looking anything but. He looked ticked off. He looked like he knew she was right. And she was. Houston Hayes was a control freak.

But she was a people pleaser, and she wanted to see him happy—truly, deeply content in a way he just wasn't. And she knew now what she wanted. She wanted Houston, not just his body, but all of him, his heart, his soul, the intimacy he had hinted at when he was lying on her table, drugged up.

An affair wasn't enough for her, she realized, and she wasn't a woman who could walk away, heart intact. If she had a fling with Houston, her heart would be squashed like an orange in a juicer. Unless she could convince Houston to give a real relationship a try.

Unless she could reach inside his heart, past the rigid aloofness, past the mentor-student relationship they had, to the real Houston Hayes. The one who wanted children and cared about the pain of his geriatric patients.

She wanted that Houston, and she wanted him to care about *her*. That didn't seem likely, but heck, she'd never know unless she tried.

"You know, Houston, I've changed my mind." The way to his heart wasn't through his pants. She didn't know which path to take instead, but she just knew instinctively that if she wanted something more she had to be his friend first.

Not an easy task, but she had always been friendlier than she was sexy, yet he seemed to have no problems getting turned on. Maybe he wouldn't be able to resist her cheerfulness either. She'd wear him down with perky instead of passion.

"Changed your mind about what?" He sat back, surly.

"I don't think it's a good idea for us to continue with an affair. It wasn't right of me to come here like this, while you're injured and try and take advantage of your vulnerability." She patted his knee and felt guilty for intentionally arousing him when she now could no longer in good conscience act on those physical feelings.

"You said you wanted one night, and that's it, and I should have respected that. I was just trying to get more bang for my buck, so to speak, and that wasn't right. I apologize, Houston."

He gaped at her. "Excuse me?"

Josie did feel relieved. She wasn't a seductress who had men on a revolving-door basis. She was just Josie, and she was happy with herself the way she was. A good friend, a caring doctor, and if anything were to come about between them, it had to be because he liked her the way she truly was.

She added, "I can't believe I acted like that. Geez, I was almost on the verge of getting on my knees and pulling your, you know, into my mouth. I'm so glad I stopped myself."

His boxers bulged, the vein in his temple pulsed. Josie heard herself babbling and realized she wasn't making it any better. He looked like he was watching a man being beaten to death with a feather duster. Total disbelief.

"Since you want us to be platonic from now on, I

think we should really try to be friends. We're co-workers, and it's impractical to think that we can go totally back to the way we were before, but I'd love to be friends."

Josie stood up and swung his legs back onto the sofa with the practiced ease of a doctor, her touch as impersonal as she could manage. She set the remote control on his lap and smiled, telling herself to think of him as any other patient. The one you would go the extra mile for, but still just a patient nonetheless.

"Friends take care of each other, you know. So is there anything I can do for you to help make you more comfortable?"

Something that didn't involve dealing with the massive erection that was straining in his boxers.

Celibacy wasn't what she'd had in mind when she'd shown up at his condo, but a couple of weeks of squirming would be worth it if in the end she could convince Houston to give an actual relationship a try. A relationship based on more than the powerful sexual attraction that raged between them.

He stared at her, an ugly scowl marring his good looks. He shook his head, his words slow. "No, there's nothing you can do."

"Okay." Determined not to make a mistake, to be supportive of Houston's recovery and resist any further urges to lift her skirt in his presence, she settled herself back on the left-hand side of the couch. Tucked in next to his feet, she started to chatter about her day, the cases she'd seen, and the weather, while he stared at her—frowning, brooding, silent—until his mother returned twenty minutes later.

Then Josie went into the kitchen to help Francesca unload the bags, more than aware of Houston's eyes on her backside as she went. She wondered if she was the only one thinking about the twin bull's-eyes on her panties and what he could be using for target practice.

Chapter Ten

Houston watched Josie saunter off into his kitchen like she owned the place, her curvy backside twitching beneath that too-short skirt, reminding him of the view he'd had earlier.

What was this *just friends* crap all about? One minute she was suggesting they have a no-holds-barred affair, and the next she was delivering a bad breakup line. He didn't want to be friends with her. He didn't even want to work with her. He wanted her for one thing, and one thing only, and he'd gotten that and it was enough.

And he was a lousy liar, even to himself.

He wanted something else, he just couldn't figure out what to call it. But it sure as hell wasn't a platonic, nurse-him-back-to-health friendship. Yet Josie wasn't coddling him, fussing over his wounds, or making weird gasping noises of horror like his sister had done.

It was the doctor in her. She was matter-of-fact about the injury, thoughtful of his comfort, but not hovering. No, she had just kept him company, just like his mother had suggested, talking about a staggering array of subjects with lightning speed and acting like she'd never once thought of him in any way other than a casual acquaintance and fellow doctor.

Despite her little bombshell statement about going

down on him, she was now being about as sexually
suggestive as a nun. He could see her in the kitchen,
talking to his mother and putting away coffee in his
pantry. No woman had ever entered his pantry before.
He felt violated, naked as she witnessed his cereal,
canned corn, and fast food ketchup packs scattered
around.

Left out and not liking it, he called, "Mom, can you
get me a water or something?"

His petty plan to break up their female gabfest back-
fired when it was Josie who brought him an ice-filled
glass, perspiration running down its side, a smile on
her lips. Plump lips that so recently had been on his.

He took the water from her. "Thank you."

"Sure." She ran her hands through her hair and
stood there, feet crossed at the ankles.

Not sure why she was still hanging around, he took
a sip of water, catching a square ice cube between his
front teeth as he ignored her.

Suddenly her fingers were in his hair and her breasts
scraping across his face, a soft, warm cotton T-shirt
pushing into his eye and nose. Houston jerked sideways, spilling some water in his lap and losing the ice
cube down the front of his shirt. "What the hell are you
doing?"

"There was a bug in your hair." She showed him a
beetle squeezed between her thumb and index finger.

Christ. He brushed at his shirt and boxer shorts,
which were sporting a nice wet spot front and center.
"You made me spill my water."

"Oh! Sorry. Here, I'll walk you to your bedroom
and help you get changed."

It was a suggestive comment, no question about it.
His brain knew it and his dick knew it, but Josie
blinked at him in innocence. She was either messing
with his head or he was still feeling the aftereffects of
drugs in his system. That was a come-on.

"I can change myself."

"Are you sure? Down one hand and one leg it will be awkward." She put her hand on his elbow to assist him up. "It's not like I haven't seen you naked before. I can handle it."

Still no sign that she was teasing him. Josie just looked clinical. Efficient, friendly, helpful, and completely unconcerned that just days before he had been inside her making her moan. That nonchalance over what they had shared, added to that bossy nurse attitude, was starting to piss him off.

"I bet you could handle it," he murmured, hoping to rock her a little.

Instead, she just laughed and patted his shoulder. "Come on. Up you go."

Like a senior citizen. The hell with that. Waving her off, he stood up, ignoring the burning in his leg as he started off down the hallway with a slow gait, a step-hop kind of walk that felt like it took forever since her eyes were on him.

Houston wanted Josie to go away. He wanted her to leave him alone to feel sorry for himself and to take her perky bedside manner with her.

Or go down on her knees and give him that nonplatonic treatment she had mentioned.

Twice daily. For an indefinite amount of time.

Limping into his room, he decided that in the matter of one week, Josie and a hungry shark had managed to turn his life upside down and leave him feeling like he'd taken a conk on the head, not a bite to the leg.

Josie went into the kitchen feeling satisfied with her behavior. It was working. She was able to control her lusty panty-melting feelings for Houston by treating him like a patient—any other old and ornery patient.

"Do you need any help, Mrs. Hayes?" Josie reached

for the empty plastic grocery bags and started balling them up.

"Oh, call me Fran. And thank you, but I've got it all put away now. Is Houston all right? I heard him go down the hall."

"He spilled his water and went to change." Which she would have gladly helped him with, in an efficient and asexual manner if he had let her, because she was in control of herself. Sort of.

The image of raising his shirt over that rippling broad chest had her questioning her powers of restraint. Given that kind of temptation she might not have been able to resist a little touch. Or two. Or sex.

"That had to go over big, spilling his water." Fran shook her head, a smile sliding across her face.

Josie leaned against the counter, still gripping the plastic bags and smiled back, shoving all thoughts of naked Houston out of her pheromone-flooded mind. "No, it didn't. He doesn't like it when he can't control things, does he?"

"You've hit the nail on the head, Josie. He's always been like that. I had a bad marriage, you know, and it wasn't good for Houston. He holds himself back, doesn't show affection. But he's very loyal to those he loves." Fran studied her in a way that made Josie uncomfortable. "Are you dating my son?"

It was so direct and sudden that Josie blushed. She dropped the bags on the counter and ran her finger across her bottom lip. "Oh . . . me? And Houston? No, not at all. We work together, that's it. I'm in my second year of my residency, and he's sort of like a mentor to me."

Oh, that sounded perverted somehow. Josie went beyond blush to a five-alarm face fire.

"I see," Fran said, with a look that clearly said she saw a lot of things, none of which Josie wanted to discuss with Houston's mother.

But the comment about her marriage brought to mind what Houston had said when Josie was stitching him up. He'd mentioned his father when he had told her he couldn't get close to people. Clearly, there was more to the story there, a bad relationship with his father that had caused the boy to grow into a man who stayed distant from people.

At first, Josie had thought Houston was aloof, unconcerned with others, professional in the extreme, maybe even a little self-centered. She was now starting to see that Houston held back on purpose, that he stayed distant from other hospital employees so things stayed neat and tidy and he never risked the chance of losing control of the situation.

"Houston, he doesn't have a lot of friends," Fran said.

Josie heard a noise and turned around, afraid Houston had caught her gossiping about him with his mother. The hall was empty, but Fran picked up on her discomfort and lowered her voice.

"He has a couple of boys he's known forever. He has his sister. He has me. That's it." Fran was a hand talker, and she emphasized now by slicing her palms through the air.

While really nervous that Houston would appear any second like he'd been beamed into the room, Josie still found herself nodding. "I thought that was probably the case."

Houston was a loner at the hospital as well, and she thought maybe they had more in common than he could ever realize. While Josie was friendly with everyone, she was close to very few people, and lately she had been feeling the same way Sara had. Lonely.

"These women, they want to date him because he is so handsome and he's a doctor. They flip their blond hair and expect fancy dinners and flowers, but no one ever tries to get to know my son, to understand him. When the right woman takes the time to see him for what he is, they'll find a good man worth keeping forever."

Fran shook her finger. "But then he's my son. I'm partial to him."

Josie wasn't sure why they were having this conversation except that maybe Houston's mother was getting tired of waiting for more grandchildren. Or maybe she figured a wife or girlfriend would keep Houston's refrigerator filled with edible food, saving her a trip to the grocery store.

Either way, she got the feeling Fran either approved of her or was politely warning her to stay the hell away.

"I . . . admire him." She did. As a doctor. As a man. As the reason behind her having three orgasms in rapid succession. "I want to be Houston's friend."

Horizontal, naked friend.

Fran Hayes nodded thoughtfully. "Good. Then maybe you can help me out by checking in on Houston once in a while. I work retail and my hours are crazy. I took a few days off, but I need to go back to work and my daughter is useless with sick people. Plus she has to bring her kids and Houston spends the whole time trying to look like he's not in pain so he doesn't scare them."

Josie had no problem picturing that. She remembered how he had spoken about his nieces.

"And when Kori came without the girls and tried to change the dressing on his leg, she ended up gagging and running outside for fresh air."

Josie laughed. "That's a common reaction. But trust me, I can handle it. I help Houston saw people's bones down: a few sutures won't bother me. Especially since I'm the one who stitched him up. I'd like to check out my handiwork."

"Great." Fran beamed at her, like they had reached a female understanding.

Josie smiled back for a different reason. If Houston protested her popping up on his doorstep, she'd just tell him his mother had sent her.

The next day Josie rang Houston's doorbell wearing denim shorts and a loose T-shirt, carrying crab legs from Barnacle Bill's in a big bag.

Houston didn't answer the door. But then, she figured he probably didn't want to limp to the door when he wasn't expecting anyone, and his mother would have a key. She tried the knob. It was unlocked and she was in luck. Which was good, because she couldn't eat this much crab in a week.

"Hello?" she called as she entered his foyer. "It's me, I brought you dinner."

There was no response and Josie wandered past his empty living room to the kitchen. Houston was sitting at the glass table, a news magazine propped in front of him, eating strawberries. He glanced up at her, then bit another berry, taking the whole thing in his mouth to the green stem.

"Is that your dinner?"

"Yes." He tossed the stem down and pointedly turned the page of his magazine as he chewed.

Like that was going to stop her. "Well, hello. How was your day? It's nice to see you, too." She plunked the bag down on the table.

"Josie." He looked at her, his expression pained. "No offense, but I'm not in the mood for company."

"Which is exactly why you need company."

"There's no logic in that statement," he said, eyeing the bag on the table.

Despite his recent ordeal, Josie had to admit that Houston looked good enough to eat. He was unshaven, scruffier than she'd ever seen him, and bare-chested. His olive-colored shorts hung loose on his waist and enhanced the surfer-bum image, which she found really sexy. Of course, he could be dressed like Santa and she'd find him sexy. And a beard could tickle in some really interesting places . . . *Knock it off, Josie.*

He kept his injured hand in his lap, and his leg was still wrapped, but he didn't look like he was in any major discomfort today.

"It makes perfect sense to me," she said, opening the bag and pulling out a Styrofoam box, setting it in front of Houston, and popping the top open. The pungent aroma of fresh seafood filled the air.

"You're not going to leave, are you?" he asked, fingers reaching for the crab before he caught himself and stopped.

"Nope. Not a chance. We're going to eat dinner and talk and you're going to tell me all about the mysterious things you said while you were on the diamorphine."

That got his attention. Houston's eyes locked with hers. "Why? What did I say?"

"You mean you don't remember?" She shook out a paper napkin and plastic cutlery and set them in front of him. "And here it was such a life-altering moment for me."

Josie took a crab leg, snapped it, and sat down in the chair next to him, feeling her mouth water. It had been a long day at the hospital and she'd skipped lunch. She took a healthy bite.

"Cute," he said, pushing his bowl of strawberries away. "But I didn't say anything."

"You said lots of things." Josie wiped her chin with a napkin. "Like suggesting I call Tim Sheinberg to take over for me since I'm not qualified."

If she had expected him to deny it or be embarrassed, she was disappointed.

He just shrugged. "Is that all? That's true."

Tempted to shove a strawberry up his nose, she snorted. "I am so qualified to give stitches. I'm qualified to do an entire range of orthopedic procedures a million times more complicated than pulling a shark tooth out of your leg."

So much for staying cheerful and friendly.

Houston stared at the table, his lip twitching, and she realized he was trying not to laugh.

She could fix that. "But after that uncomplimentary statement you went and told me how pretty you think I am."

That got a better reaction. The bronze muscles in Houston's bare shoulders tensed, his arm flexed. The vein running down to his elbow bulged as he shot her a wary glance. "Oh, really?"

"Really." If he denied it, she'd skip the berry and go right to her fist in his nose.

Houston had brought out an unknown violent streak in her.

But the lecher just shrugged again, eyes dropping to her chest. "That's true, too."

Gasping in annoyance, she stood up. He'd gone and made her embarrassed, and that had been the last thing she'd intended. She grabbed a paper plate out of the bag and slapped a crab leg in front of Houston. "I hope you're hungry, there's a ton here. I didn't judge very well."

Houston's hand landed on her waist as she leaned over the table and fussed with the food, cutting crab on his plate with the plastic knife and fork. She ignored him and sawed urgent little pieces, sending the crab leg sliding around in its buttery juices.

"You're very pretty." The cool air of the kitchen hit her skin as he lifted her T-shirt. His breath drizzled across her waist and she stiffened, holding the plastic fork so tight she snapped a tine off in the crab.

"Shoot." Josie reached forward, fishing around for the lost piece of plastic as Houston's lips landed on her flesh.

The fork went skittering right out of her hand, crab still attached to it, and crashed to a halt in the spine of Houston's magazine.

She stepped away from the kiss that was rapidly turning into nuzzling. "Stop that."

"Why?" He tugged on the edge of her shirt, trying to pull her back.

"Because you said one night, remember? We're trying to be just friends, remember?" This wasn't working. How could she resist him when every time she looked at him there was sexual promise hovering in his blue eyes?

"That was your idea. When you suggested we have a string of one-nighters, I agreed. I just asked for a week to recover."

"But I changed my mind and decided that you were right. Now I'm trying to be a friend, to help you like your mother asked me to until you feel better, so be good."

"You want to know what would make me feel better?"

Since it probably involved a laundry list of sexual positions a man with a leg injury could do, she didn't want to hear it. "No."

He laughed and popped a piece of crab into his mouth. "But then you're not fulfilling your promise to my mother. She asked you to help me. And I have some requests."

That sounded dangerous. And it looked even worse, given the glint in his eye and the unmistakable smirk crossing his face.

Sitting down so she wouldn't singe him from the heat radiating off her shorts like a space heater, she chewed her lip. "Why? What do you want?"

"Josie, I'm disappointed in your bedside manner. That's usually your strength."

"We're not at the hospital, Houston, and you're not a sweet little old lady."

He went for another bite of the crab, the fingers of his left hand rolling the piece around the plate first before pinching it. "No, not exactly."

She sighed, feeling like she was going to really regret coming to his condo in the first place. Her determination was no match for the complex and alluring Houston Hayes. "So what do you want?"

"No enthusiasm there, Josie. Now I feel like I have to beg for it." He was enjoying this altogether too much.

"Of course you don't have to beg."

"Okay." He rolled his shoulders. "After we're done eating, could you give me a massage? Because of my leg, I'm sleeping on my back, which I never do, and now my neck and shoulders are killing me."

Josie swallowed hard. Oh, sure, she could slather her hands all over his bare skin, no problem. She wouldn't even need to use lotion because her drool would be puddling down his back.

"Sure thing," she said in a squeaky voice normally only used by animated mice.

Houston chewed his crab, feeling quite a bit better than he had before Josie had shown up. He'd spent the day reading, watching TV, and trying to ignore his bundled and nearly numb hand. Which was impossible since almost everything he did involved the use of his right hand. He couldn't even take a leak without switching his methods of unzip-and-lift to his left hand.

But Josie was a nice, healthy, sexy little distraction. And if she thought she was going to show up here day after day and they were going to be platonic friends, she was naïve and kidding herself.

All the reasons to either ignore Josie or stay just casual co-workers still applied, but he no longer cared. Right now his life was a wreck, his career hanging by a repaired tendon, and at the very least he was going to allow himself to indulge in a juicy passionate affair with Josie Adkins. He already knew how explosive they could be together.

Exhausting himself with pleasure a couple nights a week might distract him from his so-called recovery and the inevitable day when he had to peel his splint off and see if his damaged hand worked.

But if Josie was going to insist on a no-touching rule, well, he was up for the challenge. He'd give it three days before she was agreeing with him that it would be much more fun to nurse him back to health naked.

Josie cast him a suspicious look and adjusted herself in the chair. "So I heard your sister wasn't so thrilled with changing your bandage."

That was an understatement. Kori had gone ashy gray under her tan. "My sister always was a huge wimp. It was easy to tease her with bugs and blood when we were kids."

Not that he had done that a lot. He had always felt more protective of Kori than annoyed by her. He'd spent a lot of time reading to her and playing games with her to distract her from their parents' fighting. Or rather from their father screaming at their mother in a rage while she pleaded with him to be reasonable.

"So who changed your dressing today?"

"Me." In a painful and sloppy job that had taken a solid thirty minutes.

Josie sat next to him, fiddling with her food, and she did it again. Gave him one of those tender looks that meant she felt sorry for him and wanted to cosset him. Wrap him up in a blanket and spoon-feed him soup.

"I can do it for you next time."

"I got it, don't worry about it." He didn't need help, didn't want help. He'd struggle through everything on his own, avoiding shirts with buttons and eating with his left hand like an ogre if he had to, just so he wouldn't have the humiliation of having to depend on someone.

He didn't want to be weak, to need to be taken care of, and the pleasure of the moment before dissolved. Pushing back his chair he stood up. Refusing to wince, he limped to refill his glass of water.

Holding it under the water flow on the refrigerator door, he balanced on his good leg. "So what else did I say when I was drugged up by you?"

Josie gave an indignant snort. "You weren't drugged up. I gave you what I would have given any patient. But let's see, you said I was pretty, and that you love my hair."

Houston took a sip of his water and felt something that could be a goddamn blush rushing up his neck. He did kind of have a thing about her wispy and adorable hair. Had enjoyed the way it brushed against his gut when she had sucked him, but hell, he hadn't meant to tell her that.

"And you called me, if I remember correctly, an absolute goddess."

His head snapped up, mortification catching him in its grip and leaving him jaw open, speechless. Josie licked butter off her fingers and laughed.

"I'm kidding. I made the last one up."

As he started breathing again, her laughter rang out, loud and unrestrained. Watching her, eternally optimistic, compassionate, unpretentious, and very much alluring, Houston was man enough to admit he was glad she was sitting in his kitchen.

And for the first time since he'd woken up and realized his career was more than likely over, Houston wanted to laugh, too.

Chapter Eleven

Josie's laughter and amusement died when Houston said, "Do you mind doing that massage now?"

Right. He wanted her to touch him.

Sloshing water over the rim of the glass as he unsteadily set it down on the table, Houston sank back into his chair with a stifled sigh. He sucked the spilled water off his hand, his lips making soft wet sounds, and Josie was nothing short of envious.

She wanted him to do that to her. Suck with soft, wet sounds. With shaking fingers, she approached his shoulders like they were radioactive, touching lightly, wincing at how warm and solid his muscles were. "Sure, now's a good time."

To torture herself.

But then she reminded herself that Houston's asking for help was nothing short of miraculous and that she should see it as a sign of trust.

Resolute, she dug her fingers into his flesh, kneading and stroking along his back, fanning out towards his shoulders. She worked the bronze flesh there, noticing it was a shade darker than the rest of his back, and that he had a smattering of cute freckles that had her mouth itching to kiss. A rush of air expelled from him in what might have been pleasure or pain, she wasn't sure.

"Is this okay? Am I pushing too hard?"

"No, that's perfect." His voice was quiet, throaty.

"Great." Josie rolled her thumbs up his neck to where the fine black hairs scattered across the nape before ascending into the thick throng of short hair.

He gave a low groan.

After a minute she settled into the motion, enjoying the feel of him beneath her fingers, as she ran up and down the warm flesh and occasionally stole into his glossy black hair. Her breasts hovered close to his back and the muscles in his arms and torso flexed and reacted to her touch.

"Did you hurt your neck, or is it just sore?"

"It's sore from sleeping on my back. I usually sleep on my side, but that tugs my leg, so I'm laid flat-out and it's killing my neck."

Josie moved down his arms, giving firm pressure with her thumbs, and he gave a soft moan of approval, which she barely noticed. She was distracted by thoughts of him suffering in pain.

She remembered the way he had looked when she'd entered the ER—covered in blood, every inch of his calf chaffed, scraped, shredded, or punctured. He had been on his surfboard, and a shark had lunged from underneath and done that to him. It made her shudder just thinking about it and what could have been the possible outcome.

"Did it . . . was it awful?" The question popped out of her mouth before she could prevent it, and she cursed herself.

He glanced back at her, his eyebrows raised. "What? Was what awful?"

Her hands stilled on his elbows. "What happened to your leg, I mean."

"The shark?" Houston didn't sound angry, just confused.

"Yes. I'm sorry, that's a stupid question. Of course it was awful."

The silence drew out and she studied the back of his head, wanting to just run her fingers into his thick black hair, lean her chest against him, and hold him to her.

Houston spoke slowly. "I don't know if awful is the right word. It's like, it happens and you just react, and then it's over." He shook his head. "That doesn't make sense, does it?"

"I think so." And she did. It had been like that when her dad had died. It happens, and you react, and later—much later—you start to deal with it.

Houston would still be dealing with the results of his accident for a long time.

"It was so fast. I thought I saw something, then there it was, on my leg, and I didn't feel any pain and I wasn't really even scared."

Josie suspected she would have been scared enough to wet her bathing suit. She wasn't aware she was squeezing his shoulders until he winced. She gentled her touch, returning to slow, smooth strokes. "Oh, sorry."

"I don't know what to call it," he said suddenly. "I mean, was it an accident? Was it an attack? People ask me what happened and I say I was bitten by a shark, and they get these horrible looks on their faces." He played with the fork lying on his used dinner plate and shook his head.

"I was on the news, you know. It's embarrassing."

"I heard, but I didn't see it." It had seemed almost rude to watch it. Invasive. "Did they have footage of you while you were in the hospital? I didn't know Acadia Inlet would allow that."

"No, they had random footage of the beach, and interviews with witnesses. They threw my hospital staff picture up there." He gave a soft laugh. "My mom taped it."

"You're kidding!" Josie laughed. "That is something my mom would do, too."

"I'm just sorry she had to worry about me." Houston reached back and tapped her hand. "Thanks, that's good. I'm going to back the chair up."

As Josie stepped away so he could stand up, she told him, "She always worries about you, shark bite or not, because she's your mother."

Pulling himself up by the edge of the table, he hovered until he got his balance. "I wish she wouldn't. I'm a big boy now."

His eyes smoldered suggestively as he turned to her, but Josie ignored the attempt to distract her. What Houston either didn't know or refused to admit was that his mother was going to worry about him until she decided that he was happy, something age and success had nothing to do with.

Josie took a risk. "She said she had a bad marriage and it wasn't healthy for you."

Anger flared in Houston's eyes, his grip on the table tightening. He crumpled up the paper plate in front of him, resting against the table with his thighs. Silent, jaw clenched, he stood there.

Josie moved around him to clear the table. "Here, let me get your plate."

When she tried to take it, he pulled his hand back. "Don't clean up after me. I don't need your help."

"It's not a big deal." She made another reach for the garbage.

He held fast to the plate. "Everything is a big deal. Josie, damn it, if you keep coming around here like this I'm going to hurt you. I don't want to do that."

Chin up, she stared him down. "I'm a big girl, just like you're a big boy. And I want to be here."

By the time he was back at work and her residency

over, she'd probably be a sobbing sack of lovesick fat
cells, but hey, you only lived once.

Which was why, with determination, she showed up
at Houston's condo the next day after her shift and let
herself in the front door again without knocking. And
was greeted with the bib-requiring sight of him bent
over the kitchen sink in black briefs and nothing else,
attempting to wash his hair.

Water was sluicing down his bronzed back as he
bent over, struggling with the little metal sprayer, his
hair piled high with an excessive amount of bubbles.
Josie had an orgasm standing in the doorway.

Well, not actually, but it sure felt close as her thighs
twitched and ached. And all moisture evaporated from
her mouth, while an equal and opposite reaction occurred in her panties. Her nipples sprung up like spring
tulips and rubbed against her white tank top. If he turned
around, kissed her, and just swiped one little finger anywhere in the area between her waist and knees, she was
going to come.

Not that he even knew she was there. He was too
busy swearing at the sprayer and trying to stretch it farther than the metal hose would allow.

"Damn it," he said, swiping at his eye as an errant
bubble slid past his dark eyebrow.

The sharp jerk made his butt tense up, the muscles
flexing and clenching, and Josie knew she had to get
the hell out of there before she was tempted to do some
spanking of her own. Given that his kitchen was tiny at
best, he was within grabbing distance and she just didn't
trust herself.

Covering her mouth to contain her drool, she backed
up and misjudged the archway to the kitchen. She
slammed into the wall with all the force of her semi-
truck-wide rear end. The bump could be heard even

over the water as Houston's wall clock rattled and threatened to hit the floor.

Houston turned, grabbing the counter for leverage, dragging the sprayer with him. Lukewarm water hit Josie in the chin and shoulder before he let go of the button and the water flow returned to the faucet.

She sputtered, wiping water off her chin, while his expression shifted from startled to amused. "Argh, Houston, you got me wet!"

"It wouldn't be the first time," he said, stretching up to his full length, favoring his bad leg.

There was truth to that, but she ignored it.

Shampoo was still clinging to his head, and a small rivulet of sudsy water slid down the right side of his cheek, but he still looked incredible. All hard and golden and broad, a confident man with a new vulnerability.

Shoot, she was an idiot. A big, Josie Adkins idiot. She couldn't resist mint chocolate chip ice cream, what made her think she could resist Houston?

"You still have shampoo in your hair," she said, because it seemed like the thing to say.

Houston rubbed his left hand over his wet hair and dropped his eyes to her tank top. A slow smile started to spread. "You interrupted me."

"Sorry, I didn't mean to. Do you want some help rinsing?" Which was a ridiculous offer to make, given her sudden state of lust-driven paralysis. That close to him, her belly pressing his butt, her fingers in his short hair, it was highly likely she'd make a fool out of herself.

"I can get it." Houston bent back over, holding his leg stiff. His bandaged right hand was tucked beneath the sink while his left hand worked the spray.

It wasn't an efficient system. With only one hand, he couldn't rub out the suds and he shot water just about everywhere but the top of his head.

"Here, I'll hold the sprayer and you can use your hand to get the shampoo out," she told him, coaching herself to be professional, friendly, nonsexual.

"I'll hold the sprayer." His voice was muffled by the stainless steel sink. "I don't trust you with it."

"What do you think I'm going to do? Flood your kitchen?" She took a step closer to him, drawing deep breaths that were completely platonic in nature.

"It's possible."

He got the water flow going in the general direction of his head, though quite a river was flowing down his back and soaking his briefs until they clung to him, damp and tight. Josie stayed clear of the butt zone, keeping a solid two feet between them before she leaned over and briskly rubbed his head.

Which vibrated his whole body back and forth. His sprayer hand shifted, sending a steady steam of water right into her chest. Damp cotton clung to her as she shrieked and tried to move out of the line of fire.

"What's the matter?"

"My shirt got all wet."

Houston didn't say anything, but his arm readjusted and sent the water back towards his head. Josie took all ten fingers and raked along his head as fast as she could without removing his scalp until the shampoo was gone.

Houston closed his eyes and tried to keep his teeth from rattling as Josie roughhoused his head. He could feel her nervousness, her body hovering behind him out of touching distance, and he wanted her. The way he did every time he saw her.

"Finished," she said in a breathless voice that completed the erection he'd been working on in his briefs.

Josie clearly was going to stick to the just-friends idiocy, but the idea wasn't sitting well with him. Hot dreams were keeping him up at night and lustful thoughts plagued him all day.

So he turned and directed the spray of water right at her already slightly damp chest.

While she screamed and threw her hands out, he smiled. "Whoops. I forgot to let go of the water."

Then a long second later, he actually removed his finger pressure from the nozzle and took in the view from the top.

Josie had fabulous breasts dry. Wet, they could make a grown man weep in gratitude.

And they were wet now, with a clinging white tank top sculpted and molded to them, her pink nipples straining against the fabric as she blinked in shock.

"That water's cold!" she said.

"Obviously." Houston took another long, leering look at her nipples.

Her arms crossed. "Quit staring at my chest."

Maybe in about a hundred years, when he'd had his fill. "I'm in my underwear and you're in a soaking-wet shirt. Do we still have to be just friends?"

"Houston . . ." She chewed her lips and looked ready to cave in and tear her top off. But then she gave him a pleading look. "It wasn't right when we did it the first time, and it would be an even worse idea now. I shouldn't have suggested another night at all. I'm sorry, but I just know it will be better if we try to be friends instead of lovers."

Better for who? He reached for her, but she held up her hand.

"I . . . I really don't want to get hurt," she added, heart in her eyes.

That hit him in the gut hard. "I don't want to hurt you."

The last thing in the world he wanted to do was hurt pretty, sweet Josie, the only person he knew who could even make him think of smiling right now when his career was crumbling around him.

"I know." She swallowed, her jaw twitching. "But I want more than you can give me."

He knew what she was asking. He wanted to answer. But the words hung in the air between them and the silence grew, and deep inside where it ached he wanted to tell her that he'd give her anything. That he'd try this time, that he'd do whatever she wanted, and that they could walk that big humongous step past just sex into something deeper together.

But he couldn't do that. Because he didn't know how to let go, how to trust her not to spit on his words, how to give up control over himself and his life to someone else.

Everything else in his future was so uncertain, he couldn't risk that, too. "I can only give you one day at a time."

She nodded, but a little sigh managed to escape her lips. "I know."

The selfish part of him wanted Josie to say it didn't matter, one night at a time was enough for her, that the affair she'd suggested was what she wanted.

But she didn't, and he felt like a total bastard. He kept saying he wouldn't hurt her, but every time he spoke to her he did just that, delivering a little drop of hurt that was rapidly filling up into a bucketful of pain. She gave and he took, and he had nothing to give back to her but sex.

He was the one to look away as a sharp pain in his leg reminded him that he'd been standing too long. "Let me get you a dry shirt."

Her fingers brushed across the damp front of her tank top. "Oh, thanks, but I'm fine. You should sit down." Her soft fluttering hands came towards him, reaching for his head. "Is all the shampoo out of your hair? I can get it with a washcloth if it's not."

Anger surged through him. Why couldn't she just

accept that he was a prick and leave him alone? Why did she have to care about him? No other woman he knew would give a rat's ass if the shampoo were out of his hair, but Josie did—and damn, she made it so hard to keep shoving her away.

"I'm fine. I'll be right back with a shirt for you." He turned sideways to move past her in the doorway, not wanting to touch her.

"I can get it," she said, placing her hand on his chest to stop him. "Just tell me where to find a T-shirt."

"I said I'll get it," he snapped at her. And confirmed to himself that he wasn't good enough for her.

She deserved someone who wasn't his father's son.

Josie blinked and watched Houston head down the hall to his bedroom, leg stiff as he fought a limp. Uncertain what had just happened, she tried to tell herself that he didn't want her help, that she had infringed on his independence. But it wasn't anything more serious than that.

Because if it was, she didn't know how to fix it.

Shivering in the air conditioning, her wet shirt clinging to her chest, she waited for Houston. And waited. Then wondered if he'd fallen down and was stuck on his bedroom floor like a tipped turtle, unwilling to ask for help.

Either that or he wanted her to take a hint and leave.

Or he'd fallen asleep.

Or was hurt and bleeding and dying of something that her medical brain told her didn't exist but her heart was sure could be an actual possibility.

After another minute she went down the hall to his room and stopped short in the door. Oh, dear God. He was trying to take his damp underwear off.

Only the sticking wet cotton, the elastic waistband,

and the use of only one hand had caused him a bit of a problem. The underwear had been rolled halfway down and now appeared to be stuck. Right across the middle of his very tight, very nice backside.

He must have heard her excited breathing. He glanced over his shoulder and cursed in a low, rude voice.

"Sorry," she said, her face hotter than hell's kitchen. "I wanted to see if you needed help, I didn't realize . . ."

That she'd get a free show.

"You want to help?" he said in exasperation, throwing his hands up in the air, the stark white bandage of the one startling against his tanned chest. "Fine. I'd love some help right now."

"What?" He wanted her to take his *underwear* off? Was he serious? She couldn't possibly touch his butt without her body getting ideas.

And he hadn't even turned around to face her yet. Who knew what she'd find on *that* side. Mercy.

"My underwear is wet, it's stuck, as I'm sure you can see, since my ass is hanging out in front of you. Can you just pull them off for me?"

His shoulders were tense, eyes stormy, jaw rigid. There was no sexual intent on his face, and he looked too ticked off to try anything funny.

"Oh, okay, of course. I'd love to help you," she said like he'd asked for help filling in a crossword, not prying off his black briefs.

He didn't say anything. He just waited. And she took a small step forward. Then another. She reached out her hands, which shook like an addict's in detox, and cringed as they landed on his skin at the small of his back.

Gritting her teeth, she slid fingers down his cool flesh, left damp by the briefs, and tried not to think about the fact that she was touching Houston Hayes's right butt cheek. Per Anatomy and Physiology it was really the gluteus maximus, and just another striated muscle.

Which didn't explain her sudden urge to squeeze.

Reaching the waistband of his briefs she tugged hard, then panicked when nothing happened. "They're stuck."

"That's the point, Josie."

Of course it was. "So . . ."

"I think you have to roll them back up, then take them down without rolling them because they're sticking."

If she looked up at him, she would die, so she kept her eyes glued to his back. She wasn't really mechanically inclined, but she thought about his directions and decided they made sense, if she wanted to stick her hands in his pants to get them down. Which she didn't.

She gave another tug. Nothing. Retreating, she unrolled them until they were back in place at his waist covering him snugly. Tapping a finger on her lip, she mulled over the problem, ignoring the hot ache pulling between her thighs and the traitorous tightening of her nipples.

"You giving up?"

"No, I'm just thinking." Still in her damp shirt, she shivered, feeling the warmth radiate off his back inches in front of her. She wanted to just lean forward, to close her eyes and fall against him, to tuck her hands inside his briefs and stroke them both to a place where nothing mattered but the pleasure they could share.

That's not what she did, of course. Because she was reasonable and rational and clearly stupid. Who cared about tomorrow when there was tonight?

Well, she did, which was why she was going to remain professional about this. There was only one way to get the briefs off and if she were at work with a patient, she wouldn't even hesitate. So this shouldn't be any different. Taking a deep breath, she jammed her eyes shut and gripped the sides of his briefs, lifted them out a little, and pulled down towards his hips.

Her breast brushed his back as she yanked, bending at the knees, expecting to get them down to his thighs where she could drop her hold and run and let him deal with the rest.

Unfortunately, they were hooked on something and wouldn't go down. She tugged a little harder and the resistance came from the front.

Oh, hell. They were caught *there*.

"Um . . ." she whispered behind his shoulder. "We have a different problem this time."

"Your fault."

Here she was trying to help and he blamed her. "What did I do?"

"You exist. You move your little finger and I get hard."

"Well." Josie let go of him and moved around to face the problem head-on, holding really tight on to her fortitude, coaching herself to stay distant.

Like that was going to work.

Breathing hard, she lifted the front of the briefs and the tip of his erection sprang free, tapping her on the wrist.

"I'm so glad we're becoming friends," she said, mortified into speech, and terrified of attacking him. "I want to help you out like this, whenever you need me to, because that's what friends are for."

Houston was damn certain that he would never ask Christian or Dennis to pull down his wet underwear. That was not what friends do. What he and Josie were doing was reserved for lovers and why the hell she couldn't see that was anybody's guess.

It was his own damn fault for getting frustrated with

both her and his Jockeys and asking for her help. Now he had a record-breaking boner and was losing his determination to respect her hands-off wishes.

She went down on her knees and any hope he had of speaking was shattered as he struggled not to swallow his own tongue. Josie's quick short gasps hit his cool skin as she peeled his pants down inch by painful inch, mouth hovering in front of his cock.

"This way is much easier," she said, her words rushing out and tickling the hairs on his thigh.

Air rushed between his legs as she freed him from the wet cotton, and his balls tightened, head aching. His body knew he was naked inches in front of a desirable woman and it was demanding attention.

So close, he was so close to her, and it wouldn't take but a shift on his part.

A little lean forward and he could bump her with his cock, rest right against her moist lips and run his fingers through her wispy hair.

The thought just about killed him.

"Josie." He grabbed her short hair, yanked her head back so she would have to look up at him.

"What?" Her nails dug into his thighs as she worked his briefs almost to his knees. Wide green eyes locked with his.

There were limits and he had reached his. "I can't do this anymore. I can't be friends." He shook her head a little, frustration pulsing through his tortured body.

"Get out, Josie. And don't come back, do you understand? Just do us both a favor and don't come back."

Chapter Twelve

A week later Josie paused in the hallway outside the recovery room to make a note on a patient's file. An elderly woman wasn't doing well in her physical therapy sessions. Josie wanted to speak with the therapist and Dr. Sheinberg about moving her to a short-term-care nursing home until she was more fully recovered from her hip replacement.

Sticking her pen in the pocket of her scrubs, it hit the shark tooth she had been carrying around since Houston's accident. She hadn't seen him since the underwear incident, and she didn't expect to. He had made his feelings X-ray obvious. He did not want to be friends. And she couldn't have just an affair.

She wanted to be able to. She wanted to be the kind of woman who could have casual sex and leave her heart out of it, but she wasn't. Her heart was already in it, and burrowing deeper by the minute, so it was probably all for the best that Houston had kicked her out of his condo, pulling her up from her knees where she had been hovering in front of his delicious version of The Full Monty.

Sure, she believed that it was all for the best. And maybe she would suddenly grow six inches and develop fashion sense. Instead she just walked around feeling like a bad hair day, PMS, and having to pull out her fat clothes had all just collided under the heading of Bitchy.

The end result of her night with Houston was that she was back to where she was before, dateless and depressed, only this time she knew what she was missing. Before she had only imagined that Houston had a hot body and magic hands, now she *knew.* And had the lost lip panties to prove it.

Even though she hadn't seen Houston, she'd heard about him. Dr. Sheinberg had come to discuss Houston's surgery schedule and the changes that were going to be made until another surgeon could be brought on board to handle the caseload.

Josie wished she were qualified to be that surgeon, but she just wasn't. Even if she held Houston's position for him, Dr. Williams hadn't been overly optimistic about Houston's future. He had been confident that in time, with therapy, Houston would have a normal life, able to drive a car and do daily tasks. But he didn't think that would extend to fine motor skills like writing right-handed or performing surgery.

With the possible loss of some mobility, and the complications from scar tissue and arthritis, Dr. Williams had said they would have to wait and see, but that returning to surgery was a long shot.

Guilt clung to her, creating sleepless nights and a tension headache that wouldn't go away. Houston was so much more talented than she was, and he had lost his ability while she just slogged on, inadequate. She couldn't even be a good friend to him without messing up and fondling his underwear.

She sighed and started walking again, flipping back through the file.

"Don't walk into me. I'm not up to it today," a familiar voice said in front of her, with no small amount of urgency.

Josie stopped dead in her tracks and looked up. There he was. Houston. Dr. Hayes.

Standing in front of her, wearing khaki pants that revealed none of the patchwork of sutures on his left leg. His weight was resting on his uninjured leg, and his right hand was still in a splint and wrapped.

His face looked a little pale under his tan, and he had dark circles under his eyes that she wanted to kiss and soothe away. Her fingers itched to touch him, and she concluded she was hopeless. Did he have to get a restraining order for her to get the message? He didn't want her.

"Dr. Hayes," she said in a voice that only shook a little. "What are you doing here?"

And how was she going to maintain a professional façade when preoccupied with thoughts of him naked and stealing another pair of her panties?

Houston grimaced. "I'm bored, so I came to check and make sure nobody's moved into my office."

It was probably meant to be a joke, but she could see he was partially serious. Trying to lighten the tension on his face, she gestured to the very small foot or two between them. "I can't believe I almost ran into you. I'm such a klutz."

He opened his mouth as if to politely dispute that, then his lip twitched. He was fighting a laugh.

Okay, so maybe she was a klutz, but surely he could see that it was his fault for being so gorgeous? It was not a reflection of her medical skills as a whole.

Besides, it had been days since she had dropped anything. Maybe even an entire week. Annoyed that he could laugh when she had spent the week *suffering*, she crossed her arms. "I know I'm a little klutzy. That's true. But it's not true where it counts, in the OR."

Eyes dropped to her chest in a completely inappropriate manner for the hospital. Not that it had ever stopped him before. "You're not clumsy in the bedroom, either."

Nor was she going to be seduced by his sensual voice. He had a hell of a nerve to even try after their last conversation, which concluded with him telling her to get out of his house. Though a part of her couldn't help but thrill that he still wanted her.

Josie rolled her eyes at him. "Except when I brought your bike down on top of me."

"That was in the hall, not the bedroom. And besides, you had a good reason." He smiled. A smile she didn't trust, full of teeth, and confidence, and shared lust-filled memories. "Your shorts were around your ankles."

They were in the hall, people passing them left and right, and he wanted to talk dirty to her after effectively blowing her off seven days earlier. Swell.

His idea of returning to just co-workers didn't exactly mesh with hers. She had never once felt the need to dissect her graceless bedroom maneuvers with Dr. Williams, and she didn't want to with Houston, either.

Of course she had never actually performed bedroom maneuvers with Dr. Williams. While she certainly had with Houston, bedroom or not.

"I need to see a patient. Excuse me."

Josie started past him, hot with annoyance and that pesky little desire that always managed to crop up whenever Houston was around.

He touched her arm, stopping her. "Tomorrow you'll be operating and I'll be assisting you. You'll have ample opportunities to prove to me how capable you really are."

"What? You mean I won't be working with Dr. Liu? I'll actually be doing the surgery with you?" Her voice squeaked a little at the end, and she clapped her mouth shut.

Finally. Her chance for vindication, to prove to him that she wasn't a malpractice suit waiting to happen.

He nodded. "But I'll be next to you watching your every move, so don't get too excited."

Without realizing she did it, her gaze dropped to his bandaged hand. He tucked it behind his back, his expression defiant.

"Are you ready to be back?" She cursed the words the minute they were out of her mouth. Being ready wasn't the issue for Houston. Being in control was.

"I mean, standing on your leg for a three-hour surgery . . . it will be painful."

His tone was icy. "I can handle it. They were just puncture wounds, for God's sake. Why does everyone insist on treating me like I'm suddenly brain-damaged as well?"

While she supposed he had a valid point, Josie was irritated. She wasn't just anyone and she didn't deserve his anger. And he needed to realize that people caring about him wasn't an insult.

Before she could stop herself, she spoke. "Maybe because some people would consider a man who chooses to stand for three hours on an injured leg to be brain-damaged."

His mouth fell open. Then he gave a tight smile while she considered all the ways he had already implied that *she* was brain-damaged, since he was the only surgeon unwilling to let her slice. It was about time he realized what it felt like to be second-guessed from here to Christmas.

"My brain is functioning just fine. It's my body I'm having trouble controlling." Those roving eyes went to her chest again and he gave a soft laugh. "Damn, I just see you, and I want you."

"I know the feeling," she said ruefully, sneaking a peek at his khaki pants, enjoying the outline of his penis against the crisp cotton. Between her anxious libido and her overzealous appetite for ice cream as a replacement for the sex she could no longer have, her body was running the show lately.

"Stop that," he murmured, stroking his thumb across her arm. "I can't get an erection on my first day back."

He could kick her out of his house, but he couldn't control that he still wanted her. And Lord, did she want him right back. He had been right. Being friends was a stupid idea. "Tomorrow, then?" she asked, leaning a little closer to him.

Houston shook his head and dropped his hand, his mouth squeezed shut tightly like he was holding back a frustrated laugh. "God, I don't know how to do this, Josie. I don't know how to go back to being professional and distant with you."

Don't. Just don't. What was so hard to grasp about that?

"Houston . . ." Emotions rose, garbled, confused, and uncertain. She didn't know what she wanted to say to him.

"Come have a cup of coffee with me." He gave a tug on the sleeve of her white coat.

"Okay." Who knew what illuminations might arise over a cup of mocha latte? Maybe talking would relax them both, so they could at least pretend when in the presence of other people that they shared a normal working relationship.

Houston walked slowly down the hall, favoring his left leg, and she adjusted her gait to his. Which was an improvement over the way she normally had to come close to running to keep up with him and his giraffe-like strides.

But she sensed his frustration and embarrassment.

"Sorry. At this rate, we'll get there in time for dinner."

Looking at his hand bandaged and held protectively across his waist, Josie said, "I guess crutches were out of the question."

He grimaced. "Yep. Crutches would be a no-no for my hand. Four weeks without movement of any kind. Down to two and a half now, actually. Thank God."

As they stepped onto the elevator to go down to the cafeteria, she watched him out of the corner of her eye. "What would you do if I said the W word?"

"W word?"

"Yes. Wheelchair."

His look of horror answered that question. "Don't even go there," he said, leaning against the wall of the elevator. "I'm not that desperate. Besides, I couldn't wheel the thing myself."

He lifted his hand to indicate why. "So, I would have to rely on other people to push me around all the time. No, thank you."

Yes, she knew exactly how he felt about people helping him. Especially chunky babbling women who helped him out of his underwear.

As they came to a stop on the first floor, he added, "I can manage for a couple of weeks. It won't take long for my leg to heal."

"Especially not with a top-notch surgeon sewing you up," she said, striving for light and friendly.

"Oh, did Mike do my sutures? I thought you did."

Friendly faded. For hell's sake. He couldn't even give her credit for a decent stitch?

Josie was about to complain when she saw the grin he was struggling to suppress. His blue eyes were dancing. The jerk was actually teasing her.

She laughed, a burst of relief in the face of her fear and tension and awkwardness. "Hey! You'd better watch what you say or I won't try to be gentle when I take those sutures out."

The doors slid open and they stepped out of the elevator. "Somehow, Dr. Adkins, I find it hard to believe you would be anything but gentle."

Josie wasn't sure what he meant, but his voice was soft and husky, his gaze locked on her. He leaned closer to her, his aftershave scent filling her nostrils and flinging her heart into her throat. They were so close to touching, had done intimate things with each other, yet there was an ocean-wide gap between them that she didn't know how to bridge.

"I'm sorry," he murmured, tips of his fingers brushing across the small of her back. "I didn't mean to tear into you like that last week at my condo. I know you were just trying to help. I'm sorry, Josie. I didn't mean to hurt you."

And because she was an idiot, who was certain she had lost at least two out of the four chambers of her heart to him, and because she understood that there were parts of Houston she hadn't seen yet, she shrugged. "It's okay."

But given that it had been a big old scoop of pain with a dollop of humiliation on top, she added, "Just don't do it again."

He gave a startled laugh. "Believe me, I'll try not to."

"No try, only do," she said in her best Yoda imitation, resorting to humor as a shield for her embarrassment. She did not want to be having this conversation in a hallway.

"I know you wanted to be friends, but I can't, because I can't separate my lust from my other feelings, and I really am sorry for that."

So was she. Because if he couldn't have feelings for her aside from lust, their relationship, such as it was, really was over.

As they approached the cafeteria, Houston shook his head, expression serious. "I wish . . . I could . . ."

Then without finishing his thought, he shoved the glass door open with his good arm and spoke in a low, warm voice. "Ladies first."

It occurred to her that if he would just see reason and fall in love with her, everything would go so much easier. But that was about as likely as her fantasies at age thirteen of all the guys in Duran Duran fighting over her between concert sets, with John Taylor usually emerging as victor.

Unfortunately she was dealing with reality these days, and Houston wanted her for one thing only. As much as she wanted to give it to him, she also wanted to respect herself in the morning.

So now they had to figure out how to reestablish a working relationship between them without any awkward feelings, and possibly coffee was a first step in that direction.

"Thanks," she said, ducking through the door. Then, wanting him to sit down and get off his bad leg, she headed for the coffeepot. "You sit down and I'll get the coffee."

Expecting him to argue, she hurried forward without waiting for an answer. She went to the large pot simmering in the corner and poured two cups of black coffee, then stood in line to pay for them. She was amazed to see on her way back that Houston had actually taken her advice and sat down. He looked relieved to be off his leg, lounging back in his chair.

That obvious relief on his face only exasperated the uneasiness she had been feeling.

"Listen," she said as she sat down across from him, placing their coffee on the table. "Are you sure you're ready to come back? I don't think anyone expects you to be back so soon. I mean, you're probably still in a lot of pain. You just had surgery a little over a week ago . . ." she trailed off as he stared at her coldly.

"I don't feel anything in my hand. It's numb," he said.

"Oh." It was a rebuff, plain and simple. *Leave me alone,* his words said.

He pulled her in, he pushed her away. Houston wanted her on his terms only, and she was getting a little tired of it. But he spoke before she could think of anything to say.

"Yes." He gave a wry and tight smile. *"Oh.* There aren't exactly any words for it, which is good because I don't feel like talking about it."

And he never would, she was sure. "Houston, I'm sorry. I know that doesn't mean a whole lot but . . ."

He held his good hand up. "No, please, don't. I'm not ready to hear condolences yet. We won't know anything for sure until the four weeks are up and the tendons and nerves have healed. Then PT, and with a little luck, three months from now you won't have to be sorry for me."

"Of course." She dredged up a smile, even though she thought he was being a little optimistic. But it must be hell to face what Houston was, and she suspected he would have to come to terms with his new life little by little.

"So, did Dr. Stanhope actually approve your return? I've heard he's a little prickly about malpractice." Josie strove to keep her voice light as she changed the subject.

Houston grunted. "Any chief of staff should be prickly about malpractice. It could bankrupt the hospital, and Acadia Inlet isn't exactly rolling in money. Stanhope just barely approved my return, and even that was with conditions."

Josie took a sip of her hot coffee, and sighed with pleasure as the warm liquid coated her throat. She was feeling cold, a chill deep to the bone.

"Maybe he was just concerned about your recovery."

Houston ran his finger back and forth over the napkin Josie had set his coffee cup on. "Maybe. But I'm not really in any pain, you know. My leg is just stiff, and the sutures are starting to itch like crazy. But nobody seems to want to believe me."

"I believe you," she said quietly.

"Stanhope forced me to agree to only six-hour shifts for the next month. That only leaves time for one or two surgeries a day. I hope you're a fast learner."

Geez, so did she. Fear of being found inadequate rushed through Josie. Here was her big chance. The opportunity to prove to Houston that she was as capable as the next at being a surgeon. To prove that despite her appearance and quirky personality, she was a brain to be reckoned with.

"I've done a lot of fractures already, you know, given my year in ER, and a wide variety of other cases." Which he had to be aware of. "But yes, I am a very fast learner."

"Good."

They settled into silence and Josie watched Houston sip his coffee, wondering if he had any idea how attractive he was. Any idea of how much she wanted him and how hard it was to keep saying no to him.

It sucked to be right. She had known it would be a mistake to sleep with him, and it had been a doozy. And now she had to pretend it had never happened, because she was determined to earn his trust in the OR. Starting tomorrow.

"So what's on the schedule?" she asked.

He stared into his mug and shrugged. "We can go down and take a look if you want."

"Not right now. I'll check in an hour or so. I've got to head back now." She had only abandoned six tasks to come and have coffee with him, and they couldn't wait another ten minutes.

Houston nodded, looking distracted. He said suddenly, "So what did I really say when you were stitching me up?"

Josie thought about his loopy sexual innuendos and smiled. "Are you sure you want to know?"

He groaned. "That bad?"

"No, not bad." Good, in fact. Very good. "But I'm not sure how you'll feel about it."

His cup went down hard on the table, and coffee sloshed over the rim. He ignored the puddle on the table and his hand and winced. "Okay, tell me. I can take it. What did I say?"

She pushed a napkin towards him and stood up, trying not to grin, with little luck. "I've really got to get back now."

"Josie," he ground out.

"Yes, Dr. Hayes?" She tugged on her scrub pants to pull them up and raised her eyebrows.

He gave her a pained look. "What did I say besides commenting on your hair? Come on, put me out of my misery."

Josie decided to tell him the truth, and see where things went. Nothing ventured, nothing gained. "You didn't say much," she said with a shrug.

Then she couldn't prevent herself from staring down at him with a little smile. "You just asked me to take your trunks off, mentioning that I'd seen you naked before. You reprimanded me for calling you Dr. Hayes when I had called you Houston when we spent the night together. And you told me if it wasn't for your father, I would be the woman you would want to be with."

Let's see what he did with that.

Josie turned, her sneakers squeaking on the tile floor as she sashayed towards the door, her nicely curved hips hugged by her scrub pants, and Houston wanted to crawl under the table.

Oh, hell. It was worse than he had thought.

Not only had he made his lust and longing for her perfectly clear, he had actually brought up his father? Good God. He was never doing drugs again.

It explained Josie's showing up at his condo day after day, though. He had confessed feelings for her, and Josie was a nice person. She cared about him, wanted to take care of him.

Only he couldn't have her taking care of him, because that was a complication in his life he didn't need. Life was challenging enough without having to guard his heart against a Josie invasion.

Starting with simple tasks like cleaning up his own clumsiness. Trying to mop up the spilled coffee on his left hand without use of his right was damn near impossible. He ended up turning his hand over and rolling it back and forth across the napkin, which ripped and stuck to his skin.

He cursed under his breath in frustration. Every day since the accident had been a constant struggle. Total hell. He couldn't even zip his pants without three or four attempts and ten minutes. Forget about buttoning a shirt. Or cutting food with a knife and fork. Showering was like participating in a comedy act, with all the stops and starts and slips and spills.

And wet underwear was impossible to deal with.

That's why he had to come back to work. He couldn't sit around his condo one more day and discover all the things that he wasn't capable of doing anymore. And maybe never would be.

He stopped his thoughts there ruthlessly.

He would get better.

It was out of the question *not* to.

Where would he be if he couldn't be a surgeon?

It was just time, that's all. He needed time to heal. In two weeks he could start PT, and then he would regain the majority of his mobility, enough to do his job as well as he always had.

In the meantime, he was going to have to learn to use his left hand if he wanted to function without the help of his mother. At thirty-three, he was a little old to have his mother buttoning his shirt for him. And Josie couldn't touch his underwear again and expect to keep her own clothes on.

And that wasn't going to happen. Because most important of all, he had to learn to ignore his ridiculous feelings and his overactive hormones and pretend that Josie Adkins was just another orthopedic resident.

That's all.

Which was about as likely as Houston going back in time and beating that shark off with his board.

Chapter Thirteen

Josie was nervous. Okay, make that terrified. She had seen this surgery done half a dozen times by Dr. Hayes, but today she was going to be holding the scalpel.

She shouldn't be intimidated, she told herself firmly as she walked down the hall to meet with the patient. During her stints in ER trauma, she'd done minor solo surgeries as well as several under the tutelage of Dr. Sheinberg.

She knew the procedure inside and out. Dr. Hayes was going to be right next to her guiding her through the whole surgery, every step of the way.

Maybe that was part of the problem. She knew that despite his allowing her to operate, he was only doing so out of necessity. He had never trusted her, and probably still didn't. But she was his ticket into the OR.

Without her as an excuse, he would probably just be seeing patients and viewing X-rays, which he clearly did not want to do for a number of reasons. Mainly that Houston did not yet want to face the future and his possible inability to operate.

Staying at home day and night would leave him nothing but time to think about the future in all its grim possibilities, ranging from a teaching job to the lowest of the low for a surgeon—being a professional malpractice expert. Here at the hospital, he could pretend he was simply recuperating, assisting in surgery until he could take his rightful place front and center in the OR.

So Josie was stuck with the unpalatable position of getting to do what she had wanted to for three months, but for all the wrong reasons. Houston might be letting her operate, but not because he wanted to, and she was going to have to do a bang-up job to prove to him she belonged in orthopedics.

And to herself.

Because a nagging little voice in the back of her mind pointed out ruthlessly that she didn't actually belong in surgery, but she ignored it. There was no sense in having doubts this late in the game. She had a promise to keep and a boatload of student loans to repay.

Taking a deep breath, she entered the pre-op room where Ruby Frenske was waiting to be wheeled into surgery. Josie liked the setup at Acadia Inlet Hospital. Each patient was pre-oped in their own room, sitting up in a comfortable easy chair that was then rolled on wheels directly to the OR.

It made the patients feel less panicky than a gurney would, and Ruby was reclined back in her chair, holding her husband's hand and looking fairly relaxed.

"Good morning, Mrs. Frenske." Josie had met Ruby several weeks earlier when she had been to Dr. Hayes's office for pre-op testing.

Tuesdays and Thursdays were Houston's office hours, where he saw his patients pre and post surgery. Josie had only had the opportunity to pop in two or three times but had really enjoyed the chance to interact with the patients.

She recalled that Mrs. Frenske had been in a great deal of pain and had been using a walker, even though at seventy she was still relatively young to need that level of assistance.

"Good morning, Dr. Adkins." Ruby's voice was a bit slurred from the medication she had been given to relax her.

"Are you all set, ready to go?"

"Yes, as ready as I'll ever be."

"Do you have any last-minute questions?"

"No, I don't think so."

"Well, okay then, I'm going to get scrubbed up. Dr. Hayes and I will see you down the hall in a minute or two. The nurse will bring you on down." She squeezed Ruby's arm in reassurance. "When this is all over, you'll be much better off, trust me. When you're walking on your own, you'll be glad you had the surgery."

Ruby nodded, her eyes a little unfocused. "I hope so."

"How are you, Mr. Frenske?" Josie noticed that Ruby's husband looked worried as he sat next to her, clutching his wife's hand.

"I've been better," he said gruffly. "Hey, who's doing the surgery with you, Dr. Adkins? Ruby and I saw on the news that Dr. Hayes got attacked by a shark."

Josie fought the urge to wince. Oh, that would just thrill Houston. "I can't believe they put Dr. Hayes on the news."

"Oh, yeah. Every time someone gets bit by a shark they stick it on the news. The bigger the bite the longer the coverage. They showed Dr. Hayes's picture and said his name and everything." He pushed up his glasses and added, "Seventh bite this year."

Ruby made a sound of contempt. "Fred keeps count, Dr. Adkins. I think it's just gruesome. Is Dr. Hayes all right?"

"He's fine." Josie spoke forcefully. "In fact, he'll be sitting in on the surgery, assisting. You're his patient after all, and he wants to keep a close eye on you."

Or on Josie. Depending on how you looked at it.

She smiled at the Frenskes. "And if I don't get going,

we'll never get this show on the road. See you in a few minutes."

Nervous about how Houston would treat her, Josie studied him carefully when she entered the OR.

But Houston was Dr. Hayes. He acted the way he always had in the OR, and no one would ever suspect they had spent a passionate night together. Which totally depressed her.

Of course she couldn't expect him to discuss their relationship with two nurses, a surgical assistant, and an anesthesiologist in the room with them. Or their lack of a relationship.

Nor did he appear to be suffering any emotional distress about his injury and the relinquishing of his usual position as head surgeon. Josie was starting to think that if recovery could be based on willpower and sheer stubbornness, Houston would be one hundred percent in no time.

A high stool had been brought in for him to sit on immediately to Josie's right, so when she came in, scrubbed and ready to go, he was already sitting there.

"Running late, Dr. Adkins?" he asked, his face expressionless.

"No. I was chatting with the patient."

"Imagine that," he muttered.

"Excuse me?" She looked at him, but there was nothing but cool, calm blue eyes staring back at her.

Mrs. Frenske was wheeled in then and Houston didn't answer. Still very much in charge, despite his diminished role, he began directing the attending staff to place Mrs. Frenske on the table.

The anesthesiologist spoke calmly and carefully to the patient, advising her to count to ten as he placed the mask over her face and put her under. Mrs. Frenske only got to three before succumbing to the anesthetic.

Her vitals were monitored, equipment checked, she

was positioned on her side, and the leg was scrubbed. Everything was ready.

For Josie.

Her hand shook just a little as she made the initial incision in the skin over the upper side of the buttock. Houston talked her through it, guiding her to the blood vessels that needed cauterizing to minimize the bleeding.

Sweat began to bead on her forehead.

The panic returned full force. What was she doing here? This dear sweet old woman's life was in her hands and she was a totally inexperienced amateur. Her hand stilled.

The cold room turned hot. Sweat trickled down her breastbone, her throat closed up.

Houston gave her left shoulder a tap with his splint, careful not to use his good hand, which was scrubbed and sterile, should he need to assist.

"Hey," he said. "You're doing fine. Let's go."

Quickly she turned and caught his eye above his mask. He nodded again, and she saw confidence there. He did trust her. He wouldn't have let her do this at all if he didn't.

With a deep breath, she returned the nod and concentrated on opening up the fibrous capsule and the labrum of the hip socket so she could dislocate the head of the femur.

Josie had to saw off the diseased head of the femur and enlarge the cavity of the cup-shaped acetabulum to make room for the metal cup that would hold the new artificial hip.

It was straightforward. She just had to do it.

The voice of the nurse, reading off stable BP and oxygen levels, barely penetrated her absorbed brain. She concentrated on holding her hands steady, working with precision, and moving along at a reasonable rate. She tried to mimic the confidence that Houston had and minimize the number of times she paused in uncertainty.

They were using a cementless implant, so when she carefully placed the new cup into position she secured it with screws, which required a great deal of strength and arm muscle. It probably took her twice as long as it took Houston.

But she did it, and she sighed with relief.

As the nurse wiped the sweat from her forehead, she moved to the femur and began the delicate process of reaming out the long axis of the bone, using a broach instrument for the final shaping.

Houston murmured, "Good, there you go. You've got it."

Josie tested a trial stem for fit, and decided on the correct size to use. Suddenly unsure, she looked to Houston for assistance. "Larger?" she asked through her mask.

"What do you think?"

"Larger. It's not sitting in the canal snugly enough."

He nodded again, shifting on his stool. "I think you're right."

From there it was a matter of fitting the stem and head prosthesis components together with a hammer, then reassessing the fit. Josie tested the hip to gauge its range of motion and stability.

The components were rechecked and the stem secured in place. She made sure there was no debris left in the area.

As Josie was backing away to allow the surgical assistant to close the wound, she felt an enormous relief surging through her.

Thank God it's over, was all she could think. *And I never want to do that again.* Horrified at her unreasonable thoughts, she watched as the anesthetic was reversed, and Mrs. Frenske was readied to be transported to the recovery room to begin the process of adjusting to her new hip.

Josie swallowed hard. The surgery had only taken two and a half hours, yet she felt like half her life had gone by since she had stepped into the OR. The intense concentration and physical demands had her whipped, and fear had her in its grip. How could she hate a job she'd spent the last nine years training for?

Once upon a time, surgery had seemed exciting and intellectual to her younger self, when she'd been eager to prove she had brains to match the best of them. In her mind, orthopedics was logical, clear-cut. X-rays of injuries and disease—then diagnosis, treatment, prevention. Simple.

Yet why was it after a full year and two rotations of major orthopedic specialties she was feeling that she'd lost the meaning of the word *logic* in her life?

Her shoulders slumped as she pulled off her gloves and gown and threw them in the bin. She intended to follow Mrs. Frenske to recovery to make sure she was stable, but first she needed a minute to catch her breath and calm down her stomach, which was doing really athletic somersaults.

But shoot, something was wrong here, though given the eighty hours she was scheduled to work that week, she didn't have time to worry about it. She should be feeling elated that things had gone so well, she reminded herself firmly. Mrs. Frenske had been a model patient, her body doing exactly as it should, and Josie had made no mistakes.

Josie turned to leave the cold operating room, suddenly aware of Houston's eyes on her. Afraid he could see her confusion, she ducked her head as she went past him, focusing on the shiny sterile floor.

"Josie."

"Yes?" The tone in his voice drew her eyes upward in spite of herself.

He had pulled his mask off, and her gaze went to his mouth. She wanted him to kiss her. To hold her against that rock-solid chest and tell her that everything was okay.

A blush began to creep across her face. Was she really so needy? He didn't need or want her, and yet she couldn't stop herself from wanting him.

To make matters worse, he didn't smile, didn't give her praise or reassure her that she had done well.

Instead he said simply, "If you don't have confidence in yourself, nobody else will."

There wasn't anything she could say to dispute that. He had told her that before. He was right. "I know."

That look on his face, of concern, labeled her first attempt in the OR with him as a dismal failure. It didn't matter that everything had gone smoothly and that she had made no outward mistakes.

It felt wrong. Dr. Sheinberg had told her once that surgery was a calling, and she didn't know now why she had ever thought she had it. And even when she had been kidding herself, Houston had seen through her, seen that inside she was a bundle of nerves, as frightened as a dog during a thunderstorm.

She started towards the door again, needing to be alone.

"Josie." His steady, unemotional voice stopped her again. "It was a nice job."

"Thanks." Afraid that she would bawl like a baby if she turned to him, she hit the swing door with the palm of her hand and plowed forward.

She needed space between herself and the OR. And Houston Hayes.

Josie nearly ran into Shirley from the ER. "Sorry to interrupt, Dr. Adkins, but are you finished in here?"

Surprised to see Shirley out of the ER, Josie nodded. "Yes. Just closed. Did you need something?"

Shirley hovered by the door, having hastily donned a gown and cap to enter the sterile room. "There's been a bad car accident out on the boulevard. It was one of those torrential rains, you know, where you can't see two feet in front of you. Six cars collided, and we're full up in the ER. We've got an open compound femur fracture. Can we send him up?"

"Of course. Put him in three." Josie fought the urge to ask for Houston's opinion, conscious of him standing right behind her, silent and watching. She was the surgeon here, damn it. It was time she started acting as such, personal feelings be damned.

Twenty minutes later, after grabbing a cup of coffee and a muffin, Josie was in room three with Houston assessing the injury.

The man, who had arrived unconscious, was now being monitored by the anesthesiologist. He was in his forties or fifties from the looks of the touch of gray at the temples and crow's feet flaring out from his closed eyes. The remains of what had been dress pants were being cut away, and the once neat and tidy gray suit reminded Josie of a businessman. Maybe he had been on his way to an appointment, the last one of the day before he went home to his wife and a couple of shaggy-haired teenagers.

It was Josie's job to fix him and send him home to that family, if they existed. The responsibility of that nearly overwhelmed her, and she took deep breaths to calm herself down. She was a fantastic doctor. She was a competent surgeon. She had spent almost a year in the ER and had never once choked when dealing with a whole range of complicated emergencies.

That thought steadied her.

Houston was relaying to her what the attending doctor in the ER had told him. "He's in rough shape. Bruised liver, broken ribs from the impact of the air bag, plus the compound femur fracture and a lot of bleeding. So get his leg patched up and we'll send him on his way to ICU with a transfusion as a parting gift."

Josie wasn't used to Houston being so light in tone. As she began clamping vessels to stop the blood flow, she wondered why he was choosing a serious injury as the time for flippancy.

Then she realized it was probably for her benefit. He was concerned about her ability to handle an emergency like this. She certainly hadn't been giving him any reason to trust her nerves given that she'd nearly choked on a simple hip replacement.

Working steadily for the next two hours, Josie concentrated on plating and screwing the broken bones back together. She felt she was gaining on the injury, when she heard the awful sound of the monitors going off, alerting them to a problem.

Josie didn't look up, knowing that was what her support staff was for. She kept on doggedly.

"He's arresting," the anesthesiologist said.

Oh, Lord, help her. It was Josie's worst nightmare coming true. This man, whose name she didn't even know, was having a cardiac arrest right there on the operating table, with her hand still in his leg.

Houston was already moving to assist the nurse. Josie spared a glance up. "Let's defibrillate him!"

The SA held the paddles in front of the patient. Houston backed up to get out of the way. "I can't do it with only one hand. You've got to."

"I know." She swiped her hands on her gown to give herself better leverage and grabbed the paddles.

Placing one below the outer half of the right clavicle and the other over the apex of the heart, Josie took an urgent breath. "200 J, let's go."

"Clear." They shocked the man's heart, with no result.

The monitor read flat line and the eerie bell rang loudly in the cool room as they hovered over him. The surgical assistant administered CPR for one minute before Josie nudged him.

"Again." She couldn't let this man die like this. It was a severe injury, with a large amount of bleeding, but it shouldn't be a fatal injury. She would never be able to forgive herself if he died in front of her, in a room filled with strangers, without ever getting the chance to say good-bye to his loved ones.

The result was the same, and the staff all worked in unison to attend to the various tasks that needed to be done. The patient was given epinephrine and lidocaine in his IV. The positioning of the electrodes was checked, and CPR was conducted while the anesthesiologist checked for a rhythm on the monitor.

"Again," Josie said, desperation creeping into her voice.

The nurse looked to Dr. Hayes for confirmation.

He nodded. "Do it."

"360 J," Josie said. "Clear."

This time there was a response. The heart began a sinus rhythm, faint but steady. Josie's knees went weak with relief.

"We've got a pulse," the nurse announced.

The anesthesiologist sank back onto her chair, wiping her forehead. "Whew, that was close."

With a nod, Josie went back to the fracture she had abandoned. She didn't trust herself to speak, afraid she would start crying, and she wanted this procedure done right now. She couldn't afford to lose it just yet.

"I'll lend you a hand," Houston said, his calm voice nearly shattering the last of her control.

How the hell he could act so unshakable, collected, so unconcerned when a man had almost died, she couldn't understand. She just gave him a nod, afraid if she locked eyes with him, spoke, that Houston would hear and see all her inadequacies, all her failings as a surgeon.

Houston began to work on turning the last screw in place with his left hand and Josie couldn't help but notice that he only needed one hand to accomplish in the same amount of time what she needed two hands for.

Granted it wasn't complex work, and he stepped back to allow her space when she needed to restore the muscles around the femur, but it felt like another blazing football field size sign that she wasn't cut out for the OR.

Twenty minutes later she had the last suture in place and they were wheeling the man to ICU to be monitored closely for signs of distress or cardiac arrest. Josie watched the gurney go and took deep breaths.

Her hand was shaking. She wondered if it had been shaking when she had been suturing. The poor guy would have an odd-looking scar if her hand had been trembling with the needle in it.

It was the absurdity of that last thought that had her peeling off her gloves with frantic energy and heading for the locker room.

"Josie."

Ignoring Houston, she left the OR behind and barely managed to keep herself from sprinting down the hall, her breath shallow and face burning. When she reached the locker room, she did break into a jog, and didn't stop until she was hidden behind the last row of lockers. Sinking down on the bench, she buried her head in her hands and let them come.

The tears of relief. Tears of panic. Tears of horror that a man could have died today while under her knife.

She hadn't bothered to remove her gown and her hands were resting in her lap, the garment liberally smeared with blood. It had never struck her as gruesome before, but it did now. That had been a person on that table, not a patient. A person who had put his trust in her and his life in her hands.

The tears turned to sobs. What was she doing? She wasn't cut out for this. Sara had been right. She should be making jewelry and selling incense sticks in a kitschy store on the boardwalk, not pretending to be a doctor.

"Josie."

Damn it. Houston. She ducked her head and swiped at her eyes, choking back a sob. "Just give me a minute, please." Her voice was shaky and high-pitched.

If he had been decent, the least teeny bit considerate of her feelings, he would have hung back until she said it was okay. Or he would have just left her alone. Instead, Houston sat down on the bench next to her, brushing her arm with his, and setting her frazzled and tangled emotions nearly skidding over the edge.

Having to deal with him and his confident, seductive looks would be downright impossible right now. She turned away from him in irritation. "Do you mind?"

"Yes, I do." He paused. "You did a good job in there."

Astonished, she gaped at him. "Are you crazy? I almost killed him!"

She wanted to take the words back immediately. They revealed far too much of her fears, and Houston did not want to listen to her whining and pouting.

"No." Houston shook his head. "That's not true and you know it. You saved that man in there. You can't beat yourself up over something that you had no control over."

Really, she appreciated the attempt on his part to make her feel better, but right now she just wanted to be alone. Houston Hayes knew nothing about how it felt to not be up to the job, how to always scrape and fight and try and never be the best at anything. To always doubt and to wonder and to second guess.

"I was too slow. If I had been faster, he wouldn't have arrested."

"I'll say it again. You saved him, Josie. I'm sure he arrested because of an undiagnosed deep thrombosis in his calf. It traveled up his bloodstream and caused a pulmonary embolism. It was a ticking time bomb. We just happened to be there when it went off."

It made sense as an explanation for what had happened. If there was a thrombosis, the man could have arrested for any surgeon. It wasn't her fault.

But somehow that didn't make her feel any better. Josie wiped her damp cheeks and sat there hunched over, her heart sick.

"Patients die. That's a fact of medicine. You do your best and that's all anybody can expect."

But that was the problem. That was where the doubt lay. She couldn't stop herself from whispering, "What if my best isn't good enough?"

Houston shrugged. "Sometimes it won't be."

His matter-of-fact manner appalled her. "I can't believe you can just sit there and act like it doesn't matter that someone dies!"

His jaw clenched, but he took her hand with his left and gave a gentle squeeze. "Of course it matters. But I'm a surgeon. My job is to fix the disease, the illness, or the injury. That's it. Sometimes I'm not going to be able to do that. I'm not a miracle worker. I can't fix what isn't fixable."

Despite trying darn hard to ignore it, Josie was finding comfort in his strong hand over hers, the familiar scent of him as he sat close to her, body touching hers. Houston had all the poise and self-confidence that she lacked. And when he was like this . . . warm and caring and personable, she found herself unable to resist him.

This was the Houston she had come to care about, admire, and respect. One who gave his very best and cared about each and every one of his patients, whether he wanted to admit it or not. This was the Houston she was fast developing feelings for that reached far beyond admiration and attraction.

"Surgery is impersonal, Josie. Not because the surgeon is cold-hearted, but because it has to be. When you're in that OR, it's about fixing the problem. Doing your job and doing it correctly. Like with Mrs. Frenske. You do a great job, but you hesitate." He smiled a little, nudging her with his knee. "I told you before and I'll say it again. You need to display a little arrogance like most surgeons and just do it. Own it."

There probably wasn't an arrogant bone in her body. Maybe he had her share. "That's easy for you to say. Just do it. Well, it's not like that for me. I have to look in the mirror every day, and I don't see a professional, intelligent surgeon staring back at me. I have to work harder to earn respect, I have to force people to take me seriously."

Agitated, she stood up, wanting to get away from him and his perfection. "You can't understand that. You've probably never doubted yourself a day in your life. Lately, that's all I have."

God, she was going to cry. Tears were hovering, threatening, embarrassing little bastards, ready to show him just how inadequate she was. He, who was always in control, watching her spin way, way out of it.

"Josie." Houston stood, and he was going to touch her and she wanted to hide, crawl inside her own skin and get away from him.

"Don't, please. Just leave me alone. I'm an emotional wreck and you're embarrassing me."

But he didn't leave her alone. Instead he took her hands in his, spun her around until she was facing the full-length mirror between the rows of lockers.

Josie winced as she saw herself, the blood-stained gown emphasizing her roundness, making her look like Frankenstein's goony sidekick. She had dark circles under her eyes, mussed hair from the cap, and she wanted to ignore it all, to pretend that she was gorgeous and confident and could waltz into a surgery and take charge. But she couldn't.

She closed her eyes against Houston staring over her shoulder with eyes that saw all of her, inside and out.

"You are a good surgeon." His hand stroked hers, even when she stiffened at his words.

"And it's the emotion that I like about you. The way you care is really amazing. You have a way with people that I could never have, not on my best day."

"That's not true," she whispered, eyes still screwed shut, dark spots dancing behind her eyelids. "You're brilliant."

"No more brilliant than you." His hand was caressing across her stomach under the gown, intimately, caring. "I'm just older, more experienced, colder. The emotion thing scares me. That's why I'm a surgeon."

Josie felt the gown being brushed down her shoulders and dropped to the floor. She shook her head, but his hand kept moving and his voice was low in her ear, stroking her resistance away.

"That's why I told you to leave my condo last week. You scare me."

Lips touched the base of her neck and Josie shuddered, feeling too weak to pull away. He was offering comfort, and God, she needed it. "I wouldn't scare a flea," she said, catching her breath when he brushed her nipples.

"You have more power than you realize." A laugh tickled her ear. "Maybe it's a good thing you don't realize how much."

"Stop." They were supposed to be friends, not cross this line again, but he didn't even pause.

Those fingers she remembered so well from their one night together slipped between the waistband of her scrubs and her panties. She jerked back, knowing this was her last moment to halt his hand before it went any farther. But she collided with his erection pressing hot against her backside and she couldn't remember anymore why she couldn't do this, why she couldn't take his reassurance and soak in it.

"Houston . . . I don't . . ." She trailed off when his thumb found her clitoris through her panties and rolled over with firm back-and-forth motions. Reason still urged her to pull away, step forward, get out of the locker room.

But her body didn't agree, and her heart hurt too much to pretend that they were or could ever be friends.

"Shh. Put your arms around my neck. Then open your eyes, Josie."

It felt good, so deep-down good, the way he was touching and prodding and coaxing her body into desire, into wetness and longing. Taking her from hurt and scared to distracting pleasure. Muscles in her shoulders and calves relaxing, others tensing in anticipated pleasure, tightening and clenching, leaning into him.

She lifted her arms, locked them around his neck, felt her chest heaving and her breasts tingling with need, pressing taut against her shirt. Her legs spread, her hips arched, and that sound, the *yes, yes,* gasp came rolling out of her mouth.

"Open your eyes. See how gorgeous you look. How smart and caring and beautiful."

Josie didn't want to, didn't want to face herself and all her defects, just wanted to hover in the fuzzy darkness, feeling Houston rock her into pleasure. He slipped a finger inside her panties, teased around her curls, sank in briefly, sparking a flood of moisture, then pulled out.

She gave a groan of disappointment.

"Open your eyes or you can't have it." Then his tongue dipped into her ear, hot and wet, making her squirm with want, making her ache to feel him inside her.

With a shuddering breath, she dragged open her eyes. Saw her face flushed with pleasure, saw his dark look of concentration, saw his tongue retreat from her flesh, saw the bulge of his hand in her pants, the dark hairs on the back of his wrist rising from her scrubs. Then watched her own eyes go wide with shock when his finger sank deep inside her, in and out, with a lascivious little wiggle that sent forth another rush of heat from her body.

She felt vulnerable, raw, embarrassed by her body's quick reaction to him, the obvious soaking wetness of her desire saturating his finger. But it paled to the other feelings Houston drew out of her. The comfort, the want, the freedom to let go, to indulge, and to distance herself from the OR. To revel in having saved her patient's life, and to appreciate all that she had.

To enjoy a stolen moment with Houston, where he wasn't pushing her away from him.

Josie watched herself, arched against Houston, panting, biting her lip, straining forward, and damn, she was pleased with what she saw. She liked herself, her brains, her humor, her generosity, everything that made up who she was, including her less-than-perfect body.

And so did Houston.

He stroked her faster, on and on until she felt nothing but tight, hot pleasure ripping through her, urging her to abandon any reserve and just enjoy.

Then he whispered in her ear with a sort of miraculous awe, "You are so fucking sexy."

It was all she needed to hear to send her pulsing and pressing and squeezing into his hand, an orgasm ripping through her with shuddering gasps.

She held on to him, fingers gripping his thick black hair.

He didn't let go.

And if there was a punishment for coming in the locker room after surgery, then bring it down on her, because it was damn well worth it.

Chapter Fourteen

"This is a bad idea." Josie stood in front of the mirror in her bedroom and inspected herself.

A shudder couldn't be prevented.

Sara laughed. "Oh, come on. You look great."

No, she didn't. She looked as white as a polar bear in this bikini. Why she had ever thought it would be a good idea to buy a Hawaiian-print bikini was beyond her at the moment.

It had been an impulse, like a lot of things lately. Houston had invited her to the beach, a murmured invitation with his finger still inside her, and she had managed a shaky nod. It had seemed natural, her body still pulsing, while she felt sexy and capable of arousing Houston, to put on a bikini and splash around in the surf in front of him.

Now she decided she'd rather die. Slowly. Eaten alive by a thousand sewer rats than let him see her in all her Pillsbury doughboy glory.

"I look about one thousand shades whiter than every other twenty-seven-year-old woman in Florida. You look fantastic. It's not fair. When do you have time to tan?"

Sara flipped her blond hair back over her shoulder and shrugged. "Josie, it's a fake tan. It's that lotion you put on to make you look tan. I don't lie in the sun anymore without SPF 30 sunscreen on. You of all people, a fellow doctor, should know the dangers of skin cancer."

"I don't have to worry about it." Josie grimaced at her reflection and reached for her cover-up. The cover-up that was going to be staying on her every second she was on that beach.

"There's never time to go to the beach."

"This will be good for us. Fresh air. People not suffering from illness or injury. A chance to relax."

Josie certainly needed that. After the episode in the OR yesterday, she needed to lounge around in the sun and read the latest gossip magazine. She was sadly out of date on who was sleeping with who in Hollywood.

She just hoped seeing Houston wouldn't be awkward. Which it would, of course, since she had let him get her off in the hospital locker room. A blush heated her face just thinking about it. But he had invited her to the beach, and well, it was his fault their conversation the day before had dissolved into a scene from a bad porno film. He had done all the groping. She'd just let him.

"Relax. Got it." She took a fortifying breath and thought calming thoughts that didn't involve sexy surgeons or beached-whale analogies.

"Okay, slather on the sunscreen and let's go. The sun, the surf, and gorgeous half-naked men await us. Or man, in your case. You've narrowed the field to Houston. I'm still searching." Sara stepped into her high-heel sandals and tied a little sarong around her red bikini.

"You're wearing high heels to the beach? Won't you sink in the sand?" Josie pulled on grubby sneakers and wiggled her toes. When had she gotten that hole in the toe?

"Yes, but so what? The heels make my legs look longer." Sara slung a floral bag over her shoulder.

Said Sara, whose legs were already eight miles long. "Then I should be wearing six-inch heels."

Josie rushed past the mirror, afraid that if she looked again she would change her mind and spend the day inside her stuffy little apartment, standing Houston up.

It was already a gamble bringing Sara. She didn't know how Houston would react to that, or what he had planned. But he hadn't called it a date, had only said he missed the beach and wanted to go, and frankly, she needed Sara as a buffer.

Walking through her tiny living room, Josie said, "Why do I have the feeling you're on a mission? A find-a-date-at-the-beach mission?"

"Because I am. I haven't had a date in six months."

Josie could sympathize with that. "Working crazy hours makes it tough to date."

"No, walking around in a doctor's coat looking smart makes it hard to date." Sara dug her sunglasses out of her purse as they stepped out into the brilliant sunshine. "I think I intimidate men. That's why I'm going for the frivolous look today."

Sara's logic seemed a little flawed. "Don't men like smart women?" Josie asked, then wondered why she thought she knew anything about what men liked.

"They do in theory. But it's not brains that initially attracts a man's attention. It's either looks or a bubbly personality."

Josie jumped into Sara's sedan. "You're totally wrong. I have a bubbly personality, and it hasn't done a thing for me."

Sara snorted. "You're sleeping with Dr. Houston Hayes, aren't you?"

As Sara pulled out into mid-morning traffic, Josie wiggled around on the leather seat and tugged at her cover-up. "Well, only randomly, not consistently."

Sara gave her a look that suggested it was a stupid comment. "You're still ahead of me. I'm not sleeping with anyone. I think it's because I'm serious and smart. That scares men."

"I'm chatty and clumsy and smart. Apparently that scares men, too. You know, I don't think I care anymore what men think." Josie was surprised to find that she actually meant it. She didn't need anyone's approval. She was a skilled doctor and a good person and she was happy with her life, aside from her nervousness in the OR. She had a lot to be grateful for.

Sara hooked a left into the parking lot by the beach and threw the car into PARK. "I totally know what you mean, but Josie, I'm just lonely. I feel old."

That wasn't Josie's problem. Hers was that she felt stuck in adolescence, unsure of herself, babbling and clumsy. "Sara, I think you have an old soul, you know? You were probably responsible and mature at birth. But I know what you mean about feeling lonely."

She felt it in spades. More so since she'd met Houston and had slept with him, because now she wanted more. A relationship. And he wasn't willing to give it.

"I don't want to be responsible. I want to be a sexy siren." Sara took off her glasses and put them in a soft pink case, tucking it into her beach bag.

Josie looked at her in amazement. "You're scaring me."

But Sara just laughed. "I want to see if men react differently to me."

"Well, you'll have to go it alone. I've spent my whole life trying to convince people I'm not a bit of fluff. I'm not about to start flashing a siren smile." She grinned as she undid her seat belt. "Besides, I don't think sirens can be short. It's written into the contract or something."

They started towards the water, Sara wincing as the hot sand slid over her feet, the sandals sinking just as Josie had predicted. Despite the fact that she looked like a twelve-year-old tomboy next to Sara, Josie was glad she had worn her trusty sneakers.

Josie scanned the Thursday morning crowd, looking for Houston. Given that it wasn't even ten o'clock yet, the beachgoers consisted mostly of families with little kids running around with colorful pails and water noodles.

She spotted Houston immediately, lounging in a beach chair, shirtless, his chest golden bronze. His right hand lay in his lap, while his leg with the sutures jutted out in front of him, the butterfly bandages gone and the black sutures visible even from where she stood.

He had his eyes closed, so maybe he wouldn't notice the pink sexual flush that raced over her body, the way her heart picked up speed, and the heavy, eager breathing.

Sure. And maybe she could borrow Calista Flockhart's jeans.

Houston was wondering if Josie was going to show up at the beach or not. He wasn't even sure what had possessed him to ask her. But he had a growing desire to return to the beach—he missed the water—and he had wanted to share it with her.

He didn't want to be alone when he came back to the ocean for the first time since the shark took a swipe at him. He had wanted Josie with him.

Watching her come apart for him in front of the mirror had reached something deep down in his gut, had made him feel both protective of her and proud. He admired her, respected her as a woman and a doctor, and he had wanted to make her feel better about the surgery, make her understand it wasn't her fault. Whether he had been successful or not, he didn't know, but he had distracted her.

And he had wanted her with him on the beach. Of course, somehow or other his sister and mother and Christian had managed to horn their way in when they heard he was going to the beach. He appreciated their concern but now he wasn't going to have Josie to himself and that was a shame. He'd been looking forward to coaxing her off the beach and up to his condo where he could make her scream and moan and come, again and again.

The thought had him shifting in his beach chair.

"What's the matter with you?" Kori said, sprawled out on a towel at his feet. "You look like you're in pain. I knew you shouldn't have come back this soon."

"What does being at the beach have to do with anything?" Houston flicked the sand with his foot, sending it skittering across Kori's arm to annoy her, tired of being cosseted and treated like he had an infectious disease.

He was all but healed and was hoping Josie could take his sutures out today. He wanted people to stop walking on eggshells around him. He wanted his life back the way it had been before.

"Hey!" Kori frowned at him, brushing the sand off. She glanced past him, shielding her eyes against the sun. "Oh, look, Mom's here with Larry."

"Who the hell is Larry?" Houston craned his neck around and saw his mother wearing a black tank suit, a floppy hat, and little white shorts. A gray-haired man Houston had never seen before had his hand on her elbow.

"Um . . ." Kori was suddenly interested in squeezing sunscreen into her hand. "Mom's friend."

His mother had a friend named *Larry?* "Since when?" He had the sneaking suspicion, given his sister's wandering eyes, Larry's hand on the elbow, and his mother's coordinated outfit, that friend really meant boyfriend. Which he didn't think he liked at all.

"Since a while."

As the pair grew closer, Larry leaned over and whispered in his mother's ear, giving her behind a soft tap. She laughed and swatted at his hand.

"What a yahoo," Houston said in disgust. His mother had never dated, not since his father had left fifteen years earlier. He couldn't see why she would have waited all that time and then would hook up with Larry of the beach grope.

"Actually, he's really nice. He's very good to Mom." Kori shot him a worried look. "Just give him a chance."

"So you've met him before?" Now he was seriously annoyed. He wasn't important enough to his mother to introduce him to her boyfriend?

"Yes, quite a few times. And before you overreact, Mom didn't tell you because she was worried about your reaction. She didn't want you to get upset."

Too late. And there was no further chance to discuss it. His mother and Larry were upon them and suddenly his mother was giving nervous, fluttering introductions and he was forced to smile and nod politely while Larry shook his hand and clapped him on the back.

"It's great to finally meet you, Houston. Your mother has told me so much about you. How's the leg?"

"Better. Almost healed." Houston gritted his teeth and forced his hand to unclench.

His mother, clearly nervous, touched his shoulder. "Where's your hat, Houston? You'll be broiled like a fish."

He'd already been chewed on like one, what was a little broiling? "Mom. Do you think I surf with a hat? I don't need a hat."

His mother put her hands on her hip. "And what's so great about surfing? It got you bit up by a shark, didn't it? I'd be happy if you never set foot in that ocean again."

Larry guided his mother forward with a hand on her waist. "Have a seat, Fran, and leave the poor boy alone."

His mother sank into the chair next to him like she was perfectly used to Larry giving her directions. Houston wanted to put a fist in his face.

"And Houston's accident was one in a million. Surfing isn't any more dangerous than walking across a busy street. You're more likely to get struck by lightning than attacked by a shark."

At least the man had a modicum of sense. Houston felt a shred more tolerant towards him until his mother said, "That's true, Larry," ignoring the fact that Houston had been telling her the same thing for over a week.

When Kori's kids came running out of the water with Christian and launched themselves at Larry with an enthusiasm normally reserved for a purple dinosaur, Houston wanted to grab a sand pail and puke in it. Clearly everyone just loved Larry.

Then he saw Josie. Walking across the sand with a soft little welcoming smile on her face, her body hidden by a voluminous white T-shirt. And he felt comforted. Like just being with her took some of the pressure off, made him relax and want to sit back and enjoy life.

"Hey," he said, reaching out and brushing a finger across her hand when she stopped in front of him.

"Hey." She twisted the toe of her dirty little sneakers into the sand. "I brought my friend Sara with me. I hope you don't mind."

Houston said hello to the tall blonde who waved from behind Josie. "No, I don't mind. I've got my whole family with me."

And Larry.

Houston made introductions, very aware of Kori and Christian's raised eyebrows. He wasn't exactly known for bringing a woman to a family outing. His mother didn't look all that surprised, but then she was probably too busy giggling with Larry to notice.

"Have a seat," Kori offered, patting the towel next to her. "Sorry, we're out of chairs."

"That's okay." Josie sat on the towel and crossed her legs, her friend Sara squeezing in next to her. "It's just nice to get out of the hospital and finally make it to the beach."

"I don't know how you do it, being a doctor, I mean. The hours would kill me," Kori said. "Just taking care of my two girls wears me out."

"Oh, raising children is much harder than being a doctor," Josie said, earning her a beaming smile from his sister and making Houston superfluous to their conversation.

They were off and running, both chattering on with barely any breaks for air. Houston felt compelled to be polite and talk to Sara, who was hugging her knees to her chest and looking a little uncomfortable.

"I've seen you at the hospital before with Josie. You're a doctor?"

Sara nodded. "Pediatrician."

"Aah. Immunizations and ear infections."

Sara gave a little laugh. "That's a big part of peds, that's for sure." She dug in her bag and emerged with a pair of glasses, putting them on and blinking hard. "That's better."

"Afraid you'll lose them in the water?" he asked politely, wishing his sister would shut the hell up so Josie would look at him.

"Kind of." Sara leaned back and bumped his knee. "Oh, sorry."

"No problem." He just wished he had invited Josie to a beach on a tropical island where no other humans were present, and her bikini was nothing but a couple of coconut shells.

Josie was enjoying her conversation with Kori, but she'd be a lot happier if Houston wasn't sitting directly behind Sara. Very long-legged and beautiful Sara, wearing nothing but a teeny-weeny red bikini. Sara who was blond and blue-eyed and was laughing, soft and throaty, at something Houston had said.

God, what had he said? The guy wasn't known for stand-up, so what exactly was so funny? And what was the matter with her that she was totally jealous of her friend?

Out of the corner of her eye she saw Sara bump against Houston's knee. It looked like an accident—she was sure it was an accident—but hell if she was going to watch anyone else touch his knee while she was sitting there.

And since there was no way to nudge Sara out of the way and not have Houston and his family think she was a lunatic, she stood up. "I'm getting really hot sitting here. I think I'll just jump in the water for a minute."

Houston's niece stopped piling sand on her father's feet and looked up. "I want to go in the water, too."

Christian sighed. "We just got out, Miranda. Let Daddy have a three-minute break."

"I can take her," Josie offered, anxious to get away, and not really sure what she'd do in the water by herself anyway. Swim laps back and forth while Houston chatted with Sara? "If she'll go with me, that is."

Miranda didn't strike Josie as a shy child, and her response confirmed it. She stood up, kicking sand over both her parents and her sister, and grabbed Josie by the hand. "I'm ready. I can swim really good, I'm in the Trout group at swimming. If you sink, I'll save you."

The adults all laughed. Christian grinned. "She gets her modesty from Houston."

* * *

Houston watched Josie and Miranda jump a wave, holding hands, laughing, and he was sorry he had come to the beach in the first place. Sorry he hadn't been able to leave Josie alone, had pulled her back into his life after he had shoved her out.

Larry was bouncing Kori's other daughter, Abby, on his hip, announcing that he was taking her for her own little dip in the water. Abby looked perfectly at ease with Larry, and Kori didn't blink at Larry's announcement. Like she was used to Larry being around.

Houston sighed, pulling forward to unstick his back from the nylon beach chair. Kori was probing Sara for free medical advice, asking for the early signs of chicken pox.

His mother was still sitting next to him and they sat in silence for a minute, watching Josie run back and forth in the surf, chasing Miranda.

It was painful to watch.

Josie was adorable. She was pretty and kind, intelligent and outgoing.

She was six years younger than him, and shared none of the cynicism he had acquired in the last few years.

He was jaded.

She was still untouched and naïve.

There were a million and one reasons why he shouldn't get further involved with her. Starting with the fact that they worked together and ending with the sad truth that he had nothing to offer her.

He shifted in his chair again and pushed up his sunglasses with his left hand. That was the biggest reason of all to stay away from Josie. He was in for a rough road ahead with his injured hand.

Two more weeks in the splint, then months of physical therapy. And still no guarantee that he would even be able to bend his thumb and finger ever again. His career would be gone.

Anger started to churn inside him. Hell, not only would his career be gone, but everything would be a nightmare. Without sensation or movement, he would have to do everything left-handed, including eating and writing.

He couldn't think about it. His hand had to heal. There just wasn't any other option.

Without his career, there was nothing left.

Surfing, his only other solace, was beyond his abilities right now as well.

All he was capable of was sitting here and watching the water. Watching Josie.

Miranda splashed Josie, who shrieked and covered her face.

Josie was still wearing her bulky T-shirt but the water had drenched it until it clung to her, outlining a bikini top hugging those lush breasts. He knew her breasts, had tasted them, touched them, and he wanted her, the way he always did. Fierce and demanding and unrelenting.

His mother waved her hand in front of her face. "Whew, it's hot."

He grunted. He didn't want to talk to his mother. He just wanted to be left alone to brood and feel sorry for himself.

She patted his arm. "Why are you frowning? It ruins your pretty face."

He raised his eyebrow. Only his mother would think pretty was a compliment to a man. "I want to be in the water and I'm stuck on the beach."

That was the truth. Part of it, anyway. No need to mention the rest. That he was warring with himself and his desire for Josie.

"Ah. I see. The cute little Josie plays in the water

without you. You'd rather play with her than sit with your mother."

Now how had his mom figured that out?

"I meant surfing."

His mother, who looked incredible for her sixty-two years, adjusted the strap on her black bathing suit and gave him a look. The don't-give-me-that-load-of-you-know-what look.

"Don't lie to your mother, Houston, it's a sin."

It wouldn't be a wise idea to delve into all the ways he might have sinned with Josie.

He turned and studied his mother. "So what's the story with you and Larry?"

The question got quite a reaction. She bit her lip, adjusted her hat, took a deep breath, then put her hand on his arm again. That hand scared him.

"Honey, I'm going to marry Larry."

"What?" He sat up straighter and gaped at her. "But you said you'd never get married again after my father."

That hand stroked softly and he felt something way beyond alarm. This was not what he wanted to hear, not when everything in his life was changing, morphing, shaking him up and twisting his realities around.

"I thought that I wouldn't, but that was a long time ago. I've forgiven your father, moved on."

"You shouldn't forgive him. He doesn't deserve it. He treated you like shit, every single day you were married, and he can never make that up to you," he said in a harsh whisper, conscious of Josie's friend three feet away from him.

But his mother just shook her head under her big-ass floppy hat that made him feel like he was talking to a 1950s film star. Or an Italian Joan Collins. He'd never seen her wear anything like that before and it bothered him that everything was changing.

"What your father did to me was wrong and I was glad when he finally left. But I decided years ago it's not worth carrying anger around with me over it. I feel sorry for Hal. He's bitter, alone, full of hate, and I'm happy, with the greatest children and grandchildren a woman could ask for. My life is full of love, and Larry has added to that."

She pinned him with a stare, her dark eyes just a touch vulnerable. "I want you to be happy for me."

That hit him in the gut. "Of course I'm happy for you, Mom, if this is what you want." Even if it was a putz named Larry.

"I want you to let go of all that anger, too, Houston. Until you do, your father still controls your life." She leaned closer to him and cupped his cheek. He remembered being so short he only came up to her waist, how she would hug him to her hard, tell him how much she loved him. How she'd apologize for his father's behavior, let him know that she loved him too much to ever let him walk in his father's footsteps. That he was better.

And here, on the beach, with her familiar rose scent wrapping around him, he still saw the worry in her eyes. It made shame cling to him like the sticky beach chair.

"You grew up too soon, Houston. You became a man way before other boys did, because you had to. You took care of me and your sister, and I'm grateful to you for that. You're the best son a mother could ask for, and I love you."

Houston felt his throat close up and he swallowed hard. He'd tried to take care of his mom and Kori, had hoped he'd done all right, but he hadn't been much more than a determined kid when his father had left.

"But you don't need to take care of us anymore. Kori and I are fine. It's time for you to take care of yourself." Her head swung towards the surf and she smiled. "And maybe take care of someone else."

"What do you mean?" He forced the words past his lips, which felt frozen despite the pounding sun.

"She's in love with you, you know."

"Bullshit." The word flew off his tongue, the pain in his chest more pronounced as he looked out again at Josie, who had Miranda on her shoulders in the water.

He wasn't deserving of love from Josie. He hadn't done anything to earn it, and she was sweet and kind and he was just going through the motions in life.

"So many swear words from you lately, it's ugly," his mother reprimanded. "And don't bother arguing, you know it's true. And I know if you think about it, you'll recognize you feel the same way."

Not. He liked Josie, he cared about her. He wanted to have sex with her for seventeen consecutive days, but he did not love her.

"She'd be good for you. Help you relax. You were always so serious, and that's my mother's guilt. It's my fault."

"It's not your fault, don't say that! And there's nothing wrong with the way I am." Nothing wrong with being a lonely workaholic.

Houston wiped sweat off his upper lip, cursing again that he couldn't go in the water to cool off, and shook his head. "Just because you're suddenly in love with Larry doesn't mean the whole world needs to be paired off. There's nothing serious between Josie and I."

And if he said it out loud, maybe he'd believe it.

Chapter Fifteen

Josie balanced Miranda's slippery four-year-old body on her back and made her way to where Houston and his mother were sitting talking. She bent over and pretended to shake Miranda off, who squealed in delight, before setting her down in Kori's lap.

"Whew, you wore me out, kiddo."

Fran stood up. "I think I'll go check on Larry and Abby."

Josie raised an eyebrow at Houston as his mother walked towards the water. "Did I drive her away?"

"No." He patted the chair next to him. "Sit next to me. I think she just wants to be with Larry. They're getting married, she informed me."

Given the sour look on his face, this wasn't happy news. "Oh?" Josie moved around Sara, who had settled back on her towel with a paperback book, all plans of chasing down single men apparently forgotten. "How do you feel about that?"

Houston looked hot and uncomfortable as the sun crept higher in the sky. The arch of his wide shoulders and his chest were glistening with sweat, and the tips of his black bristly hair were damp.

"It doesn't matter how I feel."

That was a typical Houston answer but it disappointed her nonetheless. She wanted him to trust her, to confide in her, and it just wasn't happening. She tugged her cover-up shirt lower so that none of her thighs were showing and fought off a sigh.

"Why are you wearing that baggy T-shirt still?" he asked, plucking at the hem with his finger.

"Because." Several explanations ran through her mind, about how cottage cheese belongs in the fridge, not on the beach, but they all sounded a little whiny so she lied. "I burn easily."

"Liar," he murmured under his breath.

Josie didn't want to have the "your body is beautiful" conversation again, so she changed the subject. "Are you getting your stitches out on Monday?"

Being that close to his leg, she had noticed the wounds had healed nicely.

"Yes." He turned his leg a little and inspected it. "I can't wait. The sutures have been driving me crazy for the last two days. I thought about taking them out myself, but I can't reach the ones in the back." He frowned. "Besides, I'm not that great with my left hand."

"I can take them out if you want."

"That would be awesome. If you do it now, I can get in the water. It's driving me nuts to have to just sit here and bake while everyone else can go in the water."

"Sure, I can do it now." It was better than having the bathing suit conversation any day.

Houston flexed his leg. "It'll be great not to have to sleep with them pulling tonight."

"Should we walk back to your condo?" Josie had all sorts of ideas about what they could do once they got there, none of which involved medical procedures. "Unless you have scissors in your swim trunks."

He pretended to pat down his sides. "Left them in my other trunks. Just let me flag my mom down and tell her where we're going." He rolled his eyes. "She worries about me, you know. If it wasn't for Larry, she'd be hovering over me right now. She didn't even want me to come to the beach. Between the heat and the horrible shark flashbacks, she's waiting for me to pass out or something."

His lip was twitching in amusement, but Josie had to wonder if he was upset staring at the water. Somehow she thought she would be if a shark had ripped into her.

"Are you having flashbacks?" she asked in concern.

"No."

Well, she was. Flashbacks of his mouth on her breasts, his fingers inside her, the way her thighs had clenched as he moved in and out of her body, slowly and powerfully . . .

Then Houston said, "What was that?"

"What?" She looked around, startled out of her erotic thoughts by his serious tone.

"That." He pointed in the direction of the water.

"I don't see anything." She leaned forward, alarmed. Maybe Houston was having flashbacks. Or maybe there was another shark in the water. His mom and his niece were out there somewhere, unaware of the danger.

"Right . . ."

His hand landed on her waist and tickled her. "Here."

She screamed in surprise, her heart racing, part from fear, part from the feel of his hand on her, so darn close to her nipple. "Oh, geez, you scared me!"

Turning to see him laughing, she swatted him on the thigh. "That wasn't funny. I thought there was a shark out there."

That grin turned her heart upside down. She had barely been capable of functioning around Houston when he had been cold and aloof. A relaxed, laughing, joking Houston was just more than one woman could be expected to resist, and she had the damp bikini bottoms to prove it.

"No, no sharks out there. There might be sharks out here, though."

The humor had left his voice, and the grin had fallen away to be replaced by a deep sensual searching gaze. His thigh was against hers, the hair on his leg tickling her. She sat frozen as he traced a finger down her arm with his left hand.

Those ice-blue eyes had darkened to the color of denim. "If I bite you, Josie, it's an accident. Just like that shark that got ahold of me."

He was warning her again that he might hurt her. Josie just looked at him head-on. "I'm tougher than I look."

They were staring at each other so intently that neither one of them saw Miranda until she was already crashing through the air towards Houston with the speed of the Concorde.

Josie and Kori both gasped as Miranda crashed into his chest, Houston grunting at the impact. Josie leaned forward, reaching out as Miranda wobbled on Houston's lap, his hands struggling to steady her. Then the child shifted, the brunt of her weight landing on his right hand with the splint, and Houston lost his tenuous grip on her.

With a shocked cry, Miranda sailed backwards off his lap into the sand, and while three sets of hands tried to grab her, all came up short. Miranda thumped onto the sand, Kori gasped, and Houston cursed.

"It's okay," Kori hastened to assure him, pulling Miranda to a sitting position. "She's fine. Sand is soft."

But Houston looked horrified. "I'm sorry, cutie. Are you sure you're all right?"

He petted Miranda's long dark hair with his left hand. She nodded and put her hands on his knees. "I want to sit on you."

"Of course you can. Just give me some more warning next time."

Christian gave his daughter a stern glare. "Miranda, be careful. Uncle Houston is hurt, remember?"

"As if anyone could forget," Houston said under his breath. With great care, he scooped Miranda up onto his lap. "I don't want people treating me like glass. I'm exactly the same as I was before."

Silence met this statement. Doubt hung in the air around them. Josie saw the frustration on Houston's face, and ached to comfort him. Everyone studiously avoided looking at his injured hand.

Fortunately, unaware of the tension, Miranda broke the silence. Wiggling on Houston's lap, she looked at Josie and tucked her wet hair behind her ear. The little girl pointed to Houston's leg. "My Unca Ouston got bitted. They had to sew up his leg."

Houston bounced Miranda up and down on his right leg, making Josie a puddle of dripping emotion. He looked so damn sweet and she was so totally gone for him.

"She knows, squirt. She's the one who sewed it up."

"Really?" Miranda's eyes went round, clearly impressed. "Was it gross?"

Josie laughed. "No. It's my job."

"You're surrounded by doctors, Miranda," Christian said, resting his elbow on his raised knee as he lounged on the sand next to his wife. "Sara is a doctor, too. Maybe some of their smarts will rub off on you."

"I'm going to be a princess when I grow up," Miranda said with total confidence.

"You can't be a princess unless your father is a king, or your mother is a queen. You'd be better off going to college."

Miranda was unconcerned. "Then I'll marry a prince."

This led to an argument between father and daughter. Josie listened in amusement as daughter appeared to be winning, listing the many benefits of being a princess.

Then Houston said without warning, "Josie, let's go back to my place now, okay?"

All conversations ground to a halt. Three pairs of adult eyes swung towards them in interest.

"Uh, sure." She stood up, suddenly realizing she was abandoning her friend. "Sara, you don't mind, do you? I'll be back in fifteen minutes or so."

Of course, that was probably not the best way to phrase it.

Christian's eyebrows shot up and he looked ready to laugh. "Is that all you need?"

Kori bit her lip and giggled, nudging her husband. Josie imagined her face was turning six shades of purple, which wasn't a good color with her light brown hair.

"Take all the time you want," Sara said with a shrug.

Houston scowled. "She's going to take my stitches out."

"Um-hmm." Kori didn't look convinced.

Josie just knew she looked guilty. She had seen Houston naked and they all knew. Right now they could probably tell that she was already having sexual thoughts, that just the idea of being alone with Houston had her body stirring to life like an oven turned on to preheat.

"Let's go," she said in what she hoped was a convincingly casual voice.

Houston stood up next to her, placing Miranda back in the chair. He pulled a T-shirt on over his head and patted the pocket of his shorts. His keys jingled. "I'm ready. Kori, tell Mom what I'm doing when she comes back."

That brought a further snicker from the crowd.

"I don't think she wants to know *that,* Houston," Kori said.

"About the stitches," he said through gritted teeth and turned around and walked off, leaving Josie to trail behind feeling something like a faithful dog. A Jack Russell terrier, that's what she was. Short, white, round, and easily trained.

And she was just waiting for him to throw her a bone, wasn't she?

If the sutures weren't driving him crazy, infuriating him when he was already pissed off, he would tell Josie to stay at the beach and just retreat into his condo alone. He couldn't think: he was churning with emotion over his mother and her impending marriage, the way he'd almost hurt his niece, and the look of Josie playing in the water and how it had done painful things to his chest.

He shoved his front door open and held it for her. "Let me grab a pair of scissors."

Rummaging around in his kitchen, he searched while she stood in the foyer.

"I'm dripping on your tiles."

Glancing over at her, he said exactly what he was thinking, not bothering to worry about the consequences. "That's because you're wearing that stupid huge T-shirt. Take it off."

"But . . ." The word sailed out of her mouth in a breathy voice.

Houston watched her politeness war with her modesty. She had a bikini on under there and he wanted to see it. He hoped politeness would win.

It did.

As his hands closed over the scissors, she stripped off the shirt, leaving her curvaceous body covered by nothing but a strategically placed palm tree or two. Damn, he wanted to pluck himself a coconut.

He took a step towards her.

"Scissors?" She held out her hand, having tossed her wet shirt out onto his front step.

Right. His itchy, irritated leg. Not unlike the rest of him.

A minute later he was seated on his couch, his leg on the coffee table while Josie perched next to it. Bending over him, she ran her fingers across the evenness of her stitching.

Houston knew from a medical standpoint the wounds had healed well. The skin looked tight and shiny pink and with a little luck and some aloe, the scars would fade in time.

It wasn't his leg that worried him, that kept him up at night, and chewed a hole in his gut.

"Why exactly are you smiling?" he said, gripping the arm of the couch as she started cutting and pulling the first set of sutures.

"I'm admiring my work. Have you ever seen such straight sutures in your life?"

He grimaced. "I didn't stop to think about it."

She snipped and pulled. "You're really lucky, you know. For a lot of reasons, besides having me stitch you up, that is. I mean, here you are, a week and a half later, none the worse for the wear, your leg almost completely healed."

Houston knew that Josie spoke without thinking. That to her, she looked at his leg, saw it was healing, and did consider him lucky. Maybe he should, too, when he thought about the alternatives of being bit by a shark. Like losing his leg or his life.

But his splinted hand lay in his lap and the intense frustration rose palpable in him again, a living breathing anger so that he couldn't stop himself from speaking tightly. "Too bad I can't say the same thing for my hand."

Josie looked up, green eyes stricken. "Houston, I'm

sorry, I didn't think. It was a stupid thing to say. I'm notorious for sticking my foot in my mouth."

Her fingers stroked across his leg, bringing him immeasurable and frightening comfort. He wanted to sink into Josie, into her warmth and compassion and cheerful optimism and rest there for a minute. Let down his guard and relax his shoulders.

"It wasn't a stupid thing to say. I'm just feeling sorry for myself." It was mortifying to realize it was true. "I shouldn't have made you uncomfortable."

Her face fell in relief and a grin turned up the corner of her generous mouth. "I'm getting used to it."

He gave a snort of laughter. "Josie, I . . ." *Want you, need you, possibly love you, will you strip and stay naked with me for the rest of my life?*

He buried his head in his hand for a minute, smoothing out his eyebrows before forcing himself to meet her curious gaze. "I want you to understand why I'm the way I am, why I have trouble getting close to people. My mom saying she's getting married today—it really threw me. You see, my father abused my mother, until he did us all a favor and left when I was fifteen."

Those words had never crossed his lips in his thirty-three years of life, and he was ashamed at the catch in his voice.

He didn't know what he expected Josie to say, maybe pity or horror, but it wasn't what she did. With a nod of her head, she leaned closer to him, touching his knee with her soft fingers, her sweet warm scent surrounding him. "I lost my father, too, at fifteen. It made me so angry."

It threw him for a minute, made him pull back, stop and think. Of course he was angry with his father for hurting his mother, but she had forgiven him. Maybe somewhere deep inside he was also angry with Hal Hayes for never being a father to him, for forcing him

248 *Erin McCarthy*

to miss out on all the things that other kids took for granted and got to do with their dads.

He didn't want to feel anger anymore. He wanted to be the better person like his mother and let it all go, leave it firmly entrenched in the past. He didn't want to become bitter and selfish, the very things he despised in his father.

Josie was between his legs, hair damp and sticking out, skin cool and smelling like the ocean. Her left nipple was visible between two palm trees on the print of her bikini top.

His hand reached out, shook a little, cupped her breast, and held the firm giving swell of her body. "You know, you're damn near perfect."

Chapter Sixteen

Where was a tape recorder when she needed one? It wasn't likely she'd hear she was almost perfect too many times in her life. Though this time was toe-curling enough to last her quite awhile.

Josie shivered at Houston's touch, at his words, at the insecurity she saw on his face. He was as vulnerable now as she had been after surgery the day before, and she hoped she could give him comfort the way he had her. She wanted him to trust her, confide in her.

"You done with those sutures yet?" he asked, plucking at her nipple.

"No." Not even close. He had extensive embroidery all over his calf, and she'd only removed about a third of it.

Not that she could concentrate with his finger gliding, stroking, dragging her into desire. A moist want heated up the bottoms of the ridiculous bikini she was wearing, and her hand trembled a little against his leg.

"So hurry up."

"I can't when you're doing that." His finger had worked its way under the wet triangle of her bikini top, distracting her.

"What am I doing?"

Fondling her, that's what. "Touching me."

Shifting a little so his finger fell away from her

breast, she focused on the scissors in her hand and snipped another stitch.

A toe pressed against her clitoris through her wet bottoms. Josie jerked back and gave Houston a dirty look, exasperated. "Are you trying to make me hurt you? I have sharp scissors in my hand!"

He looked unconcerned, resting his feet back on the tops of the sandals he'd kicked off, his expression mild but his eyes lit with lust. "But you know what? I trust you, Josie, to take care of me. And I've noticed you don't drop things around me anymore. I wonder why."

If he was teasing or not, she couldn't tell, but his words made her warm, and it wasn't just from sexual stimulation. She'd actually been stupid enough to fall in love with him, which was sure to go over big.

"You don't make me nervous anymore." It was true. While he still sent her blood pressure into the abnormal range, and could talk her into joining a nudist colony with at most a little coaxing and a box of chocolates, he didn't intimidate her any longer.

"So it wouldn't make you nervous if I untied the strings of your top?"

Okay, so she wouldn't even need the chocolate as an inducement. A little coaxing and she'd be naked.

"No, that wouldn't make me nervous." Horny with hurricane intensity, but not nervous.

She added, "But I still think you should let me finish removing these before you take any string untying action."

As it was she wasn't being particularly gentle, but was tugging and dropping half-inch bits of thread on his coffee table with double her usual speed. Yet it didn't seem to be bothering him or the erection growing steadily in his swim trunks spitting distance from her mouth. Or tongue distance, she thought, then berated herself for not behaving professionally while she worked. He was just damn close, that's all.

And she was almost naked, wearing nothing but a couple of overpriced triangles on her breasts and a swatch of nylon across her butt, leaving the rest of her as bare and expansive as the I-95 highway.

"I kind of like the idea of seeing you between my legs with no top on."

Josie ripped out a stitch and willed her nipples not to harden . . . *too late*. Geez, was there really any good response to a statement like that?

Emotions far too close to the surface for comfort, she went with humor, relieved she was two-thirds done removing the sutures. "I don't mind if you take your shirt off."

The corner of his mouth lifted, but he didn't laugh. Before she could react, his hand was on her back and the ocean-blue strap to her top, tied into a droopy bow, gave way as he jerked it loose.

"Would you like that? If I took my shirt off? Do you like me, Josie?"

Um, that would be a yes. Her bikini crept forward, gravity urging her breasts out of the loosened restraints, top inching up, stopping only when the fabric caught on the undercurve of her breasts. Josie was very, very aware that once the bikini top gave, it was an ensemble that would only work in two circumstances. A topless beach on the French Riviera or a strip club. Which made her wonder how good it would feel to imitate an exotic dancer's moves in Houston's lap.

Minor shifting caused the triangles to give up their valiant hold and bounce up over her nipples like the retraction of a bungee jump. Houston let out a rush of air, his head shaking just slightly.

Josie swallowed the suddenly enormous amount of saliva collecting in her cheeks. "You know I like you."

"Put the damn scissors down and stand up."

"I'm not finished. There are still two one-inch segments to remove." But she shot up anyway when he prodded her with his toe again, sharp pangs of fiery desire darting through her at his nudging touch and demanding tone of voice. The raw need on his face set her arousal to a razor-sharp edge.

"Leave the sutures for later." He rose off the couch and flexed his leg, bending it several times and brushing his kneecap right across her, on that last bit of intact bikini, the wet bottoms that were clinging to her mound.

"Ah, much better, even if you're not finished."

A gasp ripped out of her mouth when his hard knee nudged against her again. A wicked, acquiescent, encouraging kind of gasp that had her dropping her eyelids in both embarrassment and poignant pleasure, as he forced her legs apart.

She teetered on the edge of the coffee table. "Houston, are you sure we can do this? I don't want to hurt your leg or anything. Are you in pain?"

Not that he would admit it. And not that she thought he was. But she didn't want to hurt him when she fumbled her way through a seduction.

"The only pain I have is in my trunks from wanting you." The indignation in his voice was real, not exaggerated.

Josie bent her legs and slipped back to the floor, with more tumbling than grace, landing right between his knees, wishing she'd thought to pull her top off since it was swinging across her breasts like bizarre nylon jewelry. But she ignored it.

Because for once, she wanted to throw him off balance, make him stumble and trip on his words and quake with need the way she did. Make him forget about his mother's marriage and his father and his torn-up hand and understand that he could deny it or call it whatever he wanted to, but there was much more between them than explosive sex.

"Good. Then I can do this."

She reached inside his still damp swim trunks and touched him, smooth and half-hard.

"Josie!" He took a step back and was halted by the couch.

Josie smiled, pressing a kiss above his waistband, running her tongue along the tuft of dark hair there. With more courage than confidence, she pulled the trunks down to his knees.

"Josie." He sounded shocked, which renewed her determination and aroused her so completely that she was breathing hard before she'd even touched him.

Breasts falling forward and brushing his thighs, she lifted her arms and took him into her unsteady grasp. Felt him thicken and jerk beneath her fingers. Felt the intensity of his desire for her.

Holding the smooth length of him with two hands, she pressed her lips right on the tip of his shaft and allowed herself a little lick.

He shuddered. "Crap, don't do that."

She licked again.

Knees squeezed her shoulders. "Damn it, stop that."

Licks gave way to gentle sucking. God, it felt good to do this, to take him into her mouth and taste with intimate strokes of her tongue.

"My mom might come up here looking for us."

His voice hitched and through the corner of her eye, Josie saw the fingers on his uninjured hand dig into the couch, searching for a hold. The tone of desperation in his voice amused her. He was the one who couldn't stay on task with the sutures earlier. Now he expected her to believe he was worried about getting caught?

Houston just didn't like being in the passenger seat.

Lick, lick. "We'll hear the front door." Mmm, he tasted good. Salty, like a fresh French fry. Her nipples tightened, rubbing against her loose top, her body echoing the hardening of his.

"Stop it, Josie."

She peeked up at him, still running her tongue along the smooth ridge of his penis. Houston's eyes were closed, his mouth a thin line, his arm muscles bulging and tense as he gripped the couch.

"Why? I told you I'll stop if you're in pain," she murmured, confident of his reaction to that statement.

"And I told you I'm not in pain!"

"Then shush and let me suck you."

"No," he said, while holding very still.

Between pulling him in and out of her mouth, she carried on with their conversation. "Let me," she said, filling up her mouth, "do this." She pulled back. "Just this one time, Houston. I really want to feel you come inside my mouth."

He just groaned and she slid him past her lips and deep into the back of her throat again. Her jaws strained, but he was so hot, so good, that she sucked in the hollows of her cheeks and refused to let him go.

The original thought had been to take it slow, take her time to taste him, please him, make him ache the way he did to her every time he touched her. But Josie couldn't hold back, couldn't halt her own rising desperation, her own body's squirming and wanting and urging. She picked up speed, the moisture of her mouth slicking his flesh as she drew on his hard shaft, his breathing deepening into low guttural groans.

She wanted him, she loved him, she needed to help him see that surgeon or not, he was successful.

She wanted to feel the hot surrender of him into her mouth as she pressed her breasts against his questing fingers. Wanted to feel his weight crash against her as he throbbed and thrust his way through a surrender into her mouth. Anticipation and taste and the little growls he was spitting out had her sliding and shifting, holding onto him, reaching for his testicles, digging into his thighs.

Intense, burning want spiraled through her stomach,

and she sensed the tightening, the familiar building throb between her thighs that hinted an orgasm could be near.

If she stood, or pushed him back on the couch, she could sink onto him and surrender to a blistering climax. It would be a selfish choice. Or she could stay put, taunt and tease herself, and give satisfaction to Houston first.

Or maybe she could do both. When she nipped at his flesh, he swore with a jerk of his fingers, pinching the bud of her nipple. The sharp flash of pleasure sent her body racing ahead before she was ready, and Josie paused with her tongue on him to moan with her orgasm, to rock against his leg and rub at her swollen clitoris.

"Fucking, *yes*," he said, shaking her shoulder with his tight grip.

"Sorry," she said, sucking in air, ripples shuddering through her, regret rising that she might have messed up the rhythm of his pleasure. "Sorry, geez, I'm sorry, I didn't mean to come, I swear."

"What made you come, Josie?" Houston asked, his erection still hovering in front of her mouth, his voice tight.

"Doing this to you . . . sucking . . . I really like it."

Leaning against his stomach, she closed her eyes and shivered, her legs buckling under her. Houston tugged her head back so she was looking at him.

The heat of passion in his smoky blue eyes stirred her own desire back to life. He looked ready to consume her, to have her fast and hard and now.

"Get up. We're going in the bedroom now, before I take you in my living room again."

"Okay," she whispered, giving one last kiss to the head of his penis. He jerked away from her, giving her arm another insistent nudge.

Josie stood, wobbling like an eighty-year-old arthritic, digging into Houston's forearms for balance.

"Oh, God, Sara, I totally forgot about her. I have to call her, she'll be wondering what happened to me."

"She'll figure it out." Houston bent and pounced on her breast like a wild animal with its prey.

Only Josie imagined when bitten by a lion, no gazelle ever wanted to scream in pleasure. She did, and only managed to stay silent by squeezing her eyes shut and thinking about the ruptured Achilles tendon surgery scheduled for the next day.

"No, I need to call her." And he was really going to believe her by the way she leaned into his touch and whimpered.

But he stopped licking delicious patterns across her skin and lifted a phone off the end table a few feet to his right. "Hurry up."

"Absolutely." Josie dialed and swatted at his hands as they came towards her.

"Hello?"

"Sara, it's Josie. I got a little tied up here at Houston's and I'm not sure when I'll make it back to the beach."

Sara snorted into the phone. "That's code for you're about to have sex."

"Shh! What if his mother hears you?" she whispered, then clamped down on a moan as Houston came up behind her and started shoving her bikini bottoms down.

"I don't think she'll mind. She's getting some action too, you know. I'm the only one who isn't."

Josie felt guilty, especially since Houston was bending her over the couch and slipping his finger inside her. "I'm sorry, Sara," she managed, breath hitching. "Did you change your mind about your beach plan?"

"I talked to one guy and it turned out he's married. It

will take me another six months to get up the nerve to do this again."

"Oh, sweetie," Josie started, but Sara cut her off.

"I'm hanging up now before this conversation qualifies us for having participated in a threesome. You are clearly busy."

Houston's teeth sank into the tender flesh of her backside and she yelped, dropping the phone and flushing with embarrassment. Sara had known what they were doing. Well, not exactly, but the general idea and that was bad enough.

"Your mother . . ." she said, though she had no idea why.

"My mother is busy with Larry." Houston retracted his finger and trailed her body's moisture up between her cheeks, her muscles giving a tight jerk at his invasion. Then relaxing, accepting, wanting him.

Houston's mother and Larry were shoved to the back of his mind in a little compartment he had stamped Later. He would be happy for his mother if it killed him. But later.

Now he was going to take Josie to his bed and keep her there until he forgot that he wasn't worthy of her and she forgot that he was a surgeon about to lose his job.

"The bedroom. Now." Houston hadn't closed his blinds against the midday sun and the brilliance was hurting his eyes, but that was only part of it. He had promised her the bedroom the first night they'd spent together and they had never made it. It was almost symbolic to him, that when they stepped into his room, they were reaching a new level in their relationship.

So he led her down the darker hall, to his bedroom where she had only been once, the time when she had tried to help him out of his underwear and had nearly made him come in them instead.

Every second or so, he turned around to drink in the sight of her, naked since she'd kicked the skimpy bottoms off her ankles before following him. Houston wanted to hold Josie, to take her lushness in both of his arms and stroke her bare back. To feel all that gorgeous heat pressed against him. When he stopped in his bedroom and tried to do just that, his splint hit the base of her spine, and he'd had enough.

With a curse, he went for the bandage with his increasingly dexterous left hand, ripping at the tape that held the wrap together.

"What are you doing?" Josie moved in beside him, her hip resting against his, the swim trunks preventing him from feeling her soft curls pressed over his thigh. But her breast rested warm and full along his elbow and he didn't resent her inquisitive fingers stilling his.

"I want this off, I want to touch you with both hands."

The smooth damp strands of her short hair moved across his shoulder and Josie lay her chin on his chest. "I thought you had another week to go."

"I do, but I just want to touch you without it being in the way. I'll put it right back on." He dropped his desperate plea, let it slow into a coaxing seductive request as he felt her responding to him.

Her body went taut alongside his and her hot little pants blasted across his chest, tightening his nipples. Josie took his hand into hers and caressed the bandage and the palm of his stiff hand.

"Let me take it off then." She kissed his fingertips one by one, lingering over the injured two.

That's not what he had wanted—Josie to study his pale and motionless hand, lying there looking like a dead plucked chicken.

But here, now, this one time he wanted to be free to trust her, to believe in a future that included both his career and a woman he had come to understand he could love. He closed his eyes for a second, his jaw clenched.

"Okay."

"The finger and thumb won't work right, you know," she warned him softly as she began to undo his splint. "Three weeks immobile is a long time, surgery or not. That's what the physical therapy is for."

"I'm a doctor, Josie. You don't have to tell me all that." But he wasn't really all that annoyed.

He was enraptured by the vision of her poised over him naked, entirely uninhibited. He knew she wasn't happy with her body; why, he couldn't understand, but she wasn't. Yet there she stood, confident and caring as she unwrapped his hand with light and efficient movements, not seeming to notice that he could see just about every inch of her bare flesh.

"What doctors know and what doctors feel are two different things." The last bit of tape and wrap was off, and Josie caressed his white and drawn fingers.

He had long red scars from the laceration and the surgery, and his hand was stiff and awkward. Ugly. Marred and mocking.

Josie put her tongue on it and traced a bumpy scar.

His heart about leapt out of his chest. His cock felt strangled in his shorts. Because Josie's touch wasn't pitying or curious, but was sensual, arousing, the touch of a woman who wants to know every inch of a man.

Then she massaged the stiff palm with her thumb, before placing his hand on her waist. "Now you can hold me with both hands."

Delicious. That's how she felt as he drew her in. He was holding her, but not close enough. With a nudge, she came forward, her breasts splaying across his chest while his erection found a place to nest between her receptive thighs. It was as good as he could ever have imagined—better, softer, his heart tripping along with

mach speed while his breath jerked and halted on sighs
and deep, reaching, languid pulls.

His uninjured fingers were racing across her dewy
skin, while the other two just rested in place. He couldn't
feel them, didn't care, wanted only to caress and stroke
and love Josie to a place where she would be his and
only his.

"You feel perfect," he murmured in her ear, brushing his lips against the pink lobe.

They were still hovering in the door of his bedroom
and he walked backwards, coaxing her with him until
he felt the cool sheets at the back of his knees. He hadn't
made his bed, not since the accident, and it was just a
matter of shoving the top sheet out of the way until
there was a soft surface to spread Josie out on.

Poised beside his bed, he held her firm, bent his
head and kissed her. All the frustration and feeling and
fascination he felt poured out onto her sweet plump
lips.

"Oh," she moaned, ransacking his hair.

Houston had never liked women's hands in his hair,
but Josie was different. She was more, everything, day
to his night, and he leaned and pushed and coaxed until
she was on his bed, thighs spread.

Her breathing was shallow, cheeks pink, eyes wide
and cloudy with desire, and he had never seen a more
beautiful woman. "I've never felt this way before," he
murmured into the pale depths of her inner thighs.

"What way?"

Sharp pain rippled through his head as Josie dug
into his hair and held tight. When Houston glanced up
past the curve of her belly, he saw she was arching in
pleasure, shifting to urge his tongue away from her thigh
and to her clitoris. Bucking, like she needed something
to ride.

The room was muted, the sheet cool, his vision in
sharp focus. His nostrils filled with the loam scent of

their sweat-glistened flesh, their desire that connected them here, right now, in the most intimate touch possible.

With a little flicker right across her damp folds, he murmured, "I've never been so fascinated by a woman. I think the first time you bent over I was gone."

And hadn't recovered himself since.

Chapter Seventeen

Josie pried her tongue off the roof of her mouth and spoke. "So being clumsy was a good thing then?" If it kept his tongue stroking over her, she'd drop an entire boxful of scalpels.

It was different this time, more intimate than when they had indulged in quick, hard passion on his living room floor. Josie understood Houston better now, saw beneath the cool professional mask to the caring and vulnerable man he was.

He laughed, nose tickling her thigh, hot breath lapping across her already sensitive inner flesh. "Good for me, anyway. I don't know about you."

If he only knew. She wanted to confess how she felt, that their relationship could grow and move forward one tiny step at a time, and that she was willing to try. But she didn't want him to tense, to retreat, when right now he was wide open to her, connected, caressing in his care. Heart in his eyes.

Houston cared about her, she could see that. He might not believe it, and maybe it wasn't love yet, but it was *something*. Real and growing.

"It's good for me, too, since it got me here."

Houston touched his tongue to her again.

"Oh, yeah. Right there, it's very good." She indulged in a little moan as she watched his dark hair bent over her.

This was the kind of position that normally bothered her, especially midday with light pouring in his large glass windows. But with Houston, she felt sexy, seductive. Those curves that had plagued her since early adolescence, those soft white hills compacted on a frame too short for them, were the very curves that fascinated him.

"What did you think of my friend, Sara?" she heard herself asking, just because she wanted to hear him compliment her again.

His fascination and lust were addictive.

And she still needed that reassurance, just like he needed convincing that he was still successful even if he never entered the OR again.

Houston paused. "What about Sara?"

"Did you like her? She's very thin." Josie arched her hands above her head and wiggled her hips to get him moving again.

He sucked on her inner thigh, pulling her flesh hard with warm lips and dragging another moan from her as the ache sharpened deep inside.

"Are you asking to be spanked again?" His voice was calm, but hard, tight with desire.

"No. Why?"

"Because you know it makes me mad when you put yourself down, when you compare yourself to someone else."

"I'm not putting myself down." Josie was sorry she'd spoken, sorry he was using his tongue to talk instead of more delicious activities.

The little nibbles along her thigh were not enough, distracting reminders of what else he could be doing.

"I barely noticed Sara. I don't notice any women but you anymore."

She would have gladly paid him money to hear him

say that, and yet he was giving her that for free. "For claiming that you don't have a good bedside manner, you're doing a really fabulous job."

He laughed, a husky chuckle that tickled. "Now are we going to continue this conversation or can I get back to what I was doing before you brought your scrawny friend into it?"

"Sara's not scrawny, she's gorgeous." Josie thought to expand on that but Houston had taken the initiative to give another long lingering lick, sinking into her. "Oh. Never mind."

"Good idea."

Then he went to work in earnest and Josie fell slack, caught in the tightening frisson of pleasure as his mouth moved over her again and again. Slick, hot movements that paralyzed her, kept her frozen, fingers curled in the sheet, eyes drifting closed.

Over and over, his hot tongue invading her, her belly tense, her nipples aching. When she was a split second away from shattering, he pulled back, wiping his shiny moist mouth with thumb and index finger while she let out a cry of disappointment that grew into a moan when he stood up.

Houston shoved his swim trunks to the floor and walked across the room, away from her, giving her a great view of his broad back and tight buns. But nice ass or not, he was walking away from her and she was quivering with want.

"Where are you going?" Josie loosened her death grip on his gray sheet and followed his progress to the dresser. She wanted to roll on her side for a clear shot of him when he turned back around, but she was afraid any movement whatsoever would send her flinging into an orgasm.

"I'm getting a condom. Feel free to touch yourself if you need to until I get back."

Josie gasped, heat stealing over her neck and face.

"I think I'll be okay." She couldn't imagine doing *that* in front of Houston. Well, in front of anyone. But especially Houston, with his perfect hard body and oh-so-knowing stare.

Houston started back to the bed, condom in place, wicked look in his eyes. "Damn, that's too bad. I'd have liked to have seen that."

"Sorry, but I don't think you'll be seeing that anytime soon." But her embarrassment was forgotten when Houston reached the end of the bed and put one hand on either side of her ankles, leaned over her and kissed her right where his tongue had been.

Where she was still slick and burning.

Then he swirled his tongue up around her hipbone, leaving a moist trail behind as he ducked into her belly button. His tongue was invasive there, penetrating, and she fought against it, against the tight hot ache below, where his hard chest would press and retreat in a painful tease.

But he ignored her squirming, continuing north until his nose nudged the underside of her breast and his tongue could flicker back and forth, making her nipples tighten with jealousy.

Then he took her hand and with his fingers aligned over hers, slid them between her legs. Josie jerked in embarrassment as she felt the moist plumpness of her body beneath her touch.

"Stop, let go."

"Shhh," he coaxed, holding her fingers firmly against herself, all while his tongue did delightful wet things to her breast.

She wiggled under him. "I can't," she said even as she arched into the contact.

She shook her head even when he sank his finger and hers deep inside her, where her body enclosed around them in a wet warm pulse.

"See how good that feels? See why you drive me so

wild?" He nuzzled into her chest. "Damn, you feel so incredible."

Out, then in, he moved their index fingers, the rest of her clasped hand pressing into the shallow dip just below, and she had no air to speak, no words to use.

Houston slid their fingers across her tight clitoris. "We're in this together, baby, you and me."

"Oh, God," she said, appalled at how good it felt to trace their touch over her again and again, shocked and thrilled and desperate for him to take away the painful pull that pooled in every inch of her. "Houston," she murmured, a ragged plea so throaty it was a wonder he didn't think he was in bed with a man.

"What?"

Back and forth his tongue went on her nipple, while the hard muscles below his ribs rocked her inner thighs. She was hungry, irrational. "More. Inside me, please."

Josie's trembling request took every last ounce of his control and threw it against the wall where it shattered like thin glass. God, he loved her, every inch of her, and her generous giving heart, and he could give back tonight, anything that she asked for.

"Whatever you want, sweetheart."

Houston shifted between her legs, searched out her slick opening and sank in with a steady thrust that tore a groan out of him. Her body wrapped around him, tight muscles caressing his cock, as he pushed deep inside her.

"Houston." Josie stared up at him, eyes out of focus, her fair skin flushed to a rosy glow, as he left whatever shards of delusion he still retained behind.

Josie was amazing. He was in love with her. And she was his.

He pulled back until only the tip of his head was still inside her and they were both groaning in disappointment. For a long agonizing second he hovered there, then drove into her with a reckless hard push that ripped a curse from his lips and had Josie jerking on his chest hairs.

The little painful stings were nothing, barely noticed. He ignored the tight trembling in his injured leg and the bizarre lack of sensation in his right hand, as he reveled in the feeling of letting go, pouring into Josie all his appreciation and want.

He was very close to coming as he set a fast rhythm, wound too tight and racing towards an explosion. "Should I stop?" He wanted her to come first, with her soft legs wrapped around him and her breasts rolling with his every thrust.

The look of horror on her face would have been laughable if he hadn't been grinding his teeth together in ecstasy. "No! I'll die if you stop."

And as if to hold him in place, her fingers were suddenly on his ass, squeezing hard, urging him forward with a little smack like a rider to a horse.

Nothing had ever turned him on like that demanding sexual swat from Josie. His gut twisted, his balls drew up and he knew he only had seconds before he was exploding into her. "Want it that bad, do you?"

"Yes!"

And damned if she didn't give him another tap, gripping his flesh and holding on as she jerked her hips up in an electric orgasm.

Houston let go, abandoned all control, fell over the edge with her, pushing hard, harder, driving himself and all his thoughts and feelings and passion forward into Josie.

They pulsed and bucked and held on, and Josie fell back slack, her fingers curling against his sheet, her upper lip dewy and her green eyes wide-open emerald pools.

"I love you," she said.

And ruined any chance he had of rescuing his heart.

* * *

Josie lay in her own sweat and tried not to groan. And not from pleasure this time, but from the sheer stupidity of blurting out how she felt to Houston in the midst of a glass-shattering orgasm.

It was the equivalent of bringing up marriage on the first date.

Not that Houston was recoiling in horror. He wasn't. Was looking pretty damn pleased, actually, but neither was he repeating her words back to her. Not even a "Ditto" or a "Right back at you, babe."

Nothing but a small sigh, a crooked smile, a finger lazily drawn across her nipple, as he settled his weight next to her on the bed.

"You're so different from me," he mused.

Yes, she was stupid, he was smart. She loved him, he didn't love her. Josie lay very still and tried not to cringe. "Oh?"

"You're so soft." That finger wandered down her stomach and rounded the curve of her hip. "I'm hard."

Boy, was he ever. From head to toe, everything was firm, including his penis still encased in the condom, resting against her. "Umm-hmm."

"Your skin is so fair, so pale, like the moon. I'm dark."

His manner was so relaxed, soothing, that Josie allowed herself to believe he didn't mind her heartfelt blurt. She gave a little laugh, turned up on her side towards him. "You're like a roasted marshmallow."

His breath brushed her bare shoulder as he laughed with her. "I'm not sure that's a compliment." He twined his fingers in hers, sighing, eyes drifting closed. "And you talk with your hands, and you talk a lot. I'm quiet."

Alarm awakened in her. Why was he pointing out the obvious unless it was a precursor to the Why This Won't Work speech.

"That's true," she said, because she was naked and

feeling satisfied with him and the world and she didn't want to ruin the moment. And she wouldn't argue with him if the time came for that speech. It would break her heart, but she would not beg and she would not coax and—damn it—she deserved a man who loved her, cherished her, wanted her with his whole heart, not a man who's been talked into it.

"I love those differences in you."

She sucked in a breath, appreciating how difficult that must have been for him to say, to even mention love and her in the same sentence. She could actually hear the emotion in his voice.

The tears she'd been holding back rained down her face. Going up on her elbow, she leaned over to kiss him and halted an inch from his lips.

He was asleep.

Gorgeous and naked, his hand still resting on her stomach.

When Josie woke up, Houston was standing beside the bed, peering down at her. Struggling to keep her eyes open, she yawned. "Did you just *blow* on my face?"

Shifting on the balls of his feet, he grinned. "Must have been the wind."

"The wind needs to brush its teeth." Not that he had bad breath. She just wanted to tease him.

Josie stretched her arms above her head while Houston cupped his hand over his mouth, doing an obvious breath check. She laughed. "I was kidding. You don't have bad breath."

"Since we're being honest, I really did blow on your face. I was trying to wake you up."

It occurred to her sex-and-sleep-fogged brain that he was wearing his swim trunks again and had the scissors in his hand. Oh, Lord, he didn't really expect her to drag herself back to the beach, did he?

"Is your leg bothering you?" Rubbing her eyes, she gradually became aware that she was naked, flat out on the bed, her legs spread as wide as the Atlantic Ocean. She tried to work up some embarrassment, but just couldn't muster it, not after the way he had touched her before.

Though she did cross her legs at the ankles.

His eyes followed the movement, the scissors slackening in his hand, jaw clenching. He took a step towards her. "Don't bother hiding from me."

And he dropped the scissors on the bed, lifted her ankle and tossed her leg back open again. "Much better."

Though her mouth went moist and her breasts tingled, she merely raised an eyebrow at him. "Find me a shirt to wear and I'll take out the rest of your sutures."

His hesitation was gratifying. Then he pulled a T-shirt out of his drawer and gave it to her. "When you're done, put your bikini back on. We'll get something to eat, then I want to go back to the beach. I want to go in the water."

The urge to shriek no or to pester him with a million questions was enormous, but Josie pulled the soft gray shirt on over her head and bit her lip to prevent spontaneous word eruption. Houston wouldn't want her to question his actions and really, there wasn't any reason he couldn't go in the water, it just seemed like he shouldn't. Her worry would be smothering and it was unfounded.

Besides, she was pretty sure he had seduced any resistance out of her. For anything he might ask. Sex on the roof? Sure, why not?

When her head popped through the neck hole and she took a deep cleansing breath, sniffing the aftershave and laundry detergent smell of his wrinkled shirt, she gave him a bright smile. "All right. Though let me throw my bathing suit in the dryer first. Nothing is grosser than putting on a wet suit."

Houston leaned forward, held the back of her head, and pressed a soft kiss on her lips that made Josie sigh.

"You're the best, Josie."

Closer and closer he was getting. Soon, he was going to have to admit to her that he loved her. She'd be ready with tears and oral sex when he did.

Two hours later Houston and Josie were stepping back onto the beach and he was trying to unstick the words from the back of his throat.

I love you.

It wasn't that hard to say. It wouldn't hurt. She wouldn't laugh. The sky wouldn't split open and a tidal wave wouldn't crash over his head.

But he still couldn't seem to get his mouth to open and form the words.

Houston didn't expect his family to still be at the beach since he had left them there at noon and it was six o'clock already. Having spent the day making love, sleeping, and eating an early dinner, time had slipped by. But now there would be no distractions on the beach. Just him, Josie, and the ocean. They could even hang around for a sunset.

Maybe by then his tongue would have dislodged from the roof of his mouth.

"You got that board okay?" she asked for the third time.

Houston knew it was Josie's way of saying she was worried about him surfing again, without actually coming right out and saying it. He appreciated her concern, but he was glad she wasn't listing all the reasons why he shouldn't go in the water.

Because he didn't really care if his hand was still numb and he really should put it back in the splint. He was free today, of the sutures, of the splint, and he wanted back in the water. The cool, murky blue water, where he could float and feel the surf roll over him, a soothing wet massage.

Josie should share that with him. It felt right.

"I got it." He adjusted his board in his left hand, enjoying the familiar feel of it, and slowed down his gait to wait for Josie, who was breathing hard as she tried to keep up with him.

The beach was almost empty. His condo community was small—a number of the residents were seniors—and the beach was private. He wouldn't normally go there to surf, would head to the Inlet where the waves were. But this was just to get back on the board. For fun. And because he'd forgotten what normal was anymore.

At the edge of the water, where the sand was damp beneath his feet and the cry of the seagulls mournful, he stopped and rested his board in the sand. "I love the ocean."

I love you.

The words stayed in his head.

He stared out towards the horizon, watching the sun radiate off the surface of the water, and caressed Josie's hand. "It's so powerful and majestic. I can't imagine living anywhere else."

"Me, either. It's so beautiful, so warm, like the sun will never stop shining." She took a few steps forward and let the water rush over her bare toes, then laughed. "Of course, I guess the sun never will stop shining. It's going to rise every day, east to west. I just meant when it looks like this, it's hard to imagine that it's ever raining or cloudy or cold."

Houston liked listening to her talk. Josie seemed to think out loud, like a perpetual stream of consciousness, and he enjoyed standing back and listening.

Josie suddenly jumped back away from the surf, the

smile falling off her face, expression wary. "Isn't this the time of day when sharks feed? And come in close to the shore? Is this where it happened?"

It honestly hadn't occurred to Houston to be afraid to get back in the water, even though he knew firsthand what happened when man interfered with the shark and their natural instincts. He figured odds were in his favor that he wouldn't be the victim of a freak attack twice in one lifetime. The ocean was a part of his life he wasn't willing to give up.

"No, it was at the Inlet, where the surfing is better."

He sank down onto the sand and patted the spot next to him. When she started to bend at the knees to sit beside him, he pulled her so that she ended up in his lap. Josie kicked off her dirty little sneakers and he debated wiggling his T-shirt off her himself or standing back and enjoying the show as she peeled it off.

Her arms wrapped around him, and there was fear on her face. "Are you sure you should go out there? What if it's still hanging around? Sharks have a huge range they swim in."

He wanted to laugh, but didn't dare. "It wasn't stalking me, Josie. I was out in his turf. I probably looked like a seal, and it was feeding time. He took one bite and let go. The shark was just a juvenile bull instead of full-grown, so it was probably the mistake of an inexperienced hunter."

Josie leaned her head on his shoulder and shuddered. "Hunter. Yuck."

He didn't answer, just pulled her in closer to him until she was nestled against his chest, her hair tickling his chin.

A warm breeze danced around them, sending a fine spray of water over them. It popped into his head that Josie's time at Acadia Inlet was limited, and that when she was finished with reconstructive orthopedics, she would probably move on to another hospital. He had never given any thought to the possibility of her leaving the area, not since they had become involved. The idea of her moving out of his reach, where he couldn't see her, hit him hard.

Hoping he sounded casual, knowing he probably sounded needy, he asked, "So, how long will you be at Acadia Inlet? Will you stay in the area?"

There was a moment of silence. "I'm not sure, but I'll be staying around here. I don't want to be more than fifty miles or so from my mother. I'm all she's got. I'll be doing pediatric ortho next, and I'm really looking forward to it."

Relief made him kiss the top of her head. "Good plan."

"Thanks." Her fingers tickled his chest, played with the hairs there. "What about you? What are your plans?"

Hell if he knew. His gut reaction was to snap at her, tell her there were no plans but to get better. But Josie deserved better than that. She deserved the truth, and he needed to speak it out loud.

"I'll tell you a secret, Josie, that I have trouble even admitting to myself." Pulling in a tight breath, he stared off into the endless ocean. "I don't know how to make plans because I'm afraid my thumb is never going to bend again. And I'm scared. I'm really damn scared."

Josie felt tears prick her eyes again. Part sorrow for Houston, that he was facing an uncertain future, and part joy that he had confided in her something so personal and painful.

She stroked his chest, nuzzled her mouth in his neck. "I wouldn't think you were normal if you weren't scared."

His breath expelled onto her head in a quick burst.

"And I'll tell you a secret, Houston." A deep, buried secret that she hadn't wanted to acknowledge was real until now. "I don't want to be a surgeon. Isn't that just completely stupid? I really thought I did, I thought it would be solving puzzles, looking at X-rays, and making diagnoses. I knew I wanted to be a doctor, to follow in my father's footsteps. Then he died of cancer when I was fifteen, and I felt like I had promised him I'd be a surgeon. But I really think it's not for me."

His grip tightened on her, and she pulled back a little to see his face. "I'm a really confident, happy person, you know, and I loved med school, but since I started my residency all I do is doubt myself. I feel *lousy* about myself."

And talking about it now made her feel vulnerable, but he had confessed his doubts and fears, so she was glad she'd come clean with hers.

"You're an excellent doctor, Josie, never doubt that."

Of course he had to say that since she was sitting in his lap. On the other hand, Houston wasn't known for sugarcoating the truth. It made her feel better.

She stroked his hand. "It will work out, Houston. You'll heal."

"And you'll be a stellar surgeon."

Maybe these were delusions they were feeding each other, but sitting on the sand—close, confessing—felt so intimate and solid, and gave her hope that somehow, they would work things out between them. Everything would work out.

Half-joking, she said, "Since we're confessing and telling secrets, you know what else I'm afraid of? Garbage trucks."

Houston laughed. "Garbage trucks? Why?"

"I'm always convinced someone is being caught and compacted in that metal press when they push the button. Very scary." She gave an involuntary shudder just thinking about it. "I think it was watching *Terminator* at age nine that did it."

He brushed his lips back and forth over her forehead. "I'm afraid of food poisoning. Does that count as a confession? It's an irrational fear of salmonella."

Josie snorted, starting to enjoy herself. "When I was twelve, I stole a lip gloss from the drug store on a dare, then felt so bad I put it back on the shelf after I had used it once."

"You naughty little girl."

Houston urged her to her feet and she rose, hands on hips, using the heel of her foot to brush sand off her leg. "What about you? Didn't you do anything you'd like to confess?"

He helped her brush the sand off with a few well-placed strokes across the back of her calves and thighs, and one light swat on her rear that had her smacking back at him.

"When I was sixteen and Jenny Stanislaski used to call, I'd have Kori tell her I wasn't home because I didn't want to talk to her."

"That's terrible," she said in mock horror.

"Hideous," he agreed. "Now take your T-shirt off so I can see that bikini."

His thoughts were never far from having her naked, and she was not complaining. "I wasn't planning on going in the water."

Houston touched the bottom of the shirt, brushing his fingers across her bare thighs. "You mean you're going to let me go in the water all alone? Unprotected? Lonely and scared?"

Shifting, devious fingers stroked across the tight nylon front of the bikini bottoms. She swallowed hard, determined not to lean forward into his touch.

"I thought you weren't scared."

"I might be once I get in."

"Right." He looked just terrified. "Come on, then."

She shucked the T-shirt and held out her hand.

He gave a wolf whistle, then grinned at her when she shot him a stern look of disbelief. A bikini had really been a bad idea.

"Every time I look at you, I want to pick a coconut."

Confused, she looked down at the print on the suit, gasped when he plucked at her nipple.

"Got one."

"Houston! Get in the water."

"Okay." With a sharp turn he grabbed his board and ran off into the surf, flopping down on the surfboard as soon as he'd cleared the shore.

His hand trailed in the water for a minute as he drifted out a little, and Josie could almost feel his relief at being back in the water. He rolled over onto his back as she stepped into the warm ocean, the silty sand covering her toes.

"Come here," he called, lying loose-limbed, legs dangling.

Making her way to him, Josie smiled. God, she was happy. Ridiculously happy. And he was more relaxed than she had ever seen him.

"Get on with me."

"How?" The board didn't exactly look stable.

"Just climb on the bottom. I'll keep it from tipping."

Sure. Josie gripped the hard white surface and hauled herself up, pausing as she tried to figure how to swing her leg up and over. Sliding back into the temperate water as her hands strained, her breasts caught on the board, squeezing painfully. She wondered again why exactly she had the stupid things in the first place, since they were nothing but trouble.

Grappling for balance, she tipped forward and about scraped herself out of her bikini top. That had to be giving him quite a view. "Uhh. I'm stuck."

"Don't try to sit or stand up. Just inch forward on your stomach."

It was good advice that worked, her progress steady until she was inching up between his knees, past his thighs and right over his soaking swim trunks that had a suspicious bump. One that hadn't been there before. Startled by the lilting motion of the board swaying back and forth, she held onto his legs and dropped her chest down right about where that bump was.

He groaned.

This was interesting. She started to enjoy herself, despite the fear factor, and began a slow, leisurely soldier-crawl up the board, hugging her body to his the whole way up. Skin touched, hips rubbed, breasts pushed into his chest, and finally her bikini bottoms came to rest right smack on his trunks. Her mouth hovered over his.

The board gently rocked, rolling all those parts of her over him.

"Can you come down to the beach and do that every day?" he asked, voice husky. "I think I just had an out-of-body experience."

Then he kissed her.

Chapter Eighteen

Houston was whistling as he strode down the hall the next day towards his office. Josie had put his splint back on, and he was still in career limbo, but he didn't care. Not much, anyway.

Not when he had Josie to be with on the backside of every day. Not when he was so content he was feeling like a Top-Forty love song. If he wasn't careful he might actually start humming.

Even though Josie had spent the night, those three little words hadn't managed to force their way past his lips. He'd meant to tell her, but he'd never quite gotten around to it. But it would happen, when the time was right.

Josie wasn't going anywhere. They were together. He was breaking every rule he had, starting a relationship with a co-worker, but what the hell. He was tired of being alone, and he'd found that his life could alter at any given moment. It was better just to enjoy what he had while he could and worry about the future later.

As he went past Tim Sheinberg's office, he glanced in and saw Tim flagging him down. "Hey, Houston, do you have a minute?"

He was on his way to several patient appointments, but he was early. His eyes had snapped open at dawn, and after a while he'd gotten up and come to the hospital, leaving Josie sleeping in his bed.

"Sure, Tim. What's up?" He propped himself on the door frame.

"How's Dr. Adkins doing in the OR?"

Dr. Sheinberg was sitting back in his chair, casual, but the question wasn't innocent. Houston sensed that.

He also knew he hesitated a fraction of a second too long. "Fine."

That was probably a slight exaggeration. Josie had the skills—she did—but she moved too slow, her decisions weighed and mulled over too long. He knew why now, but he was in an awkward position.

Protect Josie, hoping she came around eventually, or tell the truth and possibly protect the patient.

"Come in here and close the door." Tim sat up straighter.

Shit. Houston followed the directive and sank into a chair across from Tim, forcing himself to stay relaxed. "Is something wrong, Tim?"

Clearly there was. Tim's fingers drummed on his desk and he fussed with his tie. "Look, Houston, we've known each other a long time, and you're a damn good surgeon. By the book. And we're friends, right? We've hit the bars together a few times, hung out."

Houston's concern deepened. He did like Tim, and he respected him professionally, but he had no idea what this was about. "Sure, we're friends. And I came to Acadia Inlet based on your recommendation."

Tim nodded, studying him carefully. "Tell me straight, Houston. Are you screwing one of my residents?"

His face went hot. Words of denial were on his lips. And indignation that anyone could refer to what he shared with Josie as screwing around. He clamped his mouth shut and said nothing.

Tim sighed. "Look, normally what you do with your dick is none of my business, but we've got a problem here. We've got a second-year resident who already has a strike or two against her on her record. She's a great doctor, with an incredible rapport with the patients. They trust her, and she delivers the kind of personal care I haven't seen in a long time. But you and I both know her surgical skills are average at best."

Houston wasn't sure he knew that, or maybe he did and didn't want to admit it. Or hear it out loud.

Either way he didn't like that all his thoughts, all his concerns about getting involved with Josie, were suddenly rearing up, just when he'd convinced himself they wouldn't.

"She just needs experience."

Pinning him with a hard stare, Tim snorted. "What she needs is to get her act together and prove she's capable. And she needs to not be having an affair with you. Look, if this blows up, you'll get singed a little, but it's Josie who will burn. Even if she's just a bit of fun for you, do you want that on your conscience?"

Houston raked his hand through his hair and tapped his foot, frustrated and furious with himself. "She's not just a bit of fun. She's more than that, and I don't want her to suffer for this, Tim."

Then Tim smiled, an approving grin on his tan, rugged face. "Glad to hear it." He swiveled his chair and faced his computer screen. "So, we'll just fix it, all right? If you're not working together, there's nothing improper about you seeing each other. So as of today, we're transferring Dr. Adkins to St. John's up the road."

"What the hell is this?" Josie read the words in front of her again, as if somehow they were going to mysteriously change into something more palatable.

Sara stopped chewing her sandwich long enough to ask, "What?"

Josie bit the cherry tomato from her salad, wishing it were Dr. Houston Hayes's head. God, she had trusted him. She had told him that she loved him. She had let him have sex with her on a *surfboard*. She had told him her fears, and he had turned her in. The sharks were biting, and not in the water.

Damn it, she felt tears forming right in the hospital cafeteria. "I've been transferred to St. John's."

"Transferred? Why? Can they do that without asking you?"

Josie's hand shook as it held the paper with the damning words on it. "I didn't think so. But listen to this. Just listen."

"Dr. Sheinberg wrote this, of course, and that's all fine." It was Houston who had sold her out. Used her. Made her feel that he could actually care about her.

And now this.

Anger and hurt pooled in her stomach. She whispered so no one else in the cafeteria could hear.

"Dr. Adkins is a highly qualified physician who shows advanced knowledge of general medicine as well as orthopedics. Her communication skills are superb in regard to both colleagues and patients, and she works well with other members of the surgical team."

Josie took a deep breath.

Sara blotted her lips with her napkin. "What does that have to do with a transfer? All that sounds great."

"I haven't gotten to the bad part yet."

Her voice began to tremble as she continued to read. "However, staff surgeon, Dr. Hayes, finds that Dr. Adkins displays a lack of confidence in her abilities in the area of reconstructive orthopedics and recommends Dr. Adkins for the pediatric orthopedic residency at St. John's Hospital."

Sara's mouth fell open.

Josie's sentiments exactly. How could he do this to her? Forcing her out of Acadia without even discussing it with her? It was comparable to smearing "don't trust this woman with a scalpel" all over her permanent record.

"The transfer will be effective October first, according to this little gem Dr. Sheinberg presented me with."

"Houston recommended a transfer?" Sara asked. "He didn't. He couldn't."

"He did. He could." Josie threw her head down on the table and fought the urge to crumple the paper up into a tiny ball and fling it across the room. Then sob.

Houston had effectively pulled the rug out from under the rest of her career.

"Josie, I don't know what to say. Maybe he thought he was doing you a favor."

She snorted, not bothering to look up. "Yeah, right. I don't call sabotaging my career doing me a favor." Her words were muffled through her folded arms. "This is my punishment for getting personal with another staff member."

His punishment to her. His way to push her away after getting so close the night before.

Control. He always had to be in control, and she threatened that.

It was a toss-up which was the biggest mistake— sleeping with him, or falling in love with him.

"Your elbow's in your salad."

Josie jerked up and saw a big glob of ranch dressing on her sleeve. Fabulous. Swiping at it with her napkin, she decided what she had to do. "I'm going to go talk to him."

"Do you really think that's a good idea?" Sara pushed up her glasses and frowned. "I don't think talking to Dr. Hayes is really the best thing to do right now."

"You're right." Josie gripped the paper and narrowed her eyes. Talking was too good for him. "I'll strangle him."

Sara shook her head. "That's not what I meant. I meant that you're not exactly in the right frame of mind to have a rational discussion with him about this."

"Rational?" Josie lost it. "You call this rational?" She waved the report around in front of her face. "Houston Hayes doesn't know the meaning of the word rational. I was *born* rational."

"You sure don't sound it right now."

Josie took a deep breath. Maybe Sara had a point. But this was about much more than her career. This was about her heart. And the fact that Houston persisted in ripping it into little pieces and stomping on it with his tanned feet.

"Okay, I'm better now. I only want to castrate him, not kill him."

"Don't do that," Sara warned. "You might regret it later."

Hurt chased through every inch of her, choking off her breath, pounding in her head, and sending a vicious searing pain into her stomach. "I'm never having sex with him again, so it doesn't matter. Certainly not on a surfboard."

Sara's mouth dropped. "You had sex on a surfboard? Holy moly, did that work? I've got to find me a surfer."

It had worked, and then some. "Why? So they can coax you out of your clothes, feed you lies, then ruin your life with cold calculation?" Damn it, tears were in her eyes and her voice warbled like a drunken parrot.

Josie squeezed her eyes shut briefly and fought for control. "I'm going to see him, and I will be calm and rational."

Even if it killed her.

Picking up her half-eaten salad, she tossed it in the garbage.

"Good luck," Sara said. "And no throwing things or leaping over the desk and throttling him."

"I would never dream of doing such a thing." The bit about strangling him had really only been a momentary fantasy. She had never intended to *act* on it. Though a slap wouldn't be out of line.

Grabbing the offending printout, she left the cafeteria with a wave to Sara. With each step she reminded herself to be reasonable, calm, and intelligent.

Sailing into his office shrieking like a fishwife would not aid her cause. Which was to insist Houston revoke that stupid, prickish, self-serving statement about her and cancel the transfer.

By the time she stood outside his door, she was almost in control and looking mostly professional. Except for the salad dressing stain on the elbow of her blouse and the hideous scowl she was sure was on her face.

The waiting area had three elderly patients waiting to be seen and the receptionist looked tired. When Josie approached her, the girl sighed. "I'll give you every cent I have if you take over my job for the rest of the day."

"That bad?" Josie asked in sympathy, feeling for the girl, who barely looked eighteen. At least Josie was adequately paid for bearing the annoyances of her job. This girl was likely just making enough to pay her bills.

"I've been on hold with an insurance company for twenty minutes about a patient's bill, Dr. Hayes is running a half-hour behind, and I broke a nail." She held the offending finger up. "I just had these done yesterday and it cost twenty-five bucks."

"Then neither of us is having a good day. I have a bone to pick with your boss."

The receptionist grimaced. "Don't leave him in too bad of a mood, I'm begging you. Once you leave, I'm stuck with him for the rest of the day."

Josie forced a laugh that almost had her gagging. "I'll do my best."

The chart was out of the holder to the examining room on the left, which meant Houston was inside with the patient. She propped herself against the wall and prepared to wait. The clock on the wall read one-twelve. She had thirty-eight minutes left on her lunch. She could wait him out for thirty-seven if she had to.

It was a mere five minutes later when the door opened and Houston came striding out, the file in his hand to slide into the slot on the wall. He came close to colliding with her, but stopped himself just in time.

"Josie! I'm glad you came by. You want to go to lunch?" He reached towards her, like he was going to kiss her right there in the hall, and she jerked away.

"I need a minute of your time."

His eyebrows rose. "What's the matter?"

Everything. "I need to talk to you in private."

He shuffled the folder, looking puzzled and inno- cent, "I'm almost finished. Can it wait until over lunch?"

Shaking her head, she held up the transfer paper. "No, it can't wait. I want an explanation for this."

"What is it?" He peered at it without recognition, then glanced at his watch.

"My marching orders. Transfer to St. John's, effec- tive October one. A week from now."

That got a slight reaction. His jaw clenched. "What about it?"

Despite the growing anger in her, she forced herself to remain calm. She was an adult. She would handle this like one. "Clearly you knew about it. Now I would like to know why you found it necessary to undermine my skills."

He glanced left and right, leaned closer to her, his voice wary. "What are you talking about?"

"I'm talking about the fact that you told Dr. Sheinberg that I'm a sucky surgeon and I should give it up and slink back to med school." Okay, that was an exaggeration. So sue her.

"What? Get in my office." He went for her elbow but she jerked away.

Hell if he was going to guide her around like she was being an obstinate child.

His jaw clenched. "We need to clear this up, but five minutes, Josie, that's all I've got. I have patients waiting. Please, let's do this in my office."

"Then you better start talking fast." The urge to start screaming right there in the hall was great. But she wouldn't because she was reeking with maturity.

Nudging past him, she walked into his office. He followed her and held his hands out in a placating manner. "I'm not sure what you're so upset about. Tim and I talked and we decided it was better for all parties involved if you were transferred before our relationship became common knowledge. I never once said you were a sucky surgeon and need to go back to med school. If that's what it said, I was misquoted."

Misquoted. She'd misquote him.

Tears started to roll down her cheeks, and she swiped at them in anger. "So you and Tim sat in his office and decided what was best for *me*? That takes a lot of freaking nerve! And how exactly did Tim know there was anything between us?"

He rubbed his jaw. "Apparently he has eyes and ears. People are talking. We didn't have any choice."

"You could have transferred!" She imagined that one had never crossed their male minds. "How could you do this to me? No resident gets transferred without a good reason, like a serious screwup, and everyone is going to wonder what I did. How could you do this, knowing it would hurt me? Last night . . ." she lost her voice for a minute.

Houston tossed the folder in his hand onto the desk and brushed her hair off her face. "Oh, sweetheart, this is coming out all wrong."

When he kissed her forehead, she shuddered, wanting to let the anger deflate, wanting him to convince her that she was wrong. Her shoulders slumped, she bit her trembling lip.

"I wasn't trying to hurt your career, I was trying to help, to protect you."

For a second, she had wavered, had fallen into the closeness of the night before with Houston. Had wanted to trust him, believe in what she had felt from him in his arms, read in his eyes. His words made her snap. He could call it anything he wanted but help.

"That's a load of you-know-what, Houston!" She waved the paper under his nose again, and moved away from him, not trusting herself if he touched her again. "This is your way of pushing me away. Last night I got too close, I saw parts of the real you, and I made the whopper mistake of telling you I love you. And now you're putting distance between us."

"That's not what I'm doing!"

Was it, he wondered? No, of course it wasn't. He just wanted her to be happy, not have to pay for his mistakes. Houston tried to touch Josie, soothe her, but she swatted at him.

He was in deep shit, and he knew it. Josie was furious, and beneath that was a naked pain that he had caused and it made him feel ashamed. "I didn't mean for Dr. Sheinberg to imply you were lacking in skill. And maybe I should have spoken to you directly first, but this is the only thing we can really do at this point. As a surgeon, my responsibility lies with the patient, not you. Even if no one found out about our relationship, we shouldn't be working together anymore. We distract each other. You wouldn't be happy."

And he suspected she would never gain confidence in her abilities while he was in the OR with her.

But Houston was a little scared. His apology had somehow turned into a defense of his position, and Josie looked beyond angry. She looked devastated. He'd never seen her like this. And damn it, those tears were killing him. He'd told her he would make her cry sooner or later and she wouldn't listen to him, and now here they were. He hadn't meant to hurt her, but somehow he had.

"How dare you tell me what would make me happy! You don't know anything about it. I love surgery," she said inanely in a shaky voice, bottom lip trembling.

He had no idea how to fix this when he wasn't even sure what he'd done wrong. They had created a problem together, and he and Tim had taken steps to fix it. She wasn't being reasonable.

So he just kept focusing on the obvious, not sure what else to do. "You don't love surgery. You hate it. I've watched you. I worked with you every day for three months. You love medicine, yes, but not surgery. You pursued it because your father wanted you to, exactly like you told me. Maybe pediatrics will be a better match for you."

"That is none of your business and totally irrelevant to what we're discussing. Knowing about my father didn't give you the right to make that decision for me."

"I wasn't making the decision for you." Well, maybe he had. "But there wasn't a choice. For both of our careers, I had to do this."

"How can you do that? Compartmentalize like that? Separate totally, knowing what you were doing would hurt me. You warned me, and I didn't believe you. You're much, much colder than I ever gave you credit for."

And that very iciness she accused him of settled over him as a cold shield. Her words tore inside him, and he shrugged in a protective gesture. Hurt before you're hurt. "You didn't seem to think I was cold yesterday when you were in my bed."

Her finger came up and there was a firmness to her voice he'd never heard. "Don't do that, Houston. Don't turn this back to sex. I will not tolerate that."

She was right. But he didn't know what to say. He needed Josie in his life and didn't want to lose her when he'd just found her, but how could he agree with her when he'd suggest a transfer for her all over again? "As a man, not a surgeon, I want you to be happy. As a surgeon, and a colleague, I want to protect you. Can't you see that?"

"Happy? What do you know about my happiness?"

He dropped his arms to his sides when she rebuffed his touch again. "I know that you're not happy. I know that every day I look at you and wonder how you can't see what I do. That you have all these choices and the ability to do exactly what you want to do, yet you pound away at something you don't like. But this wasn't about happiness, this was about keeping your career intact."

From his perspective, he couldn't imagine having a choice and choosing to do what you didn't enjoy. But if Josie wanted to be a surgeon, he'd do whatever it took to ensure she became one. He waved his right hand in the air in front of her and gave her a small smile.

"I have no choices right now. I can't do what I love. And to watch you struggling through each day, it makes me unbelievably sad for you. And downright envious for me."

He'd gotten a reaction. The anger fell away from her face. Josie chewed her lips for a second, then took a deep breath. "Did you do this to hurt me?"

"No, of course not. The opposite, in fact."

"Do you want a long-term relationship with me?"

The very words made his chest feel tight. That's what he wanted, he did, but hearing her say it like that, so final, so serious, so angry with him, he panicked. He wasn't good enough for her, he couldn't be what she needed. One day at a time, that's what he wanted. To enjoy being with Josie and not planning, thinking, worrying about the future.

"I'm not very good at relationships, and I'm facing the hardest time in my life. Right now I'm almost crippled."

Just saying the word made him cringe. But when you couldn't drive and couldn't write, there was nothing else to call it.

Josie didn't show any sympathy. She huffed, blowing her bangs out of her face. "So your hand isn't fully functional yet. So what? You're also a control freak. And I'm overweight and insecure. We all have faults, Houston."

This wasn't a fault. It was a potentially permanent disability. "It's not the same thing."

Josie was losing him. He had already drifted, distanced himself, pulled away from her. And she couldn't do this anymore. Her heart was shattering.

There was only one reason she would stay.

"Just tell me, Houston, honestly. Do you love me?" she whispered, hoping against hope he'd give the answer she wanted.

His face tensed. His shoulders went rigid. His jaw worked. And while his eyes spoke volumes, showing care and concern, his mouth didn't move. She gave him a good long moment to speak, then she turned in defeat, biting her lips to hold back a sob.

A sigh did escape as she took a step towards the door. "I'll be starting at St. John's on Monday. I hope your hand heals."

"Josie! You're not just going to walk away, are you?"

Yes. Because she'd never had him, any more than she'd had John Taylor in her Duran Duran fantasies.

"We can work this out," he insisted.

Her hand hesitated on the doorknob, then she steeled her resolve. No. This was it. She deserved better. The whole enchilada, and the extra hot sauce.

"Good-bye, Dr. Hayes."

Chapter Nineteen

Houston tried not to be annoyed by the therapist's small talk, but he wasn't having much luck.

They'd been doing this therapy for four weeks, and he'd struggled through every session. It had been five weeks since Josie had walked out of his office, and it had been a long, miserable autumn, every single lonely second his own damn fault.

He had screwed up and there was nothing he could do to fix it.

Nothing.

It felt like he was walking a tightrope and was about to pitch off and hit the ground with a resounding smack. He wasn't even sure what had gone wrong and when. It just all had and here he was, stuck in this chair listening to Frank, the physical therapist, tell him about the wonderful cookout he and his wife had thrown over the weekend.

Houston had spent the weekend brooding inside his condo with thoughts that never strayed far from a certain pixie-haired doctor. The same doctor who had painfully avoided him her last few days at the hospital at all costs and who he'd only seen four times in four weeks, each time more difficult because it meant she truly wasn't going to forgive him. She wasn't coming back to him.

It was over.

"So, are you having a good fall, Dr. Hayes?" Frank asked, as he packed ice on Houston's hand. "Geez, I can't believe it's almost Thanksgiving."

No, actually he was having the most hellish fall of his entire life and Thanksgiving loomed ahead of him as a reminder that everyone else had someone. His mom and Larry. Christian and Kori. He had no one. "It's been okay."

Frank started massaging his index finger and thumb and Houston tried to ignore the fact that he barely felt it. Outside of his daily therapy sessions, he had been ignoring his injured hand, relying on his left hand the way he had been for the past seven weeks.

He couldn't move his thumb and index finger. They wouldn't move. He knew that. He didn't have much sensation either.

And that was something he wasn't ready to deal with just yet.

Except that he couldn't ignore it. It followed him everywhere. He had adjusted, learning to drive with one and a half hands and scratching out shaky words with his left hand, but he sure in the hell couldn't do his job. He'd been doing office appointments, but referring all his surgeries to the other orthopedists.

"Okay, let's try and give it a bend and see how you do."

Frank pushed back on his wheeled chair to give him more space. Houston glanced around the room to make sure none of the other occupants were paying attention to him. There were only two other patients in the room with therapists and they were both preoccupied with their own bodies and their failings.

Houston stared at his hand and tried to bend his index finger. He willed it to bend. He squeezed as hard as he could.

The lower half jerked half an inch, and the tip didn't move at all.

"Okay, that's good. Very good." Frank handed him a soft ball. "Now see if you can squeeze the ball."

Houston took the ball, sweat forming on his forehead. He couldn't squeeze the ball and he knew it. They had been trying this every day for a week, with no results at all.

He couldn't take it today. One more failure and he wasn't going to be able to ignore the problem anymore. "Can we just skip this one for now?"

"You're not going to be doing yourself any favors if you do. You know you've got to work it if you want to regain some mobility."

Frank was right, of course. But his cheerfulness drove Houston nuts. Gripping the ball tightly, he tried to squeeze. Nothing happened. He tried again.

Nothing.

"Give it another try," Frank urged, leaning forward to offer assistance.

Houston stood up from his seat. He was sick to death of people having to help him, of being helpless. He couldn't take it another second, this burning and building frustration.

Transferring the ball to his left hand, he kicked the chair out of his way. "I can't do it! I can't squeeze the goddamn ball and you know it."

He hurled the soft ball at the wall behind Frank with all his pent-up anger and fear. "Aahh! I can't squeeze it and I'll never be able to."

The ball hit with a soft thump, then tumbled down the wall to the floor.

Frank retrieved the ball while Houston stood there panting and feeling like a two-year-old who'd just thrown a tantrum.

"Feel better?" Frank asked mildly.

"Yes. No. I don't know." He sank back into the half-turned chair and ran his fingers through his hair, taking a deep breath in exasperation. "I'm sorry, I don't know what the hell I'm doing."

Frank shrugged. "Hey, don't worry about it. You're going through a tough time. Though I'm thinking this isn't just about your hand, is it?"

It was about his hand, his life, Josie, everything.

He was a disaster. A physical and emotional wreck. With a useless hand and a useless heart.

He was in love with Josie. He knew that as clearly as he knew his thumb didn't bend. Yet he hadn't told her. He had stood there like a dumb ass and let her walk away. Protecting his vaunted control hadn't been worth losing Josie, wasn't worth facing every day alone.

He loved her. Her generosity, her smile, her chatty run-on sentences. He loved everything about her. And he wanted her back.

The question was, would she take him? Him, a man with little to offer. Not particularly good at relationships, frightened to be a father, and facing unemployment.

But he'd never know unless he tried.

When Frank handed him the ball a second time, he took it. He gave it his best effort. He really did.

"It's going to take time, Dr. Hayes. Weeks of therapy."

But his hand didn't move.

"Are you using your hand at home, Dr. Hayes? Because part of what you need to learn how to do is adjust how you use your hand. You shouldn't be ignoring it, but neither should you expect it to do what it did before. You've got to relearn some things, change."

Easy for Frank to say. But Houston heard the words, really heard them for the first time, and knew they were true. He couldn't ignore the problem or sit around waiting for a miracle anymore.

After twenty more minutes of exercises designed to manipulate his fingers into movement, Houston felt sick to his stomach from concentrating so hard.

It was a relief when Frank massaged his hand again and rested an ice pack against it to reduce any swelling or pain that might occur from the intense activity.

"Well, see you tomorrow, Dr. Hayes. Same time."

"Thanks, Frank."

Houston stood up, rolled his neck to alleviate tension, and went to meet with Dr. Stanhope, the chief of staff.

He knew what he had to do.

It was time to resign.

Then he was going to go to Josie on his knees and beg her for a second chance.

Josie grabbed the last tissue in the box on the couch and blew. Fluid leaked through onto her hand as she coughed, nostrils completely plugged. Tossing the used tissue wad onto the towering pile with its brethren, she shuffled across the living room to wash her hands.

She had a cold. Which seemed an appropriate representation of her feelings for the last five weeks. Exhausted, miserable, teary-eyed, and foggy-brained.

It still amazed her that she had gotten through those first few days at work after the scene in Houston's office without bursting into tears. But she had, and her residency at Acadia Inlet had come to an abrupt and quiet ending. She'd started at St. John's and had found almost immediately that she really enjoyed pediatric orthopedics, a lot of which dealt with correcting musculoskeletal birth defects and problems arising from cerebral palsy. She was enthusiastic that she had found her orthopedic niche.

She was also hopeful that in a year or so she could transfer to the children's hospital in Daytona to finish the remainder of her residency. Which meant she could leave the final remnants of her life in Acadia Inlet and forget that she'd ever met Houston Hayes, let alone fallen in love with him.

And that should happen in about eighty years. She couldn't forget him. She thought about him every day and wondered if she had made a mistake walking away from him. Or if she had somehow imagined that he'd ever had feelings for her at all. Now with hindsight it almost seemed that way.

He had been attracted to her, no doubt, but maybe she had been nothing more than a challenge to him. A conquest. An attraction to explore, knowing he would tire of her. He'd said as much to her the day he had propositioned her by the X-ray box. Maybe if he hadn't gotten attacked by that shark, they never would have gone beyond the first night, their agreed-upon one-night stand.

But they had, and she had the scars on her heart to prove it.

She scrubbed her already dry and chaffed hands while the water ran. The splashing masked the sound, but she thought for a second that her doorbell was ringing. Maybe it was her mother appearing out of nowhere due to maternal ESP, and bearing soup and the expensive tissues that had aloe in them. The kind that Josie was going to invest in from now on since her nose had suffered severe epidermal damage. Which meant it was beet red and missing the top layer of skin.

Or it could be the woman next door coming to complain about Josie's 3 A.M. coughing fits.

"Coming," she said, shaking water off her hands before wiping them dry on her sky blue pajama bottoms.

Grabbing a tissue out of a fresh box on the way past and tucking it into the waistband of her pants, she opened the door.

And wanted to close it again.

Houston was standing there wearing jeans and a black shirt. His hands were tucked into his front pockets and he was studying her intently, a little smile at the corner of his lips. As usual, he had cornered the market on gorgeous.

"Hi."

"Hi," she croaked, then capped it off with a sniffle.

Her mind, dulled by decongestant, couldn't wrap around why Houston was standing on her doorstep, but she was painfully aware that she wasn't exactly looking her best.

Apparently he noticed, too. "Are you sick?"

"Yes, I have a cold." Thanks for noticing. Josie turned around and shuffled in her slippers over to her glass of water on the coffee table so she wouldn't hack on him.

She took a sip and swallowed, her ears popping.

"Have you taken anything? Are you pushing fluids? You're not going to work, are you?"

Josie flopped onto the couch with a big sigh, exhausted. She couldn't deal with him right now, not when she'd spent all this time convincing herself she'd be okay, that eventually she'd get over him. And now, when she was sick and vulnerable, he was waltzing into her apartment and acting like he actually gave a damn about her.

"Houston, is there a reason you're here? Can I do something for you?"

He stopped in the middle of crossing the room and looked taken aback. "I came to see how you are."

Houston watched Josie shoot him a glance of disbelief and wondered how he was supposed to proceed from here. It had seemed so simple. Go to Josie, apologize, confess his feelings, coax her out of her clothes and back into his life.

He hadn't counted on her looking at him like he was an ugly alien.

"You've seen me. I'm not so good."

That was obvious. What he was supposed to do about it wasn't. "Can I get you anything? Do you have any Gatorade? You need to replenish your electrolytes."

Josie just looked at him. Then carefully, she pulled a tissue out of her pants and wiped her red and raw nose.

He was going to have to say something. Tucking his hands behind his back, he frowned. "I resigned today."

The tissue tumbled out of her hands, landing between her thighs. Her jaw fell open. "You did? Why?"

It didn't hurt as badly as he'd thought to admit the truth. "I'm not capable of conducting surgery at the level I was before. My thumb is never going to have a full range of motion, and I have no interest in retraining to compensate for the loss."

Sympathy filled her eyes. Different than pity. Warmer, softer, a flash of the way she used to look at him emerging. Maybe, despite everything, she still cared.

"Houston . . . I'm sorry."

He nodded. "Me, too. But I can't give up medicine, it's too much a part of me. I haven't decided what exactly I'm going to do, but I'm hoping an orthopedic practice might have use for me."

The idea had stolen over him after he'd left the hospital, and what had just been a thought now cemented. He knew that's what he wanted, what he should do—continue to use his orthopedic skills without surgery. He could still be a doctor and help heal patients, just in a different way.

"And I want you to join me." Now that came out of nowhere, but damn, it was a good idea. "We'd be great together. Complement each other."

Josie gaped at him. "That sounds about as much fun as a liquid diet. I can't work with you, Houston! I can't even look at you."

And to prove her point, she buried herself behind another tissue.

Shit, he was screwing this up. Why the hell had he brought up work first? Dropping down on the floor next to her, he touched her knee. "Jesus, sweetheart, I'm sorry. I'm not doing this right. What I really came here to tell you is that I love you. Josie, I really, really love you, and I've missed you like crazy."

It wasn't even hard to say it. The words rolled off his tongue, true and fierce.

Josie didn't look impressed with his liberation. She spoke through the tissue. "Wow. And it only took you five weeks to say it."

"I'm not always in touch with my emotions."

She snorted, then threw her crumpled tissue at him, bouncing it off his nose before it rolled down his chest. "Why are you doing this to me? I gave up my residency at Acadia without a fight, and I just want to get out, get away from you, repair my heart and dignity and here you are, trying to reel me back in with a bunch of BS."

"It's not BS!" He'd never been so damn serious in his life. He loved her. He was desperate for her to say the same. He'd never wanted anything so much as he wanted her to forgive him. "I do love you. And even with a half-functional hand, I'm a better-off man than I was before I met you."

He stroked her knee through her cotton pants. "You helped me heal, Josie, both emotionally and physically. I thought that I couldn't ever love anyone because of my parents, and that loving meant giving up control. You showed me it doesn't have anything to do with that." He squeezed her knee, trying to get her to look at him. She seemed incredibly absorbed in peeling apart two tissues that had stuck together.

"My physical therapist told me if I adjust and shift the way I use my hand, it will be better for me than to keep trying to use it the way I always have. When I re-alized that, I realized the same was true for us. I can't make my feelings for you fit the selfish way I've always approached women. Loving you makes me happy, and I want to spend forever taking care of each other."

He'd done it. He'd laid it all out there. And it felt damn good. Burrowing his head into her thigh, he kissed her leg, the warm cotton of her pants smelling light and fruity, like Josie. His Josie.

"I knew how I felt five weeks ago and I should have told you, but I was scared. Thought you might squash me like that garbage truck compacter. I'm sorry."

Sorry he'd hurt her. Sorry he'd wasted time.

Josie stared down at Houston's dark head leaning over her lap as he kissed her, and wondered if she were hallucinating. If so, she was never taking Nyquil again. She couldn't prevent her fingers from smoothing the tips of his coarse black hair any more than she could prevent her heart from leaping to enthusiastic attention.

And then he begged. "Josie, please, honey, I love you. Please forgive me. Please."

Oh, God. Tears pooled, knowing what it must have cost him to say those vulnerable words. She stroked his head, his cheeks. "It's okay, it's okay. I forgive you."

He sighed, nuzzling his nose across her thigh before lifting his head. "Thank you."

Fingers found their way over hers, and he locked their hands together. He stared at her, eyes trailing over her face, jaw working, and Josie let the wave of tenderness wash over her, soaking her, comforting her.

Then she sneezed.

Right into his face.

Groping for her tissue, eyes watering, Josie groaned, "Geez, I'm sorry!"

Houston wiped his face on his shoulder and laughed. "I love you," he said with great affection.

Why was a mystery, but she wasn't going to question it. "Houston, are you saying you want a long-term relationship? With me?" Better be clear on that.

"Yes."

For the first time in her life, words failed her. Then burst forth in a rattled rush. "Are you sure? I can't do this again, you know, I can't get all worked up, then have you change your mind and yank it away from me. And I understand why you and Dr. Sheinberg arranged the transfer, even if you should have consulted me. I know you were protecting me. But working together? I've really enjoyed working with kids. It's been going really, really well, and I haven't dropped anything or screwed anything up. I'm totally confident. And so I was really thinking more about pediatric orthopedics . . ."

She paused for air, which could only come through her mouth because of her inflamed nasal passageways.

He looked up and smiled. A grin, really. And his hand was on the go, ascending upwards from her knee and sliding sideways, probably being sucked into the gravitational pull of her eager inner thighs.

"You are a goddess. That's what I said in the ER right? It's very true."

His kisses were shifting, too, marching to meet his hand, and Josie pushed his head to stop him. But he was stronger and determined.

"You didn't actually say that, remember . . . and what are you doing? I don't look like a goddess, I'm sick. I have bad breath and excess snot."

Which was such a sexy thing to bring up. Josie clapped her hand over her mouth, then had to spread her fingers so she could take in oxygen.

"You are a goddess. A love goddess. A sex goddess." His fingers had found their mark, stroking across the apex of her thighs, while his lips reached the bare skin between her pants and her shirt.

"More like the goddess of cold products." But her body was stirring, reacting to his touch.

Underwear and pants were no match for Houston. He was already inside both, sliding down in her curls, rolling across her clitoris, coaxing moist heat from her body. "Do you really forgive me? Do you still love me? Will you be with me, give me a chance?"

Uhh, yeah. *Please.* Walking away from him had been the hardest thing she'd ever done. "Are you really okay, about your hand, and everything? How's your leg?"

Kissing across her abdomen, he nodded. "I'm really okay. And my leg has healed with minimal scarring, thanks to my wonderful doctor."

Josie closed her eyes, overwhelmed.

"Are you going to answer me, sweetheart?"

"Huh?" She bit her lip, then dropped her mouth open when she couldn't breathe. Houston's finger had slipped inside her and her nipples were hardening, her body tightening.

He bit her stomach lightly. "Do you love me?"

Josie swiped at her nose desperately, heart racing. Trust her to mouth-breathe and sniffle her way through the most romantic moment of her life. "Yes."

While he smiled in triumph, Josie reached into the basket she had sitting on her end table. Straining to feel around in it as Houston held her prisoner with his tongue on her navel, she felt the sharp poke of the shark's tooth.

Fingers closed around it, she struggled for breath, struggled for composure. She wanted Houston now and for forever and she was going to have him. And she was a damn good doctor and her father would be proud.

"First of all," she managed to say, valiantly ignoring his roving fingers, "I don't want to work with you, Houston. I want to love you, live with you, be your friend and lover, but trust me on this, I do not want to work with you anymore. I'm not at my professional best with you."

Houston laughed. "What's in your hand, honey?"

She held up the shark's tooth. "It came from your leg."

Houston watched the light reflect off the shiny dark surface of the inch-long tooth. It touched a part deep inside of him that Josie had been hanging on to that stupid thing for two months. "You know, in a weird way that bastard bull shark brought us together. I say we keep the tooth. Make it into a necklace for you."

He grinned up at her, enjoying his perch between her legs, the soft give of her thighs beneath his elbows. "With a shark's tooth necklace and that tropical bikini, you can be a regular beach bunny when you watch me surf."

Josie laughed, dabbing at her nose. "Forget that. You're teaching me how to surf."

"It's a deal. We'll do it together, you and me, everything from now on."

Josie gave him a sweet smile, with all the goodness of her pure heart in it, and he felt his gut relax.

Then he sat up and with a quick hook of his thumbs beneath her waistband, peeled her pants down. For five weeks he'd been missing her, and every inch of her luscious body. "What are today's panties? Hearts, maybe?"

That would be appropriate.

"No," she said, her breath hitching.

A big green shamrock was stretched taut across Josie, cupping her, outlining that feminine arch of her body, the erotic dip between her soft silky folds. His gut wrenched. He groaned.

And he started towards that enticing clover. "Oh, yeah, perfect. I'm feeling damn lucky today. For more than one reason."

Wildly romantic and super sexy . . . that's
THE PREGNANCY TEST
by Erin McCarthy,
available now from Brava . . .

She covered her face with her hand. "God, I think I'm blushing. This is just so unbelievable."

"But in such a good way." Damien put his hand on the small of Mandy's back and herded her in the direction of the hotel shop.

Good thing it was a short walk, because now that he had been given the green light by Mandy, he was more than a little eager. He was on fucking fire.

Mandy hung back in the store, hovering over by the imported magazines displayed both in English and Spanish, her cheeks a charming pink. Damien didn't feel any embarrassment whatsoever. He strode over to the counter and asked the clerk, "Where are the condoms?"

Why waste even five minutes looking for them?

The man, in his late twenties, grinned at Damien and pointed behind him. "Individual or a box?"

"Box." No sense in having to repeat this shopping expedition if things went according to plan.

The clerk slapped the box down on the counter, and Damien studied the busty Hispanic woman in a bikini on the front. The carton was bright yellow, the bikini a violent orange, and while the label was in English, the small script was in Spanish. He hoped like hell these weren't novelty condoms. He wasn't wearing anything with parrots on it.

"Would you like some Mamajuana, too? Good stuff." The man pointed to a bottle of what looked like alcohol, shelved next to the rum.

"What is it?" Not that he had any intention of getting drunk. He wanted to remember every second of this.

"You drink it. We call it Dominican Viagra." The clerk winked. "Helps you last, if you know what I mean. If this doesn't work, they say you should just go and kill yourself."

Did he look like he needed Viagra? What the hell. He was so hard he could moonlight as a woodpecker. Damien shook his head. "I don't need any help, thanks." He handed over the six hundred pesos for the condoms, which he shoved in his pocket, and turned to find Mandy. She was biting her lip, arms over her chest, staring vacantly at a display of T-shirts.

"Have fun!" the clerk yelled with a knowing grin.

And people thought New Yorkers were rude.

Fortunately, he'd forgotten how to blush. But Mandy looked like she'd spent too long in the sun, so he took her hand and hustled her outside to the quiet walkway that led to the main lobby.

And kissed her eagerly.

"Damien," she protested, trying to pull back. "There are people around."

"No, there aren't. Not a single one." The path was deserted, everyone still down at the buffet, and it was lush with foliage, and thick with humidity in the glow of faux gas lamps.

But she was still darting her eyes around, hands pressed on his chest to hold him at bay. So Damien dropped his mouth to her forehead and gave her a soft kiss. "My room is in the first building on the right."

"Then it's closer than mine. I'm by the adults-only

pool." But she didn't move in the direction he had pointed to. She worried her lip, and Damien watched her, waited for her to say what was on her mind. "I just want you to understand that I don't usually . . . I don't sleep around. I thought Ben really cared about me, and well, I've never really fancied one-night stands. But that's all this can be, because I can't get involved with anyone until I've sorted out my own life."

Damien brushed a hair back that had caught on her lip. "This isn't a one-night stand. It's not just about sex. It's about being together, enjoying each other, if only for a few hours." It was about loosening the suffocating chains of loneliness and reaching out for something simple and uncomplicated. "But I'm not looking for a relationship, either."

He couldn't believe he was about to admit this, but he wanted her to understand, wanted her to know what this—she—meant to him. "I haven't been with a woman in three years."

"You haven't been in a relationship in three years?"

"Yes, but I also haven't had sex in three years."

Understanding dawned in her eyes. "Oh. Oh, my." She stroked his forearm. "Since Jess?"

He nodded, not willing to say any more. "That's been a conscious choice I've made, and now I'm making the conscious choice to change that. Let me have you tonight, Mandy."

There was no way she was going to say no. He could read the acquiescence in her eyes, the way she leaned toward him, stroked his arms and opened her mouth. Her breasts pressed against him as she tilted her head to the side and gave a small, sweet sigh.

"Oh, I'm not a bloody idiot, Damien. I have every intention of doing this—I just needed to make sure we were clear on what it was, and that you don't think I'm some sort of swinger who sleeps with her boss in the Caribbean on every job she takes."

He raised an eyebrow. "That definitely wasn't on your résumé."

She gave a soft laugh and wet her lips, making him want to suck on both her lip and her tongue, taking turns. "What if I don't meet your expectations? Three years is a long time to wait. I'd hate to be a disappointment."

That was a joke. He'd be lucky if he got a full five seconds in her before he exploded. "As long as you don't have some sort of objection to oral sex, we'll be fine. I have it in my head that I'd really like to taste you."

Her breathing quickened. "Funny, that. I had a dream you were doing that very thing to me, and I was really quite enjoying it."

Damien's groin tightened. What the hell were they doing standing here then?

"You know, you're usually much more efficient than this. Move it, Mandy. Before I drop your sundress here on the sidewalk." And he reached for her zipper.

Mandy had taken Damien's threat seriously, and a quick two minutes later they were in his room, her beach bag tumbling to the floor as she reached for the buttons on his linen shirt.

She'd seen the way he looked in his swim trunks that afternoon and she wanted to touch that broad chest. She wanted to explore his hard flesh, make him tremble with want. She wanted to draw this all out and enjoy every blasted second of it since she was facing a future of celibacy.

Damien's own hands were busy unzipping the back of her dress. But whereas she was fumbling, overeager, nervous, he was quiet, studied, intent. Goose bumps rose on her flesh as his fingers trailed over her back. His room was at the end of the hall, remote, the sounds of the resort buffered by palm trees and flowering plants. The whirr of the ceiling fan and the uneven tempo of their breathing were the only sounds in the room.

All her doubts, all her concerns, fear about how she should behave and how he might react to her pregnancy, her body the way it was now, had all evaporated when Damien told her he hadn't been with a woman in three years. She'd seen it then, what he had been telling her. That they both needed each other, just here, just now, to touch and taste and push on each other in uncomplicated pleasure.

She wanted that. She wanted him.

Buttons free, she spread his shirt and sighed as the palms of her hands caressed hard, warm muscle. "You have a lovely chest."

His lips quirked up. "What a coincidence. I was thinking the same thing about you."

Mandy glanced down and saw that with the zipper undone, her dress had slipped a bit, only to come to a crashing halt at her cleavage. Nothing could get past her newly blossoming breasts, and her plump flesh was bursting out of the top of her strapless bra.

"This isn't my natural state, you know," she told him, pushing his shirtsleeves down to his wrists. "Every day I wake up to find they're a bit bigger, like I've taken an air pump to them."

Damien's thumb ran over the swell above the bra. "I like the end result."

"Yes, well, easy for you to say." Mandy gripped his wrist as his thumb brushed lower and lower, skirting her nipple. She gave a sound of disappointment. "But at this rate, I fully expect one day to roll over and have them clap."

He laughed, expression relaxed and amused. "I love your sense of humor."

She was about to tell him that back in England, at the Wycombe Abbey School for Girls, she'd been quite the comedic thespian, but she only had time to open her mouth before he ripped her dress down to her waist, and she promptly forgot how to speak.

Or breathe, when his head descended to her chest and his tongue traced above the rim of her overburdened bra. Back and forth it went, as if it was on a leisurely stroll in the park, and Mandy shivered, appreciating fully how much more sensitive her breasts were now. Torn between wanting to just enjoy his teasing tongue and urging him to dispense with her bra and head south to her nipple, Mandy gripped his wrists and squeezed.

Damien lifted his head, and Mandy expected him to shove her dress down, strip himself, and slide right into her standing up.

Or maybe that was just wishful thinking.

But she had expected Damien to be urgent, to take charge, to rush through to the release they were both seeking.

He was taking charge, yes, but he wasn't interested in rushing. Which had its pros and cons.

As she tugged his shirt off and dropped it to the floor, Damien pulled the clip out of her hair. He stroked in it and smiled. "I love your hair. It's just like you. Sort of free, with a mind of its own, but always in control."

Was that the way he saw her? Mandy thought that was just a lovely way to describe her, even if she felt control was the last thing she possessed. Unable to resist touching him, she smoothed out his dark eyebrows, traced his cheeks, brushed along his lips in a caress that was too intimate, but felt so, so right here with Damien. His lips pressed in a kiss over her fingers and she smiled, knowing she felt as raw and vulnerable as she looked.

Buy These Calder Novels by

Janet Dailey

Shifting Calder Wind 0-8217-7223-6 **$7.99**US/**$10.99**CAN
Chase Calder has no recollection of who he is, why he came to Fort Worth...or who tried to put a bullet in his head the night that a cowboy named Laredo Smith saved his life. Laredo recognizes him as the owner of Montana's Triple C Ranch—but according to the local papers, Chase has just been declared dead, the victum of a fiery car crash. The only person Chase can trust is his level-headed daughter-in-law, Jessy Calder. Helping Chase brings Jessy into conflict with headstrong Cat Calder, and into an uneasy alliance with the mysterious and seductive Laredo. And when another family member is found murdered on Calder soil, Chase resolves to come out of hiding and track down a ruthless killer...before the killer finds him first...

Green Calder Grass 0-8217-7222-8 **$7.99**US/**$10.99**CAN
Jessy Niles Calder grew up on the Triple C ranch, six hundred square miles of grassland that can be bountiful or harsh, that bends to no man's will—just like a Calder. As Ty Calder's wife, Jessy finally has all she's ever wanted. But even in the midst of this new happiness there are hidden enemies, greedy for the rich Montana land, and willing to shed blood to get it. Not to mention Ty's ex-wife Tara, causing trouble wherever she goes. And soon Jessy will be faced with the fight of her life—one that will change the Triple C forever...

Calder Promise 0-8217-7541-3 **$7.99**US/**$10.99**CAN
Young and beautiful, Laura Calder isn't content to live on a Montana ranch. Touring Europe with her "Aunt" Tara brings her into contact with the sophisticated world she's craved...and with the two men—and ultimate rivals—who will lay claim to her heart. Boone Rutledge is the son of a Texas billionaire and used to getting what he wants. He wants Laura...and so does a Sebastian Dunshill, Earl of Crawford, a handsome, sexy Londoner with a few secrets he can't share.

Available Wherever Books Are Sold!

Check out our website at **www.kensingtonbooks.com**

Say Yes! To Sizzling Romance by
Lori Foster

__Too Much Temptation
0-7582-0431-0   **$6.99**US/**$9.99**CAN

Grace Jenkins feels too awkward and insecure to free the passionate woman inside her. But that hasn't stopped her from dreaming about Noah Harper. Gorgeous, strong and sexy, his rough edge beneath the polish promises no mercy in the bedroom. When Grace learns Noah's engagement has ended in scandal, she shyly offers him her support and her friendship. But Noah's looking for something extra . . .

__Never Too Much
0-7582-0087-0   **$6.99**US/**$9.99**CAN

A confirmed bachelor, Ben Badwin has had his share of women, and he likes them as wild and uninhibited as his desires. Nothing at all like the brash, wholesomely cute woman who just strutted into his diner. But something about Sierra Murphy's independent attitude makes Ben's fantasies run wild. He'd love to dazzle her with his sensual skills . . . to make her want him as badly as he suddenly wants her . . .

__Say No to Joe?
0-8217-7512-X   **$6.99**US/**$9.99**CAN

Joe Winston can have any woman—except the one he really wants. Secretly, Luna Clark may lust after Joe, but she's made it clear that she's too smart to fall for him. He can just keep holding his breath, thank you very much. But now, Luna's inherited two kids who need more than she alone can give in a small town that seems hell-bent on driving them away. She needs someone to help out . . . someone who can't be intimidated . . . someone just like Joe.

__When Bruce Met Cyn
0-8217-7513-8   **$6.99**US/**$9.99**CAN

Compassionate and kind, Bruce Kelly understands that everyone makes mistakes, even if he's never actually done anything but color inside the lines. Nobody's perfect, but Bruce is about to meet a woman who's perfect for him. He's determined to show her that he can be trusted. And if that means proving it by being the absolute gentleman at all times, then so be it. No matter how many cold showers it takes . . .

Available Wherever Books Are Sold!

Visit our website at **www.kensingtonbooks.com**.